Ndalla's World

Ndalla's World

Beth Franz

atmosphere press

Published by Atmosphere Press

Cover photo by Pat Herb
Cover design by Beth Franz
Technical assistance by Lynn Damberger and Ronaldo Alves

atmospherepress.com

*for those people in our lives
(partners, friends, family members)
who help us find our way by encouraging us
to follow our heart*

Part One:
Julia's World

CHAPTER 1
Waking Up

The morning after my 35th birthday, I woke up feeling more positive, more hopeful, than I'd felt in some time. I awoke with the definite sense that everything would work out all right.

I'd spent most of the previous evening, June 19th, 1989, out on the tiny balcony of my third-floor apartment. I could say that I was called out there by the full moon, whose glorious light filled the clear night sky, and by the intoxicating sweetness of the early summer night air, and there would be truth in that. After all, I was living in Iowa City at the time, and many of us who have battled our way through some bitterly cold winters, only to have to then slog our way through the soggy, messy months of spring, hold a special place in our hearts for the first inklings of warm, dry, sweet-smelling summer air. But the truth is, something else called me out onto the balcony that night. I couldn't give it a name, but I knew exactly what it was.

At the center of what was threatening to pull me under that night was my uncertainty about where my life was headed—or, to be more honest, my fear that it wasn't really

3

headed anywhere. I was doing well enough, making sure my bills were paid, but I wasn't—what you might say—moving "forward" in my life, and I knew it. Birthdays had a way of forcing me to face this simple reality. But on this particular birthday, I could feel something else tugging at me.

Coupled with that familiar sense of disappointment in myself was something even more disconcerting. I guess I'd have to call it a kind of loneliness, even though I refused to call it that at the time. I'd always valued my solitude. It was part of who I was ... or who I wanted to see myself as. I didn't like the idea that something so ordinary as a feeling of loneliness had made its way into my make-up. And yet, I was growing increasingly dissatisfied with what had become a very solitary life, especially these last few years.

And so, after the sun went down, I put on one of my favorite records, one that featured Roberta Flack's "Killing Me Softly," turned up the volume on the stereo so that I could hear it outside, grabbed a couple of beers and a light blanket to ward off the slight chill of the night air, and curled up in the rickety old plastic chair I kept out on the balcony. My sole companion that night was the moon.

I knew from experience that this strategy would work. And sure enough, after a couple hours of sitting out there and a few more beers and a few more records, the wave of sadness I'd been fighting back all day finally washed over me, and I let the silent tears flow. It was the best way I'd found to navigate such journeys: embrace the sadness, whatever its actual cause, hold on for the ride, and hope to come out the other side. It was a few hours later, then, after I'd enjoyed a few more beers and a few more records, that I finally said "goodnight" to the moon, after first thanking her for her company, and headed inside.

That's why I was so surprised to wake up the next morning feeling so positive, so hopeful even, about things. It made no sense. But then, my philosophy at the time was that it's generally better to take life as it comes, no questions asked, especially if it involves a pleasant surprise.

So I got up, showered, went out to the kitchen, and re-discovered what I'd known last night but neglected to take care of: I was out of coffee. An hour later, I returned from the grocery store, restocked my fridge with beer and a few other items, started a pot of coffee, and sat down with the morning paper, prepared to enjoy my day off: a belated birthday present to myself.

That's when I heard a noise come from the direction of my bedroom. At least I thought the noise came from my bedroom. It could've come from my neighbor on the other side of the wall, I thought, as I finished pouring my first—and long-awaited—morning cup of coffee.

But then I heard it again. Or thought I heard it.

"Okay, third time's a charm," I said out loud, solely for my amusement. Or maybe it was to calm my nerves, which I could feel starting to get the better of me. I was just setting down my cup of coffee, for fear that I might drop it otherwise, when I heard the noise a third time.

I scanned the kitchen. My eyes landed on a "gourmet" rolling pin, the roller of which was solid marble, that looked— and felt—heavy enough to function as a weapon. I thought briefly of my mother, the rolling pin's previous owner. Neither she nor I had ever used it. The only reason I had it now was that I hadn't the heart to let it go after she'd passed. I sent a silent word of "thanks" her way, along with a quick but sincere apology for having given her such a hard time about holding on to such a worthless item, and headed for my bedroom, rolling pin in hand.

When I got there, I carefully laid my hand—the one with-out the rolling pin—on the doorknob, gave it a turn, and cracked the door open just enough to look inside and see one side of the room. I quickly pulled the door shut, blinked my eyes, and then opened the door again.

Sure enough, there was a person in my room. He was lying there, on the floor beside my bed, either dead or unconscious ... and naked! I shut the door again and looked at the marble rolling pin in my hand. Now what?

I decided to open the door one more time ... all the way this time ... and that's when I saw another person in my room. She was on the floor on the other side of my bed. She too was naked, but unlike her counterpart, she was moving, or trying to. She was holding her head and appeared to be suffering from some kind of vertigo or perhaps just a really bad hangover.

Quietly, I pulled the door shut. I was sure she hadn't seen me. I looked down at the rolling pin in my hand and thought about my two intruders. Between the unconscious—if not dead—state the man was in and the compromised condition the woman was in, I was sure I could take them. But take them ... where? ... or how? ... or ... What was I even thinking?

Better plan: I could call the police; that's what I could do. That's what I should do. But the only phone in the apartment was in my bedroom ... on the nightstand ... on the other side of the woman who was in the process of regaining consciousness.

I stood there, trying to gather my thoughts. Okay. I had the advantage. I may not have had my morning coffee yet, but I was still more capable of quick and decisive movement than they were, in their present condition, and I had my trusty marble rolling pin to protect me, as well. What could possibly go wrong? Armed with that question as my only plan of attack, I opened the door and stepped inside the room.

"You, there," I said, while holding up the rolling pin in one hand as firmly as I could even as it tried to roll out of my grasp, while pointing with my other hand, while also trying to project the most authoritative voice I'd ever managed to make come out of my mouth. I spoke in the direction of the woman, who, upon hearing my voice, tried to raise her head to meet my gaze. But it was clear that she was unable to shake off the dizziness with which she was struggling.

Her inability to bring me into focus, let alone offer any kind of response, was my cue to make my next move, but I'd just checked off the only item on my list of "threatening things to say and do," and I found myself unable to move or to say anything else.

As I stood there, momentarily paralyzed, I watched in amazement as the woman willed herself, with great effort, to stand up. Using the wall on one side of her and the edge of the bed on the other side of her, she succeeded in getting to her feet and stood there, more or less upright.

After taking a moment to catch her breath, she said, "I am Ndalla." Then she indicated the man who still lay on the floor on the other side of the bed. "This is Makei." Then I couldn't tell whether she bowed slightly or whether the dizziness that she was still feeling got the better of her. Whichever it was, she lost her balance, and she started to go down.

Without thinking, I moved forward to catch her and helped her sit down on the bed.

I took a step back once I could see her starting to regain herself. Only then did I realize that in my rush to get to her, I'd dropped the damn rolling pin on the other side of the room.

Time slowed down around me then as I took the next fraction of a second to think through my next move: I could make my way back across the room and retrieve my trusty rolling pin, or I could go ahead and use the phone, which was now within my reach, standing, as I was, in front of the nightstand. Whichever action I took, I was sure that the woman in front of me was in no condition to stop me. But which was the more sensible action?

Before I could decide, I heard the woman say, "May I ask you for something to drink?"

Her voice was weak, and now that she was sitting up, she was rubbing her forehead. Up close like this, I could see that she posed no immediate threat. Either that, or she was the best actor I'd ever seen.

"Something strong would help me clear my head," she said, still rubbing her forehead. "Perhaps you have some tea?" Something in the way her voice sounded convinced me that she was speaking the truth.

And like that, I knew what I needed to do. I crossed the room, retrieved my weapon, and headed out to the kitchen, where I poured another cup of coffee and picked up my own as well.

When I returned, carrying two cups of hot coffee, I admit: I felt a little silly with a rolling pin tucked up under my arm, but I wasn't taking any chances.

"I'm not a tea drinker, but I brought some coffee for both of us," I said, offering her one of the cups. "You said you wanted it strong, so I didn't put anything in it. You'll have to tell me if you take sugar or milk. Be careful now. It's very hot."

Her puzzled expression made me wonder how much of my monologue she'd taken in.

"Thank-you," she said, taking the cup and wrapping her hands around it in a way that made me wonder if she was cold. After all, she was sitting there, naked.

"Here," I said, getting up and reaching for my robe. "Let me put this around you."

She seemed surprised and a little confused, but she let me drape the robe around her shoulders. "Thank-you," she said again. And after a moment, she added, "You are very kind."

"I'm very confused," I countered. "Who are you? And who is he? And what are the two of you doing in my bedroom? How did you get in here? And what do you want?"

She rubbed her forehead again, and I realized just how loud my voice had become as my questions had come spilling out, one after another. I sat down beside her on the bed in an effort to convey the idea that I was willing to lower my volume and also adopt a different tone.

"I am Ndalla," she said very patiently, and only then did I realize she'd already offered that information. "He is Makei," she said, just as patiently. "If I may first drink some of this, I will then be able to answer all of your questions," she said, as if asking my permission.

I took a sip of my own coffee then. "It's still pretty hot," I said. "But yes. Take your time. I apologize for my tone. It's just that I don't understand—"

"Do not apologize. You have a right to ask such questions. The traveling sickness will leave me shortly. I assure you," she said, still rubbing her forehead. "Then I will be able to think more clearly, and I will answer all of your questions." She took a sip of her coffee. "This drink tastes very good. It will help me recover more quickly."

She took another sip of her coffee and studied my face a moment.

Then she surprised me with, "Do you have a name?"

My first thought was, *Curious phrasing!*

"Yes," I said. "My name is Julia."

"That is a beautiful name," she said before repeating it slowly, as if to see if she had it right. Or maybe just because she liked the sound of it.

"Where are you two from?" I asked, keeping my tone under control this time.

She smiled before speaking, perhaps aware of how strange her words would sound. "We are from a different part of your world, Julia, and we are from a different ... time."

"You're time travelers?" I said. *Really?* I thought. *That's the best you can come up with?*

9

But she must've missed the sarcasm in my voice. "Then you have known others?" The hopefulness in her voice was heart-breaking.

"Uh, no."

She seemed confused by my answer, so I offered, "I mean, I've heard about time travel, read stories about such things, but never actually met a traveler ... until now, I guess."

"Read stories?" she asked, the first word having apparently thrown her a little.

"Yeah, you know, in books."

"Books?"

I pointed to the overflowing bookshelves on the other side of the room. "You know, books." But she just looked at me.

So I got up, set my coffee cup down on the nightstand, walked over to the bookshelves, chose one of my favorite hardbacks, and carried it back to where she sat and offered it to her.

She set her coffee cup down beside mine and, with great care, took the book in her hands. She turned it over, very carefully, and looked at it from every angle, never once moving to open it.

"Have you never seen a book before?" I asked.

She looked up at me, then down again at the object in her hand, and shook her head.

So I took the book in my hands and held it out in front of me, fanning the pages so that she could see inside. Then I held the book open so that she could examine a couple of the pages more closely. She looked at it and waited but didn't seem to have a clue what she was waiting for it to do. Then she reached forward and, very gently, moved her fingers over the page as if taking in the feel of it.

"You really haven't ever seen a book before, have you?" I asked, taking my seat beside her on the bed.

Again, she shook her head and then pointed to the rolling

Ndalla,'" trying to get my tongue around the double consonant for the first time. "But earlier, I understood you to say, 'I am Ndalla.' I'm confused. Is Ndalla your name, or the name of where you and Makei are from?"

"I was given the name of my people when I entered the physical world for the first time," she said, matter-of-factly.

"You mean when you were born?" I said, not wanting to assume anything here.

"Yes, Julia. That is what I mean." And I heard in her tone an appreciation for my trying to make sure I understood, rather than any kind of impatience.

Not sure how to ask this next question, I opened with, "You said, just a moment ago, 'my people.' That makes it sound like—"

But before I could finish, she said, "I meant the people of my village. We are the Ndalla. And when I was born, I was given the same name."

"Doesn't that get a little confusing sometimes? I mean, how do you know whether the people in your village are referring to you or to the entire village?"

For the first time in our conversation, I saw her appear a little uncomfortable. I could almost swear, I saw her start to blush. "No, Julia. It is not confusing." And then, before I could ask another question, she stood up, coffee cup in hand. "With your permission, I will take some of this drink to Makei. He must sleep longer, but drinking some of this now will help his head begin to clear so that it will ache less when he does fully wake."

"Certainly," I said as she was leaving the room. Then, I pushed the start button on the coffee maker. *I'll just stay here and take care of my job: to make sure that we have plenty of the magic drink on hand to help all of our time travelers get over their traveling sickness.*

When she returned, her coffee cup was empty. I nearly

dropped my own cup as I took in the sight of her. She really was stunning ... and apparently very comfortable moving around in the world totally naked. "More coffee?" I offered, holding up the fresh pot.

"Yes, please."

I brought the pot over to the table, and we took our seats again. I felt her eyes studying me as I poured the coffee, and I suddenly felt very self-conscious.

"May I ask you some questions, Julia?"

"Certainly." After all, it wasn't as if the answers I was getting to any of my questions were clearing things up. Maybe I could learn more from her questions.

"Does everyone in your village have the same pale skin that you have?"

I looked at her, feeling slightly offended. I worked hard at achieving what I thought was a pretty decent tan every summer. What did she expect? Summer hadn't even officially begun.

Before I could find my voice, she reached across the table and set her arm next to mine as if to help me see what she thought I had trouble seeing. "See how much darker my skin is than yours? And Makei's skin is even darker than mine. Do you not go outside, Julia?"

"Yes, I go outside, but the warm weather of summer is just getting started. I don't know what the weather is like where you come from, but we have pretty cold winters here and pretty rainy springs. So it isn't until this time of year that we really start to feel the sun on our skin."

"And then your skin will turn dark, like mine?"

"Well, my skin will never be as dark as yours, but it will get a little darker."

"I see," she said, her tone indicating that she was certainly trying to understand.

"And your hair is different, too. May I touch it?"

CHAPTER 2
Venturing Out

The two of us stayed out on the balcony for what must've been another hour or two. I really have no idea how much time passed, nor did it matter to me. It almost felt as if time itself might be playing with me, and I wondered with a smile if that was a side effect of being in the company of actual time travelers.

When we came back inside, I helped Ndalla wake Makei up. She was extremely patient with him as it took him much longer to be able to regain himself than it had taken her. When he was finally able to bring me into some kind of focus, Ndalla introduced me to the man.

"Greetings," he said simply. Then he bowed his head a little and resurfaced with what presented itself as a very broad smile.

I bowed my head a little in return and said, simply, "Welcome to my world."

His smile broadened even more, and he seemed genuinely relieved to hear the words I'd spoken, although I'd said them in jest, a tone I was starting to feel uncomfortable using.

I left it to Ndalla to introduce Makei to the bathroom and its many mysteries. I took advantage of the opportunity to pull out a pair of shorts and a T-shirt that I thought might fit him, and then I headed for the kitchen, where I prepared a simple lunch for the three of us.

They were both ravenous. *Time travel must really take a lot out of a person*, I almost said, but I was determined to watch my tone from now on. They were two of the most physically fit people I'd ever seen, yet they could not seem to get full. I was glad I'd made that trip to the grocery store earlier that morning.

After lunch, the three of us spent the afternoon out on the balcony, where I enjoyed listening to Ndalla explain to Makei many of the same new sights she'd taken in earlier.

The two of them seemed very comfortable in each other's company, and I found myself wondering if they were a couple, but it felt somehow intrusive to just come out and ask. And yet something told me they were not. I could hear a deference in Makei's voice when he addressed Ndalla, a deference that did not seem to find its way into Ndalla's voice ... ever.

She was never rude ... either to Makei or to me. It's just that there was a kind of authority in her voice that came through and conveyed the sense that she knew herself to be in charge. And yet, she seemed a little more tentative when addressing me. Or at least it seemed that way to me, sitting out on the balcony that first afternoon.

That evening, I called and ordered some large pizzas to be delivered. Having seen how much food my two guests had put away at both breakfast and lunch, I thought I'd better err on the side of having more than enough to eat tonight.

The phone call, of course, prompted a whole new conversation about how there could possibly be a person in that little thing I called a phone. While we were waiting for the pizza, I also called my boss to explain that I was going to need some snow in the winter in your world?" I got nothing in response, so I added, "You know, that white, fluffy stuff that happens when the temperatures drop, and the rain turns to ice and snow?"

She did not answer at first. Then, after a moment, she seemed to come to herself.

"No, Julia. I think I know what you speak of, though. I have heard stories of those in our village who traveled, a long time ago, to distant lands where they saw this 'snow' on the tops of mountains. But where my village is, and for as far as the eye can see, ours is a land of warmth, a land of rich forests and open fields. Even in winter, we rarely need to wear any kind of covering to keep warm." Then she smiled and added, "But I think you know that already, do you not?"

"I think I would like such a winter, although I would still wear a covering," I said with a smile. "I used to love snow when I was young. It was magical, and I wanted to be outside in it all the time. But the older I get, the more I feel the cold in my bones," I said with a shiver. "At this point in my life, I would welcome a winter without snow, a winter of unseasonable warmth."

Her smile broadened, and I was glad to have brought that beautiful smile of hers to life once again. "I would like for you to see my world, Julia." She sat a moment in silence before saying, "I am grateful to the Forces for bringing us here to you, Julia. You have been a good host on this, our first day in your world. I look forward to the days to come."

"As do I," I said, and not just out of politeness. I felt myself drawn to this woman in a way that was already, after spending only a day in her presence, pulling at me somehow.

At some point, though, I had to admit that I was having trouble keeping my eyes open. "Listen, you two," I said, getting to my feet. "I'm going to have to call it a night."

They looked at me, and I realized, once again, that I needed to be more careful with my choice of words. "I'm feeling pretty tired. It's been a long day, and I need to get some sleep."

And still they sat there, and it occurred to me that they might be thinking that they could just sleep out there on the balcony. "I'll need you to come inside now," I said, sliding the screen door open.

"Can we not sleep out here, Julia?" Ndalla asked.

"No, that's not going to work. I need you to come inside for the night."

They got to their feet, but it was easy to see that they would've preferred not to.

"I'll tell you what," I said as they came inside. "We can leave this glass door open and shut only the screen door. That way the fresh air can still come in." They seemed to be giving the arrangement some consideration. "And," I said, "you are welcome to sleep right here, where you can feel the fresh air coming in and where you can still see outside. Will that work?"

Makei looked to Ndalla, who, once again, spoke for both of them. "If that is what you think best, Julia, then that is what we will do."

"Will you be comfortable here on the floor?" I asked. "We can bring over some of the cushions from the sofa if you like."

"No, Julia. The floor will be fine. That is where we sleep when we are in our world."

Why am I not surprised? "I will go and get some blankets for you, though."

"Thank-you, Julia. That will be all we need."

Ndalla's words—and the tone she used when she spoke them—sounded more like a dismissal than I wanted to admit, and I thought about saying something. But when I returned with the blankets, I found the two of them sitting on the floor, cross-legged and facing one another. Their eyes were closed, and they appeared to be engaged in some sort of meditation.

I set down the stack of blankets and was just about to

the sights. They seemed to me to be ready to spend time there and not be totally overwhelmed by it all, so I described it to them as best I could.

"It is the center of your village?"

"Yes," I said, satisfied that she understood. "Exactly. Shall we go?"

"We would like to see the center of your village. Have you let your people know that we are coming?"

"My people?" I laughed at the thought. "I'm no one special in the village. Uh ... town."

"But the Forces brought us to you. I thought ...." But her words trailed off.

I watched as she was clearly unable to finish the sentence out loud. So I finished it for her. "You thought perhaps I was a queen like yourself."

I could not read the look that flashed across her face at that moment. Was she perhaps still taking in the fact that I was not royalty like herself, as she had apparently assumed I was? Or was she perhaps caught off guard by the fact that I had guessed her secret?

"You carry yourself like royalty," I explained, intending it as a compliment.

Makei was helping me clear the table when we were having this conversation. Hearing the change in the tone of the conversation, or perhaps seeing the look of surprise—no, the look of alarm—on his queen's face, he quickly stepped in front of Ndalla and faced me. He made no threatening gesture, but the look on his face spoke volumes.

"I intended no rudeness," I said, lowering my eyes.

Ndalla spoke softly to Makei's back, and he stepped aside, though he remained alert to any sign of threat I might make toward his queen.

When our eyes met, she said only, "I am confused."

"You're confused?" I wanted to say, but I thought it wise

to remain silent.

Ndalla stumbled into one of the chairs at the kitchen table, apparently unable to speak. When she did find her voice, it was clear that she was speaking more to herself than to me. "The Forces would have sent me to a ... corresponding spirit ... when they sent me through time." Then she looked at me. "I do not understand your saying that you are no one special in your village. You must be, or the Forces would not have sent me to you."

I had no response to offer in the face of her unflawed logic. I took a seat on the other side of the table while Makei continued to stand guard. Ndalla seemed disoriented in a way that made me concerned for her.

After waiting as long as I could, finally I said, "I wish I could help."

I was still kicking myself for the lameness of the only words I could find when Ndalla looked up at me. She took a moment to look deep into my eyes before she spoke. "Having said that, you have helped." That beautiful smile of hers made my heart melt. "We will find our way through this mystery together, Julia. That, after all, is why the Forces have brought me to you—because it is known to them that only together can we find our way through this part of Life's Great Mystery."

Sensing the renewed assurance that not only she but also Makei seemed to feel, I got to my feet and offered Ndalla my hand. She took a moment while I enjoyed seeing a smile of what appeared to be genuine gratitude. Then she took my hand and let me help her to her feet. That wave of energy that I felt whenever we made physical contact was becoming addictive!

"Come," I said to the two of them. "Let me introduce you to your mode of transportation while you are in my world."

We went downstairs, and I showed them my small, used, blue Ford Fiesta hatchback. "One of you can ride in the front with me, and one of you can ride in the back. Or you can both their faces, but they didn't seem overwhelmed, the way I was feeling. Maybe, I thought to myself, their "forces" had managed to prepare them for all of this in some mysterious way. They seemed content to just take in as much as they could without necessarily trying to understand all that they were seeing.

As dinnertime approached, I suggested that we cap off our excursion with dinner at the same locally owned pizza place that had delivered our dinner the very first day they arrived. We sat at an outdoor table and were enjoying a pitcher of beer when I heard a familiar voice.

"So this is what you needed time off for this week, drinking beer with friends?"

"Brad," I said, setting down my beer and looking first at him and then at my two guests and then back at him. "Yeah," I said. "I got some unexpected company. I really appreciate your giving me the time to show them some of the sights."

"Ah, not from around here, eh?" he asked, speaking directly to them. "Well, welcome to Iowa City. I'm Brad," he said, offering his hand to Makei, who looked at me for guidance.

"I'm sorry, Brad. Forgive my manners. This is Makei, and this is Ndalla. They're in town for a few weeks, and like you said, they're not from around here. In fact, they're still getting used to a lot of our customs here in this country, not to mention our language."

"Wow. Not just from out of state but from another country. That's impressive. Are they connected with the university then? Like visiting professors or something?"

"Yeah," I said, pretty impressed myself. I couldn't have thought of a better way to put it.

"Well, welcome to you both," he said, turning to them and nodding, which I can only imagine they took to be a slight bow. Then he turned back to me and said, "Well, listen. I didn't mean to barge in here." He stopped. "Wait a minute. You say they're here for a few weeks?"

"Yeah, as near as we can tell. Their schedule is still a little ... hard to nail down at this point. But I'm thinking we're looking at a few weeks."

"And they're staying with you?"

"Yep."

"Well, listen, if you need more time off, you should take it. I mean, if they went to all the trouble to travel here from another country, we want to make as good an impression on them as we can. Right?"

"Right," I said. "But you've already given me the entire week off."

"That's all right. It's like I said, you never ask for time off."

"Maybe just one more week?"

"Absolutely, Julia. You got it."

After he left us, I turned to my guests, thinking I probably had some explaining to do.

But before I could figure out where to start, I heard Ndalla say, "Brad," trying on his name as she had tried on mine the day we met. "He seems like a very thoughtful and generous man. He is your friend?"

"He is."

"You are fortunate to have such a good friend." She smiled then before adding, "Even though there is much I do not yet understand, I do not doubt that the Forces brought us here to meet you for a reason, Julia. Like your friend, you too are very thoughtful and very generous."

Just after she said those words, the tiny incandescent lights that were strung up in the branches of the trees scattered throughout the pedestrian mall came on, right at dusk, casting the whole area in a soft glow that must've seemed magical to my two guests. I know it did to me.

CHAPTER 3
Settling In

I was glad to have another week off to make sure my visitors would be all right on their own in the apartment without me, but I don't think they really needed the extra preparation time. I was pretty sure they'd probably choose to spend most of their time out on the balcony, and then there was also the time they spent communing with the Forces. Those two activities alone could fill the six hours or so that constituted a typical shift for me.

Before the week was up, the three of us also took a couple trips over to where I worked. The photo shop was in easy walking distance of my apartment, and I wanted them to know I'd be close by, just in case they needed anything. I even offered Ndalla a key to the apartment and had her practice letting herself in and then locking everything up and leaving again.

"With this thing you call a key, we can walk with you to your work and then come back and let ourselves into the apartment?"

"Sure," I said. "I mean, if that's what you want to do. You don't have to walk me to work, though. You can just stay here, or you can walk down to the park, or you can take a walk around the neighborhood."

She seemed pleased to have options.

"But if you go anywhere, you'll have Makei with you, right? I mean, you won't go out alone, will you?"

"Yes, we will go together," she said. "Makei is the bravest of my warriors. That is why he made the journey with me. I did not know what I would find, but I knew that if Makei made the trip with me, we could keep each other safe." Her words offered me some comfort, but I also felt a whole new concern taking hold of me.

"Yeah, but you're not going to get into any fights with anyone while I'm at work, are you?"

She thought for a moment. "I do not know why we would, Julia," she said simply.

"Please don't," I said firmly.

She thought for a moment before saying, "I will honor your request."

It wasn't the reassuring response I was hoping for, but I realized it was all I was going to get.

My first day back at work, I knew I had to try to come clean with Brad. It was 6:00, closing time, and we'd just locked the front door and were straightening up the front counter when I broached the subject.

"You mean they're not teaching at the university?" he asked as he took the cash out of the register and put it in the bank deposit bag.

"Not exactly," I said.

"Are they students?"

"You could say that ... only they're not enrolled in any classes right now."

"Must be nice," he said with a smile, "to be a student without having any classes to go to."

"Yeah, they're kind of 'between programs' right now."

When I remained silent, unable to say anything, she sat up and resettled herself closer to me. "Tell me about your parents, Julia. I have seen many ... 'photos' of them in your scrapbook but only when you were much younger," she said, using the still new-to-her word. "But I see no 'photos' of them in your book now that you are older."

I merely shrugged. "I guess after I left home, life just started ... happening, you know? And keeping up these scrapbooks just didn't seem worth the effort. I mean, I was busy with college ... and then grad school ... and then moving here so my partner could go to grad school ... and then my parents died ... and I guess I was just too busy to keep up with the scrapbooks. That, and I just didn't see the point. Now that I think about it, it's kind of crazy that I work at a photo shop. I mean, I don't even own a camera anymore."

A moment passed before I heard her voice. "Your parents have ... passed into the spirit world?"

I looked at her and saw in her eyes the kind of heartbreak for my parents that I'd never let myself feel. Besides, my mind had already started to move in a new direction. I was wondering if I went out and got a camera, if Ndalla would let me take some photos of her.

I shrugged again, trying to pull myself back into the conversation Ndalla was trying to have with me. "Yeah. Actually, I wasn't too close to them when they died. They were on the east coast; I was moving around a lot, and a lot of things were happening ... in my life and theirs. We just sort of fell out of touch, you know? I mean, I was trying to figure out how to live my life after college, making choices, some of which I knew they didn't approve of, and then my dad got sick. So my mom's life started revolving around what ended up being his last six months of life, and then she'd no sooner taken care of his affairs than she died in an accident."

Ndalla moved closer to me and put her arm around me.

"You carry such sadness inside, Julia. I did not know."

I got the sense that she was inviting me to open up, but I merely shrugged again. Then I got to my feet. "I'm going to go get a beer to enjoy while we're sitting out here. Want one?" I asked. She merely shook her head silently. "Can I bring you anything?"

"No, Julia. Thank-you." It was all she said, and I felt like a real heel.

As I walked through the living room, I saw Makei sitting on the couch, enjoying a music video on MTV. I'm not sure when he'd discovered the music channel, but ever since he had, it was the only channel that the TV seemed to be tuned to anymore. I watched him as he sat there, totally engaged in what he was seeing and hearing on the TV, and I thought about Brad's offer. Maybe Makei was more ready to strike out on his own than I'd given him credit for.

"You like that channel, don't you?" I said as I walked out to the kitchen. I looked over my shoulder and saw him look up at the sound of my voice and nod enthusiastically.

"The music in your world ... is ...." His arms went up, as if trying to indicate something huge and powerful. But he didn't seem to have the vocabulary he was reaching for.

"I know," I said, with a smile. "I think so too. I'm going to grab a beer. You want one?"

"Yes, please."

On my way back from the kitchen, I walked over to the coffee table and set his beer down there. He was bouncing so enthusiastically with the rhythm of the music that I really didn't want to interrupt him. I heard him say, "Thank-you," but my attention was caught by something else.

"What's this?" I asked, pointing to the over-sized book on the table. "A photographic look at the continents," I read aloud to myself. "Where'd this come from, Makei?"

"I found it on one of your many bookshelves," he said,

she showed me photos that revealed a variety of landscapes: everything from what looked like the lush forests we'd just been looking at in South America to the wide-open plains and, of course, the desert country that makes up so much of the Outback. "This looks very much like my world, Julia."

I sat there, taking in the beauty displayed before me before saying, "No wonder you miss your world. It is gorgeous."

And then I happened to see some of the text on one of the pages as I was flipping ahead to get to the next photo. It talked about the reversal of the seasons in the two hemispheres. "Of course," I said, more to myself than to Ndalla. "That could explain why our solstices are opposite one another."

She looked at me as if seeing something in my face for the first time. "Are the Forces speaking to you, Julia?"

The look in her eyes was so hopeful that I was tempted for a moment to humor her and say, "Perhaps." But knowing how important a role those Forces played in her life, I didn't dare. I merely said, "I think I am beginning to see ... just how connected our worlds really could be."

She positively beamed upon hearing this. "I too feel the connection between our worlds, Julia. I am so glad you feel it too," she said, giving me a hug.

We spent the rest of the evening out on the balcony, looking at photos that reminded Ndalla of her world, and Makei spent his evening inside, enjoying one music video after another.

It wasn't until the next evening, then, that I had the chance to share Brad's offer with the two of them.

Naturally, it was not Makei who spoke. Rather, he looked to his queen, who asked, "Is the offer only for Makei to work?"

Her question caught me off guard. "I really don't think it occurred to Brad that you'd be interested in manual labor."

"Do I not appear strong enough to handle the work?"

I realized then that Ndalla was feeling somehow slighted,

overlooked. I realized that her pride had been hurt, so I chose my next words carefully. "I don't think that's it. I think Brad just made an assumption: that only a man would be interested in that kind of work."

"We will tell him tomorrow that we are both interested," she said decisively.

I didn't think that was such a good idea, but I wanted to be careful not to offend Ndalla.

"If I could make a suggestion—"

She merely nodded, her imperiousness showing.

"I think it would be best for Makei to go alone to the job. I fear that your presence might make the other men, who are not used to working with women in that way, uncomfortable."

"This is what you think?"

"Yes."

The two exchanged a look I could not read.

"We will do as you suggest," she said. "We rely on your wisdom in matters of your world." And with that, Ndalla stood up from the kitchen table and left the room. I heard the screen door to the balcony open and close.

After Makei and I cleaned up the kitchen, I decided to give Ndalla a little more time to herself, so I sat with Makei in the living room for a while. Normally I would've preferred the classical music station on the radio, but Makei's enthusiasm for the music coming at us through the TV had a way of opening me up to it in a way I'd never experienced before.

At one point, I asked him if going to the construction site on his own was what he wanted to do.

He turned to me and said simply, "I will do as my queen commands."

"But do you want to do this?"

He looked at me and, after a moment, said, "I want to do what my queen commands."

I was starting to have second thoughts about this whole

idea of his going out on his own.

"You know, when you're out there with other people, Makei, I don't think you should mention that you're there because your queen commands it. In fact, I would ask that you not mention anything about the world you come from ... or your queen. The people in my world would not be able to understand what you're talking about, and people can get very angry and even violent when they become confused and afraid."

He thought for a moment. "But you understand, and you are from this world," he said.

"There is much that I still do not understand. And if you remember, I was pretty afraid when you two first arrived in my world." But then I remembered that by the time he'd regained consciousness, I'd set down my big bad rolling pin. "Our worlds are very different, Makei. And if you're going to go out into my world on your own, you've got to promise me that you'll be very careful and not offer up any information about your world or your queen. To do so would be to put both yourself and your queen in danger."

My last word definitely caught his attention.

He sat there a moment, considering his next words carefully. "If this is what you think, then this is what I will do. My queen said when we were in the kitchen: 'We will do as you suggest. We rely on your wisdom in matters of your world.' And so I will."

"Thank-you, Makei." And it took me a moment to realize he'd just quoted her exact words.

"You are welcome." He smiled. "And thank-you for your advice," he said, restoring my confidence in him that he would find his way just fine.

"And if anyone asks where you're from," I said, as I started to get up off the couch, "you might try saying 'Australia.' For all we know, that really could be where you're from, and I think it might help people not be afraid."

"Australia," he said, getting his mouth around the sounds of it.

My mind immediately started cataloging some other advice I wanted to give him, but first I wanted to check on Ndalla, so I went over to the door to the balcony and knocked gently on the frame of the screen.

"May I come out?"

It took her a moment to say anything. "Of course, Julia. It is your balcony."

"Yes," I said, still not moving. "But I do not wish to intrude if you want to be alone."

Again, she took a moment. "I would like you to come out and join me."

I went out and sat down beside her but remained silent, determined to let her dictate the timing and the content of this conversation. I was looking up at the moon when I felt her shift her position to get close enough to me that I felt safe putting my arm around her. And still I waited.

"Since our arrival in your world, there has been much to see and try to understand."

"I'm sure there has," I wanted to say, but something in her voice suggested that my words would only interrupt what she was trying very hard to find a way to say, so I remained silent.

"Much of what we have been called upon to do here has come more easily to us than we had dared to hope it would. And that is because of your thoughtfulness, I think." She looked up at me then and flashed that glorious smile of hers. And I felt my heart melt.

"Even so," she continued, "we have been very much 'between worlds' ever since our arrival. Neither in our own world, nor fully in yours." Here she paused again and sat up so that she could face me.

"Before beginning my journey, I understood," she said,

time to heal; a time to break down, and a time to build up; a time to weep, and a time to laugh; a time to mourn, and a time to dance; a time to cast away stones, and a time to gather stones together; a time to embrace, and a time to refrain from embracing; a time to seek, and a time to lose; a time to keep, and a time to cast away; a time to rend, and a time to sew; a time to keep silence, and a time to speak; a time to love, and a time to hate; a time for war, and a time for peace.

She was amazed to hear read aloud to her something that sounded so much like, as she put it, the "soul wisdom" of her own world. She had me read the verses aloud to her several more times so that she could commit them to memory and bring them back to her people: evidence, as she put it, that we, as a people, shared the same "soul wisdom" as her own people. She remarked, "My people will be greatly comforted to hear that these words have been spoken throughout the years by your wise ones," for that is how I described the Bible to her: a collection of stories told by our wisest and most knowing elders. She was amazed at the book's thickness and the sheer number of stories it seemed to hold.

I offered the Bible itself to her, as a gift, to take back with her to share with her people. But she reminded me, gently, that no one in her world could read its cryptic markings, nor could she take anything from my world back with her. And I recalled some of her earliest words to me: "We could take nothing with us on our journey." To those words she added, on the night we sat there with the Bible between us, these striking words: "I can take back only what I hold in my head and my heart. These will be the gifts from your world to mine."

I recalled these words of hers as we lay in bed together, the next morning, when I asked her again if she was ready yet to share with me what it was that was troubling her.

She shifted her position, locking eyes with me before she spoke. "I hesitate to share my thoughts with you, Julia, but I need you to be prepared." She took my hands in hers. "I feel that the time for me to return to my world approaches." Her eyes fell as she said, "I fear that our time together may be coming to an end."

I felt my heart drop to my stomach. How could such a thing happen? This was someone to whom I felt more strongly connected than I'd ever felt ... to anyone. The thought that such a person could be yanked, just like that, out of my life left me speechless.

How could such a thing happen? It was the only thought I could hear echoing in my mind.

And then I heard a small voice inside my head answer: *As abruptly as she came into your life.* And I knew that it was possible that she could—and probably would—be taken from me.

I sat there, not saying anything until finally I asked, "Could your fear be ... wrong?"

She looked at me. "A fear is just that: a fear. It is neither right nor wrong."

"I mean, could you be wrong about our time together coming to an end? It is too soon."

"I too feel a connection I am not yet ready to sever," she said, holding me closer.

"What can we do?" I could hear the panic in my voice.

She lowered her eyes, saying simply, "If it is time, nothing." Then she looked up, and her eyes met mine before she spoke. "It is like the soul wisdom you read to me the other night, Julia. We must not try to control the flow of events that make up the Great Unfolding of Time. Rather, our lives are about moving with those events; only then can we learn what we are here to learn."

I could not argue with her. I did not want to even try. But still ... "Is there any way to know, I mean, to **know** that it's time before I just wake up one morning and find you ... gone?"

"While you are at work today, I will try to see more clearly how much time we have."

"I'm not sure I want to leave you today. What if I come home and you're not here?"

"I do not think that will happen." Somehow, she managed a reassuring smile.

"How can you know?"

"I do not know, Julia. But I do not feel that it is yet time."

She took me in her arms. "This is why I hesitated to share my fear with you. I did not want you to worry. My fear is just that: a fear." She turned away then, and I heard her say, softly, "A reluctance to face the inevitable." Then she turned back to me and managed another smile. "Please trust me. It is not time just yet. It is all right for you to go to work. This is a fear I must come to terms with myself."

But I trusted her feelings and intuitions more than I would ever be able to trust my own. And if she felt that our time together might be coming to an end, I could not bear to go to work.

"Please," she said. "I want you to go to work today. I need the time alone. I will be here when you return." I knew the word "please" did not come easily to her.

"Must I go just yet?"

"Soon," she answered. "But not just yet, I think," she said with a smile as she moved still closer to me.

Work that afternoon did not go well. I had little to no patience with customers who had a hard time making the simplest of decisions. "Singles or doubles? Gloss or matte finish? I mean, come on! These are not hard decisions," I wanted to shout.

Not only that, but one of the two big machines was misbehaving. The machine that we relied on to print the photos once we'd developed the roll of negatives in the other machine kept jamming, and I didn't have the patience to deal with a jammed machine. Not today. I hated to call Brad at home, but it was either that or tell his customers to take their business elsewhere.

"Not a problem," he said. "I'm on my way."

By the time Brad had driven the twenty minutes or so from his house to the shop, I'd come to the realization that I needed to hand in my two weeks' notice. It was a decision that made no sense whatsoever. What would I live on? I didn't know. And I didn't care. All I knew was that I wanted to spend whatever time I had left to spend ... with Ndalla. I didn't want to get up one morning, say good-bye to her, spend the day at work, only to come home and discover that she was gone, as suddenly and mysteriously as she had arrived. I wanted to spend all the time I could with her until she was yanked back out of my world. I knew that. I knew it more surely than I'd ever known anything in my life.

As soon as Brad walked in, he could see that I was not myself.

"Everything okay?" he asked.

I just shook my head, wordlessly, and gestured to the uncooperative machine behind me.

"Let me take a look at it," he said in a tone intended to reassure and calm me down.

I did my best to take care of things at the counter while Brad wrestled with the machine that we relied on to honor our sixty-minute promise to customers. I heard him swear at it under his breath only a couple times before he had it up and working again.

When he came up to join me at the counter, he took one look at me and said, "You look like you need to go home." I could feel tears starting to come. "Hang on," he said. "Give me just fifteen minutes." And with that, he disappeared into the office at the back of the shop. And sure enough, fifteen minutes later, one of my co-workers came in the front door to relieve me, and Brad asked me to join him for a minute back in the office before I left for the day.

"I'm sorry, Brad," I said as I took a seat on the only chair in the office other than the one he always sat in at the desk. It was a chair that always had stuff piled on it, but he'd managed to clean it off quickly and efficiently in the time it took for me to get to the small office.

"Nah, don't be," he said, reaching for a box of tissues and placing it on one of the stacks closest to me. "Everything's fine. Well, I mean, everything as far as the shop is concerned is fine," he said with a shrug. "You know me, Julia." And I did. Nothing seemed to faze him. He was able to roll with whatever he needed to roll with to keep things in the shop going.

"But you," he said. "What's going on with you? Everything okay?"

I just shook my head, determined to hold the tears back. "Not really," I finally managed to say. "I just need some time to deal with some things at home." Then I looked him in the eye and said, "I don't want to do this to you, Brad, but I need to hand in my two weeks' notice."

"Now wait a minute, Julia," he said as he leaned forward in his chair.

"No, I mean it, Brad. You've been great to me. Really, you have. But I just need more time right now, and it's not fair to you that I can't carry my share of the load here."

"Is this about your house guests? Something going on there that I need to know about?"

"No, Brad. It's ... Well actually, yeah. I think their time here

61

in Iowa City is almost up, and I really want to be able to spend some time with them before they leave."

"If it's time you want, you've got it."

"Yeah, but—"

"I tell you what," he said. "I've got things covered here pretty good. And now that August is here, summer traffic will start winding down. Why don't you take a couple more weeks off ... just like you did when summer was getting going, starting today? Those two weeks did you a world of good. Just like before, it'll have to be without pay, of course, but if it's time you want right now, it's yours. Come back in a couple weeks. If you still want to hand in your two weeks' notice, you can do it then. Don't decide anything right now, though. Okay? I really think you just need another little break. I mean, it's summer, for Christ's sake!" He smiled then and said, "See, that's the problem with you folks who never know when to quit going to school. You just don't know how to pace yourself."

I didn't know what to say. Brad was a good guy. If he wanted me to wait a couple weeks before handing in my notice, who was I to say no? I really did want the time right now. I would worry about the rest in a couple weeks' time. "Thanks, Brad."

"No problem. Take care."

"Call me if you get in a pinch, okay?"

"Get outta here," he said as he waved me out the door.

"You're the best," I said, wanting to hug him, and I hurried out the door.

When I arrived back at the apartment, I entered quietly. I didn't know if Ndalla was still engaged in her conversation with the "Forces." I saw Makei already working in the kitchen.

But when I walked into the living room, she wasn't there,

nor did I find her out on the balcony. My breath caught in my throat. Rather than call out or try to speak to Makei, I hurried to the bedroom. I could feel my heart starting to race. Her premonition had proven to be entirely too accurate. I knew it. But when I got to the door of the bedroom and pushed it open, I found her sleeping peacefully on the bed.

The window was open, and a gentle breeze was making the curtains dance their way into the room and back out again. As was her way, she lay there naked, the sheet folded back neatly across her stomach, her arms relaxed, one resting on the pillow beside her head, the other resting on her stomach. She could not have looked more peaceful. Tempting though it was to wake her up gently, I decided to let her rest.

While I was having my worst day ever at work, she'd probably spent the better part of her day communing with the Forces. I figured that if whatever she'd learned was allowing her to rest that peacefully, well then it couldn't have been too upsetting. I closed the door and headed out to the kitchen to work on supper preparations with Makei.

That night after supper, Ndalla asked me if I would like to take a walk with her. It was clear from the invitation that this would be a walk for just the two of us. I looked to Makei to see if he'd been offended by the slight, but I needn't have, as he simply began clearing the table.

"Sure," I said, and with that we headed out.

We walked a few blocks in silence as I waited to see if she had some particular line of conversation in mind. Finally, she spoke.

"Julia, you have said that your work at the photo shop was ... 'temporary'," she said, using a word that was still somewhat new to her. "May I ask, what it is you plan to do with your life after you leave the photo shop?"

She wasn't one to beat around the bush. Actually, we'd come close to having this conversation more than once in the last few weeks, but I'd always managed to sidetrack the talk in some way. I was pretty adept at avoiding the simple reality that I didn't have a clue what was coming next. This time, however, she seemed determined to pull an answer out of me.

"Do you have any plans, Julia?"

I decided to meet her directness with my own. "No, I don't." I wondered if this was the time to share with her the gist of my conversation with Brad earlier this afternoon, something I'd kept to myself up until now. But I didn't want to further complicate things.

"This ... 'studying' you spent so much time doing, it was to prepare you for a life of teaching and sharing stories, no?" It sounded like as good a description of what a master's degree in English was good for as I could've come up with.

"You could say that. Yes." To be totally honest, I wanted to spend more time on my writing and, to make financial ends meet, I'd probably have to get a job teaching, at least for a number of years. I wasn't crazy about that part of the picture since the teaching I'd done while I was still working on my degree, as a graduate assistant, always had a way of sapping too much of my creative energy out of me, and I knew that.

"Would *you* say that, Julia?" Her question snapped me back, and I realized that I was feeling a little defensive all of a sudden.

"Yes," I said, just to get myself started. "There's a lot that I enjoy about teaching, and I would probably have to find work doing that. But it's the other part of what you said. What did you call it? Sharing stories? Now that's what I really want to focus on." To myself, I added, *If I can figure out how to do that and still manage to pay the bills.*

"Julia," she began. But then my name was followed by a long silence.

"Yes?" I said at last.

We kept walking until we reached the small park in my

Ahhh. I see. But I chose to say nothing out loud until finally she turned back to look at me. "This, then, is what you meant when you said things would be different in your world. You will always be queen when you return to your world."

"Yes, I will always be queen. It is a commitment I made to my people long ago. It is a commitment I must honor regardless of my personal feelings in matters of love and attachment."

"Can you not be both," I asked, "public queen and private person? In fact, must you not be both? How can you lead your people if you do not allow yourself to be a person, plain and simple, first and foremost?"

I watched her hand go up to her forehead, rubbing it as if in search of answers that would not come to her.

"My people do not ask me such questions, Julia. I am queen." She tried to say it with force, but it came out sounding softer than she intended, almost as if she were pleading.

"But I have never been one of your people," I said as gently as I could. "Rather, I have been your friend. And I would be your partner if I make the journey back with you." I took her hands in mine. "You will have to decide if that feels right to you," I said. "Only then will we both know if this is a journey we will take together."

"This cannot be a matter for me to decide. The Forces have made it clear that this is a matter for you to decide, Julia."

"I will decide whether or not I will come with you only after you decide what role I will play in your world when we get there."

"But that is putting the matter in my hands."

"Then so be it," I said. "Let me know what you decide."

And with that, I lay back down and turned my back to her as though I could even try to get some sleep with such a matter hanging in the balance.

Within minutes, I had turned back over, reached up, and

taken her in my arms. "Let me help you with your decision," I said. And as I held her in my arms, I knew in my heart that I couldn't let her simply vanish out of my life as mysteriously as she'd come into it.

Over the next several days, Ndalla and Makei spent much time communing with the Forces. "Makei will stay here and watch over your things," Ndalla said to me one morning as we were making the bed together, "while you and I make the journey together."

I had started to wonder what would happen to my apartment and everything in it once I vanished, but it hadn't occurred to me that Makei would not be making the journey with us.

"He's ... okay with that?"

She stood up straight before she answered me in a tone that spoke volumes. "The Forces have made it clear that this is how it will be."

"Will he not miss being with his own people?"

"He will return to his people," she went on to explain, as matter-of-factly as if we were discussing someone's vacation plans, "but this journey that will happen soon is not his to take."

I decided to venture a question that had been playing in my mind for some time. "Aren't you ever afraid that you might sometimes misunderstand the Forces and thereby take the wrong action? I mean, how can you be so sure about such things?"

She shrugged. "The Forces make their messages very clear. If one listens respectfully, one can be sure of their meaning."

It was as simple as that then, was it?

I was just mulling this one over when she surprised me

this hardly seemed the time to have a change of heart about making the journey, nor was I in any kind of position to quibble about the arrangements, over which neither of us had any control whatsoever. This was a time for letting go ... of accepting, plain and simple. What would be, would be.

That evening, after we'd both said our farewells to Makei, Ndalla and I retired to the bedroom. Unsure just what to expect, I was nevertheless surprised to hear her suggest that we prepare ourselves for bed.

"It is all right," she said, no doubt in response to the dumbfounded expression on my face. "We should make ourselves comfortable and try to relax completely." Still unable to move from where I stood, I heard her say, "Come, Julia. I will not leave your side."

We undressed then and climbed in bed, just as we had every other night. We lay still, side by side, only our hands enclosing one another. I turned my head to look over at her. She did the same.

"Do not be afraid, Julia. We are in the hands tonight of the Forces. They will hold us and carry us, safely, across time, from your world to mine. All that is asked of us is that we declare that we are ready for such a journey."

And with that she turned and faced the ceiling again and closed her eyes. Following her lead, I did the same, half expecting that she would begin some sort of incantation, I suppose. But she did not.

All was silence. And I found one phrase repeating itself over and over inside my head: *Let the journey, for which I am prepared, begin.*

ones I was now experiencing, and without the benefit of any sort of magic drink.

"You might just want to let yourself sleep one more time," she offered. "The rest will help your headache go away."

"I don't know if I can fall asleep," I said, trying my best to rub my pounding forehead.

"Here," she said, gently pushing me back down and stretching out beside me where I lay. "I will help you relax so that your body can get the rest it needs. When you awake again, you will feel much better. I assure you." I didn't think I could feel much worse.

As I drifted off to sleep with Ndalla at my side, it occurred to me that I'd seen no one other than Ndalla herself. And I wondered about that, but not for very long, for soon darkness closed in around me, and I slept a restful sleep.

When I awoke the third time, I felt much better. As Ndalla had promised, the headache was gone. I found her beside me, still sleeping, and reached over to kiss her awake. But just as I was about to touch my lips to her cheek, I thought I heard something. Startled, I sat up.

Looking around me, I found that our "bed," such as it was, consisted of nothing but blankets on the ground at the edge of a clearing. Above us was a canopy of tree branches, and all around us were rocks and tree trunks, behind which, I imagined, hid our audience.

"You must be feeling better," she observed in response to my ability to sit up straight.

"I think we are not alone," I whispered to her.

She smiled and assured me that other than the animals that lived in the clearing, we were quite alone. "We are here in my beloved clearing. It is a very special place. I have sent word to my people that we have arrived. Even though I'm sure they are very curious to see you, they will not bother us here unless I invite them."

"For how long?" I asked.

"I am queen." There was no mistaking the imperious edge to her voice as she made this statement. "No one will come here unless I invite them, and I will not do that until you are ready to receive visitors." She smiled then. "Now that you are in my world, Julia, I think there are some things you will need a little time to get used to." I was just about to ask her what she meant by that when she said, "As you already know, my people wear far less clothing than the people in your world ... except for certain occasions. You may find yourself a little uncomfortable in such a world, at first. The two moon cycles I spent in your world helped me understand that. So I have asked Yolana to have some of the people in my village create a covering that I think will help you feel more comfortable around my people."

"Yolana?" I asked.

"Yolana," she said simply, as though the word explained itself. But then seeing my uncertainty, she added, "Yolana has taken care of my needs since before my memories begin. She and I grew up together. I do not know the word in your world for what Yolana is to me."

I hesitated but then decided to say what was on my mind. "A companion, perhaps?"

She considered the word choice a moment. "Yolana is both more and less than that to me. I do not know how to explain this. You will see for yourself when she brings our meal." And she reached out and put her hand on mine as if to reassure me. "Are you hungry?"

I hadn't noticed until she asked. "Starving!"

"Then let me call to Yolana to let her know that we are ready." And so she did ... out loud, not telepathically or anything. She moved away from me before calling out. The for you to try on," she said, holding up what I realized was my new set of clothing. She waited for me to say something.

"It's ... a lot less than what I'm used to wearing," I said, and I had no idea what animals might have given up their skins for the sake of my modesty and comfort, "but let's give it a try." I reached for the simple garment.

"Not yet," she said, pulling it back from me playfully. "Do you remember your words to me on my first day in your world, Julia?" At first, I didn't know what she was referring to, and then I heard her say, "If you want to sit a while longer with no cover on, it is all right with me," and we both laughed.

It was only after we finished eating that Ndalla handed me the garment. "Now, let us see what my people have come up with for you to wear," she said.

It was a very short, very simple, one-piece ... tunic, I guess you could say. It had no sleeves, and it didn't go down too far, about as far as a pair of shorts might have gone. It was definitely of the one-size-fits-all variety, but it came with a rope that I tied around my waist, giving it a look that I knew was more stylish than I had a right to ask for. And as for comfort, it really wasn't that bad. More than anything, though, I appreciated the thoughtfulness shown both by Ndalla, who had asked her people to create something, and the ingenuity of her people, who managed to pull it off.

"What do you think?" I asked as I stood before her, striking a pose.

Ndalla put her hand up to her chin as though the matter deserved serious consideration. "I think ... I think ... You know, if only we had a mirror ...," she said playfully.

After we'd finished our mid-day meal and had enjoyed still more time together, my new outfit having been tossed aside some time ago, Ndalla told me that she wanted to spend the rest of the afternoon in communion with the Forces. "Now that we have made the journey back to my world, it is time. Do you mind, Julia?"

"Of course not. Should I leave? Give you privacy?"

"If that is what you wish." She paused a moment, as if considering the matter. "Or you may stay and assist me, if you wish."

"Assist you?"

"Only if that is what you wish."

"That is what I wish. Tell me how."

And so, on my first day of being awake in Ndalla's world, I received my first lesson in how to consult with the Forces.

Ndalla selected the appropriate spot in the clearing, and we sat down facing one another, as I'd seen her do with Makei, back in my world, so many times. I tried to mimic both Ndalla's posture and her sense of profound calm as she settled into position, but even as I did so, I knew her graceful actions and movements to be the result of years of disciplined practice.

"If you can, Julia, try to open yourself to what is to happen here. Try very hard to clear your mind yet remain present to what you hear and see."

I knew this was not the time to ask questions, and I could not have formulated one if I'd tried. So I merely nodded, and we began. I had read and heard about meditation practices in the East and had even tried to meditate on a couple occasions ... long before Ndalla came to my world. But I never seemed to develop the patience for it. Or maybe it was the balance I lacked: being able, on the one hand, to "clear my mind" and being able to "stay present," as Ndalla put it, to all that I saw and heard. But I determined to keep myself still while imagining her to be having a much more successful time of it.

I opened my eyes from time to time. And every time I did,

statement was put forth as a question or as an assurance.

"Being with you is pleasant enough," I offered by way of response. And I was pleased to see that I'd managed to make her blush again.

After we'd eaten our fill, we headed down to the river, first to walk along the bank for a while and then to swim. This time, I was able to shorten the time it took me to get into the water, if only by a little bit. As Ndalla had indicated it would be, even the feel of the water on my skin felt more invigorating than it had ever felt before. We swam around each other and played in the water, like children, long after the sun had set.

Then we lay on the bank and looked up at the full moon.

"Does it not look as beautiful from this world as it did from yours, Julia?"

As inadequate as it felt, all I could say at first was, "Yes." But then, after we lay there a little longer, I said, "Our worlds are one. I know that now with absolute certainty. I do not know whether it is time or space—or both—that we traveled through to get here. And the truth is, it doesn't matter. I am here now, with you, and it feels very ... right to be where I am now."

She propped herself up on her elbow and looked at me. Again, she looked positively radiant. "It gives me much happiness to hear you speak those words, Julia. You have spoken the same words I feel in my heart. Thank-you, Julia, for choosing to make the journey with me."

"Thank-you for bringing me here. It's not exactly a trip I could've made on my own!" I said with a smile. She smiled back before lying back down beside me then.

It was only then, after we'd been lying there a while, totally relaxed, looking up at the night sky, that I heard her ask, "May I speak of the vision we shared this afternoon?"

"Yes, please."

She sat up before saying, "What we saw today will inform

what I will tell my people when the time comes for us to leave the clearing, and I address my people at the Ceremony of Welcome. You should know that. It is not my wish to catch you ... off guard." She smiled as she used this expression, which she'd learned back in my world.

"Will you tell them what you saw?"

"It is not that simple, Julia. What we saw is not nearly as important as what it means."

I hesitated, unsure whether I wanted to know the answer to what I was about to ask. "You know what it means?"

She put her head down and did not speak at first. "I believe I do," she said at last.

"Do I want to know?"

She looked at me then. "I cannot answer that question, Julia. Only you can."

And still I hesitated. "Tell me then. If you can."

"The vision," she began, "spoke of important times that lie ahead ... for all of us." She took my hand before continuing. "For my people. And also for ... the two of us." She smiled a moment before saying, "It is clear that there is some danger involved in what lies ahead."

"In the vision," I said, "I felt as though I was ... losing you." There. I'd finally gotten the words out. I did so, hoping that the very act of finally speaking them could take away some of the vision's tremendous power.

She said nothing at first. And then I heard the words that stopped my heart. "I felt that too." It was all that she said, so softly that I could barely hear the words. I didn't want to hear those words. I wanted her to tell me that in my ignorance, I'd simply misunderstood the vision and that there would be no such loss in our future.

"Please don't tell me that," I said, at least to myself, as I took her in my arms and held her. I cannot say whether I ever spoke the words aloud.

"Downtown? You mean, it is time to enter the village? When?"

"As soon as you feel ready, Julia. I am sure that the people of my village are ready to meet you whenever you are ready to meet them."

"They are waiting on me?"

"No," she said with a smile. "They are waiting on me, and I am happy to wait until I know you feel ready."

All of a sudden, I felt the weight of the situation I found myself in, and a wave of stage fright washed over me. "What if I embarrass you tonight? What if I say or do something stupid?"

She pulled me closer to her then and said, firmly, "Do not be afraid of that. Ever. All you need to do is be yourself." Then she added with a smile, "While you are here in my world, Julia, you should feel free to do only what you choose to do ... always."

And like that, I felt a calmness wash over me.

But no sooner had my nerves settled than I felt a very different emotion start to creep in, one I chose to give voice to. "Our time of being alone together is almost over, isn't it?" I'm sure she could hear the sadness in my voice, and I could see the sadness in her eyes, too.

"This has been a special time for us, Julia. I am glad that we could enjoy it for as long as we have." Then she brightened. "But come, let us not be sad. Let us enjoy our company tonight."

"When will they be here?"

"They are on their way here now. And I have asked Yolana to join us, too. Can I help you with your covering?"

I had no sooner tied the rope around my waist than I looked up and saw a small group in the distance, making their way to us.

"Come, Julia. Let us meet them and help them carry the

feast they have brought us."

As we approached the group, I recognized Yolana right away. Walking next to her was a man who bore a striking resemblance to Makei. The two of them, who appeared to be quite a bit younger than the other two individuals accompanying them, were carrying most of the load. The older man and woman appeared just as animated and energetic as the two younger individuals, but the baskets they carried were much smaller and, I assumed, lighter, too.

When we met up with them, all four bowed slightly, and Ndalla returned the gesture. "Julia and I are here to help carry the load," she said, reaching for the lighter baskets that the two older individuals carried and handing them to me. Then she took almost half of the load Yolana carried and some of the load that the man carried, too. She took a moment to survey the area around us before picking a spot nearby that seemed to satisfy her.

Once we set down the loads we were carrying, Ndalla introduced me to the two older individuals first. "Julia, this is a dear friend of mine and the healer of our village," she said, indicating the woman, who appeared to be a good twenty or twenty-five years older than Ndalla. There was also a certain sternness about her that I felt right away, but she smiled easily enough when Ndalla introduced her.

"And this," she said, indicating the man, who had to be at least another ten years older than the woman, "is our village's storyteller." There was a kindness about him that I felt at once, and his smile was much more ready than the woman's.

And then, turning to face both of them, she said, "This is Julia, who has traveled from her world to ours at my invitation. She is my honored guest." Then she looked at me and smiled. "And more," she added. The two older individuals bowed slightly, and I did the same.

Then she took me over to where the younger man and

"How so?"

"Well, some of the storytellers in my world write their stories down in what we call 'books' so that individuals can pick up that book—sometimes years after the storyteller has died—and read the storyteller's words as though he were still alive." I took in the look of surprise on his face but decided to amaze him a little more before pausing long enough to allow him to speak. "Others tell their stories by having people we call 'actors' perform on stage in front of everyone in the village so that we actually 'see' the story playing out before our eyes." His eyes were getting bigger. "And still others tell their stories in song—"

"Enough, enough," he said, waving his hand. "This story-teller will need to spend more time with you, traveler, if I am ever going to begin to be able to 'see' the world you describe."

I merely shrugged.

"What little you have shared with me, traveler, tells me what I already knew: and that is just how brave our queen was to travel to your world."

I nodded. "That she was." I was only one week in, and I knew I hadn't even begun to absorb the magnitude of the differences between our worlds.

"And perhaps, too, how brave you were to travel to a world you knew nothing about." He surprised me with this one. I could be wrong, but it sounded almost like a compliment.

"Corresponding spirits," he said, so softly that I had no doubt it was a comment meant more for himself than for me.

Before I could ask him what he meant, though, he'd leaned forward and gotten to his feet. Once he did so, he turned to me as soon as I'd gotten to my feet, as well. I was just getting ready to exchange slight bows with him, but he surprised me by extending his hand toward me in a gesture I hadn't seen any of his people make. "I am glad to have met you tonight, traveler."

I reached out, and he grasped my forearm. As we stood there, locked in some sort of embrace, he said, "I am glad that our queen found her way to you and also that you agreed to return to our world with her."

He smiled then, still holding my forearm. "I am only a storyteller, but I see what I see. There is much I like in you, traveler."

I was just about to ask him if he was heading back to the village alone, when I heard the healer and Ndalla returning from where they'd gone off to talk alone.

Ndalla thanked them both for coming. "Will you two be all right on the walk back?"

"Do not worry about us," said the healer, locking her hand in the storyteller's arm, and so we said our good-nights.

"Did you have a good time tonight?" Ndalla asked me once we'd followed them as far as we could with our eyes and turned to make our way back to our bed in the corner of the clearing.

"Very much so," I said. "You?"

"Very much so," she said with a smile, and I could see just how happy she was tonight.

"Thank-you," I said suddenly.

"For what, Julia?"

"For tonight. You were right. Spending time with just a few of the people from your village has made me realize that I am ready to go ... 'downtown'," I said with a smile.

"How soon?" And I could feel the excitement in her voice.

"As soon as possible," I said. She looked about to burst with happiness. And so I offered, "How about tomorrow?"

"Are you sure, Julia?"

"Yes," I said. "I'm sure."

And like that, her mind started working. "I can send word back to the village with Yolana in the morning. That will give my people the time they need to make preparations."

hear in her voice the fact that she wasn't winded at all.

"No, I'm fine." Her eyes lingered a moment on me, even as I said this.

"We will rest up ahead just a little way," she assured me.

Sure enough, about five minutes later, we arrived at a spot that opened up a view of the valley below. "Come, sit," she said, taking a seat on a flat rock that radiated the sun's warmth.

"Is that your village?"

"It is," she said, exuding pride.

I saw below me many small structures, what I would call "huts," spread out quite a bit from one another but loosely lined up along what seemed to serve as a kind of Main Street, as well as a handful of larger structures sprinkled throughout the village.

"The people down there seem very busy."

"They are preparing for our arrival, Julia."

She looked up at the sky then, and only after she spoke again did I realize that she was doing it the way I would've looked up at a clock on the wall. "The Ceremony of Welcome will occur in about one of your hours. We still have plenty of time to make it to the Meeting Place." Then, getting to her feet, she said, "Come. I want to show you something."

We started walking in the opposite direction of where the village lay below us, neither further up into the hills we'd been making our way up into, nor down toward the village, simply back away from the edge of the hillside.

In no time at all, we were standing at the mouths of what appeared to be a series of caves, either carved into the side of the hill or appearing there naturally; I couldn't tell. I hadn't noticed them from where we sat just a moment earlier.

"These caves are where the people of my village hid when our warriors went off to battle ... a very long time ago, Julia. When you sit with the storyteller, you can ask him to tell you of those times." And I thought I heard some sadness in her voice, or maybe it was just solemnity.

I couldn't think of a thing to say.

"It is all right, Julia," she said, reading whatever expression it was that she saw on my face. "My people have not been in a battle in several of what your people call 'generations.'"

"Even so," I said, trying to absorb the sobering thought of her warriors going to battle.

"It is all right that I have shown you this?" she asked, apparently taken aback by my reaction.

"Yes," I said. "I want to learn all that I can of your world." And I meant that. It simply hadn't occurred to me that battles would be a part of it.

She appeared reassured by my words, and I found myself grateful that she didn't have the power to read my thoughts this morning.

We took our time walking down out of the hills to the Meeting Place. Even so, we got there before the people assembled. It was a large, open field that the village itself spilled into. We arrived at what in my world I would've thought of as the "front" or the "stage" area, which consisted of a wide ledge that ran the width of the field so that anyone standing in the open space could see whoever stood up on that ledge, which was also accessible from below.

"Come, Julia. Let us sit here," Ndalla said, taking a seat on the ledge and letting her feet dangle over the edge. "My people will be along soon enough." I looked over the edge to gauge how high up we were. I estimated it to be about ten feet. "Are you afraid of heights, Julia?" she asked with some concern.

"No more than I am of cold water," I said with a smile. And I took a seat next to her.

Slowly, as the sun reached its zenith above us, the people from the village started to make their way into the open field, as though a bell had been rung, letting them know it was time.

CHAPTER 8

Freeing a Young Girl's Spirit

I awoke, fully expecting to have to nurse one hell of a hangover. But I was pleasantly surprised to find that when I sat up, I felt no ill effects whatsoever of the night before. In fact, I felt just fine.

I rose and looked all around the small dwelling, but it was clear that Ndalla had not returned. I went outside to search for her and was surprised to find her lying on the ground, just outside the entrance to the hut.

There must have been either a light rain or a heavy dew, as her body felt cold and damp to the touch.

"Ndalla?"

She awoke, either to the sound of my frightened voice or to my violent shaking of her. Or both. I'm not sure which.

But when she opened her eyes and looked at me, she seemed far away still. "Are you all right? Why are you sleeping outside? You are cold and wet," I scolded her as though she were a child. "I must get you inside, where I can get you dry

117

and warm."

"Julia?"

She seemed to be struggling to know her surroundings still.

"You've probably caught a cold, given yourself a fever," I continued, doing my best to maintain my "I'm-disappointed-in-you" tone of voice.

"Julia. Wait—" And she put her hand on my arm as if to force me to be still. "You do not understand. Please. Go inside. Or be silent."

"I—"

"Julia," she said sternly. "Be silent."

It was only then that I noticed a silent procession moving toward us.

Ndalla got to her feet as the procession neared. And when it arrived right in front of the dwelling, she walked out to meet it. At the forefront of the procession was the dead body of a child being carried on a litter, I assume by members of her mourning family.

Ndalla bent over and gently lifted the child's lifeless body, and the litter was folded up. Ndalla then joined the procession, the child in her arms. I watched as the procession went on in the direction it had first been headed.

I was debating whether or not to follow when Yolana came up beside me and made her presence known. "My queen asked me last night to be by your side when you awoke. I am sorry I was not here when I should have been."

"What?"

"Please. Come inside. I will explain to you what has happened and what will happen next. My queen wanted you to know. And she knew that she would not be able to be here to explain such things in person."

"What?" I couldn't seem to get my feet to move.

"Come inside. I will stay with you and answer your

Yolana went to her and helped her regain herself so that the family could be brought back in as soon after the moment of passing as possible.

The queen stayed long enough to offer what comfort she could to the family. And then Yolana helped the queen make her way back to her own dwelling so that the family could have some time alone. As was her custom, whenever she had to take the life of one of her own people, she slept outside that first night so that the spirit of the deceased could easily find her if needed.

It was just before the queen fell asleep outside for a very brief time, apparently waiting for the procession to pass, that Ndalla had asked Yolana to stay with me, to keep me inside when the procession passed, and to stay with me until she could return home again.

"I am sorry," she said again. "I stepped outside, only for a moment, to relieve myself. That's when you must have awakened and found yourself alone."

"Do not apologize," I said, trying to soften my tone. "You have done your job well. I will tell the queen as much when I see her again." Yolana was clearly relieved.

"When will I see her again?"

"Not until tomorrow."

"It would not be proper for me to join her tonight?"

"No!" Yolana said, and I could hear the alarm in her voice.

"What has been happening today then?"

"Today, the queen is helping the family honor the death of the body, and tonight, the passing of the spirit. She will stay with the family until daybreak. Sometime after that, she will return here."

"She will be exhausted," I commented, almost more to myself than to Yolana.

"She is queen," Yolana said firmly, as though I had insulted the queen by suggesting that she was human, and then I thought to myself that perhaps, in Yolana's eyes, I had done just that.

"I'm sorry. I meant no offense."

Yolana seemed confused by my apology and began to clear away the remains of my supper. "Will you need anything else this evening?"

"No, Yolana."

And with that, she started to leave.

"And thank-you, Yolana, for sharing with me all that you did. I know it was not easy."

Yolana smiled slightly. Then she paused a moment before saying, "You will let the queen rest when she arrives?"

I wasn't sure just how to answer.

"You are right. She will not have slept for two risings of the sun. She will need her rest." I assured her that I would let the queen rest.

And with that, Yolana left, and I tried to sleep, my mind filled with the mysteries that Yolana had just shared with me.

The next morning, I awoke alone, but as I came to my senses, I became aware of a commotion just outside.

I got up and went to the door and watched as Ndalla made her way through her people toward the small hut where I waited for her. No wild cheering this morning. Only what seemed to me a sincere and warm welcome for one who played such an important role in their lives.

As she came closer, I could see the tiredness in her body as she moved, and when she came closer still, I saw in her face an exhaustion I'd not seen before.

Still, she attempted a brave smile for me. Then she turned to her people one more time before we went inside.

Once inside, she collapsed, and I carried her over to the bed.

"Yolana!" But I needn't have called. She was already at the

away the remains, Ndalla took the opportunity to speak to us both.

"I must attend to something. It will take me some time." Before either of us could speak, she added, "Yolana, you will stay with Julia until I can return."

Then she turned to me. "You can stay here in the village for a few days, if you want. But before one of your weeks passes, Julia," she said, "have Yolana take you to the clearing where we—" But she knew she did not have to finish the sentence. "I will meet you there as soon as I am able," she said and then paused a moment before adding, "There is something I must attend to now. But then there will be time ... for us. I promise." These last words she spoke softly.

Then she turned again to Yolana. "I am leaving Julia in your hands, Yolana. You will take her where she wants to go and tell her what she wants to know about our people."

Then she turned to me. "I must go now." And with that, she was gone.

CHAPTER 9

Dealing with a Betrayal

Over the next several days, Yolana took me around the village and introduced me to the people of Ndalla, all of whom seemed to take special care to introduce me to the young and the old, more so than to the people who, like myself, were somewhere in between the two extremes of life.

One afternoon, I asked Yolana to help me find the storyteller. He was surrounded by a group of children to whom he was telling one story after another. I joined the group and listened with great interest. I have no idea how long I sat there. After a while, he looked my way and told the children that it was time for them to get up and move around; he said he needed a rest.

"Traveler," he said when he saw me getting up to leave, too. "Do not leave. I asked the children to go play so that you and I might talk."

I went over and sat down next to him. "How do you remember all these stories?"

I tried to recall how I'd managed to still my mind before, the one and only time I'd been able to, but then I knew that Ndalla had been there that time and had probably helped me in some way I wasn't even aware of at the time.

Nevertheless, I determined to try. The healer had referred to this as a "practice," and so I thought I should not expect total success right away. Time to begin to try, though. And so I did.

With little success, however. In fact, I had no success that night, or the next day, or that evening. But on the third day, I experienced something that I chose at the time to believe was a sign of some improvement. I'd been sitting still for some time; I had no idea how long, when I began to experience a certain sensation of "clearing" in my mind's eye.

As I'd done prior to the one vision I'd shared with Ndalla, I became aware of the sensation of the mind "clearing" itself, and I kept urging myself to just be still, trying to keep doing whatever it was that was working, even though a part of me was well aware that I didn't have a clue what it was that I was doing ... or not doing.

And I became aware of my mind continuing to clear itself, and the time of absolute stillness and silence, within and without, lengthening. And then I became aware of a source of light that I felt compelled to move toward. But as in the vision before, the further I moved toward it, the further away from me it seemed to move. And so the only logical thing to do seemed to be to stop and wait.

And as I waited, it seemed to me that the light began to approach me. It grew in size and intensity until I had to raise my hand to shield my eyes from its brightness. Just when I thought I would have to flee, so bright was it becoming, the light seemed to break upon me, and millions of little specks of light fell all around me. And as I opened my eyes to take in the splendid scene all around me, I beheld Ndalla.

She stood before me now, neither victorious as she'd been in the one vision, nor weak as she'd been in the other. I stepped closer to her to make out the expression on her face, for I could not see it clearly.

And in my straining to see her more clearly, I opened my eyes, and the vision faded.

That night, I did not try again. I'd had enough practice to satisfy me for a while. It was just as I was settling down to sleep that night that I heard Yolana call out.

I sat up and could see that she'd met up with Ndalla, who was making her way toward me. As I got up to greet Ndalla, I heard her say to Yolana, "Go to the village and get the healer and bring her and the families of the warriors to where I have left the warriors themselves at the edge of the clearing. They will need ministering to. Julia will be here with me. Go now."

Yolana waited until I had reached Ndalla before hurrying off.

It was only when I reached Ndalla that I realized why Yolana had waited. Ndalla could barely stand under her own power. And in the moonlight, I could see all too well why.

"You're injured," I heard myself say stupidly, as though she needed to be told.

"It is not fatal," she said, attempting a wry smile.

All the same, I could feel myself wince as I took in the severity of her wounds.

"It is not deep," she said in response to my eyes, focused unmoving, on a gash that crossed her mid-section. "None of the wounds are serious, Julia." And then she added, either to convince me or to amuse me, I couldn't be sure, "Trust me, Julia, I would know."

When I tried to lead her to the bed at the edge of the clearing, she stopped me.

her sleep. And I spent most of that night hearing over and over in my head the stories that both Bakka and Yolana had shared with me about a queen who took the lives of her own people, a queen so obviously loved by her own people, a queen who so obviously cared about her people.

I thought that night about what I'd heard as a child back in my old world: "No greater love hath a man than this: that he lay down his life for another." What kind of love, I wondered, did it take to do what she had done? Was it love? I knew she loved her people. Yet she could find it in her heart to kill them when killing seemed the only course of action available to her.

My thoughts wandered far that night. At one point, I realized that it might help me if I could try again to "connect" with those Forces of Life, greater than myself, to see if I could see all of this happening around me more clearly.

As I had done previously, I settled myself and began the process of trying to clear my mind. I let the images that filled my mind—of Ndalla herself as she lay there before me, of Bakka telling me his story, of the scenes of the betrayers' encampment that his story brought to mind, of Yolana telling me her story, of the scene of the little girl dying that her story brought to mind—flow through my mind. One by one, I let the images come into my mind, unbidden, and then, just as easily, I let them go. I felt the now-slightly-familiar sensation of "letting go" that, as I was coming to learn, was a crucial part of this practice. It was a sensation that, in itself, relied upon and demonstrated a trust in those Forces greater than oneself.

I kept letting go, long after I thought I had anything to let go of. Emptier and emptier became the scene before my mind's eye until there was nothing before me. Only darkness and complete stillness and silence.

And then I heard and saw something move. It was too quick, too stealthy, though. I could not make it out. I sat as still as I could, unmoving, not making a sound.

And then I saw it again. And again, I waited.

When I saw it again, I followed its movement even though I still could not make out what it was.

I was ready when it moved again. My eyes were upon it, and I could make it out. It was a wolf, intent on its prey.

Still I sat, watching, waiting. And then I saw that the wolf was not alone. It was part of a pack of wolves, all hunting together, all intent on the same prey.

I watched in fascination. I had never in my life been so close to real wildlife. I could see the moisture on the fur of their coats, and I could see the intensity in their eyes. I could actually make out the smell of their wild bodies and feel the heat coming off their bodies as well. It was as though I were among them, almost as though I were one of them.

And then, when next they ran, I could feel myself, running, faster than I've ever run. Not recklessly. Everything I did felt within my tremendous control. And yet there was something else that moved within me, too.

When the pack waited, I waited. When it was time for the pack to move, I knew it, and I felt my body move without my having to tell it to.

I felt myself a part of the pack as I had never felt myself a part of anything.

I continued on with the hunt. Not once did I feel myself tire or hesitate. There was a sureness about everything I did.

And when at last we brought the prey down, I too joined in the killing. And when it was over, I too partook of the bloody, raw meat.

And then, before I had a chance to think, I opened my eyes, and the vision was gone.

I had no way of knowing how long the vision had lasted. The fire, it seemed, had burned itself down a ways, but for all I knew, Yolana had kept it fed throughout the night.

again the "rightness" that I registered as I had moved, unthinkingly, as a part of the pack, knowing somewhere deep in my very bones that I was a small piece of something much larger than myself. And I knew I would not like to be asked to put such feelings into words.

"I understand."

She looked at me a moment then before saying, "Yes. I believe you do."

And with that, we resumed our walk.

After we'd walked a while longer in another easy silence, she asked, "Can you share with me how it is that you came to have a vision last night? Or would you rather not speak of it?"

"I've been practicing," I said simply.

She turned to me then, her face beaming. "This is good," she said, her voice conveying more than her words could how she felt.

And then, almost with a new burst of energy, she said, "Come. Let us go see my warriors and their families today."

Together, we visited with each family. And with each family, Ndalla took the time to make it clear how bravely the warriors had fought and how difficult had been their task, fighting against members of their own village. Such action, it was clear, was not taken without great consideration.

And I noticed, too, that at the end of each visit, she took each warrior aside and spoke with him privately, very briefly.

It was only after we'd made the rounds of every group in the camp that she turned to me and asked me to help her back to the clearing. And only then did I notice just how tired she had gotten in the course of the afternoon.

"I must rest before nightfall," she said softly.

I could see how exhausted she was, and a part of me wanted to lift her up and carry her back to the clearing. But I knew that she would not have such a thing, so I paced myself, going slowly enough that she could keep up but not so slowly that she would notice.

Once back at the clearing, she took something to drink and closed her eyes, asking Yolana to wake her if she did not awake on her own at sunset. But she needn't have worried about not waking up. Her body seemed to have an internal alarm clock. She awoke just before the sun touched the horizon. Yolana brought food, and the three of us ate before Ndalla made it clear that she would meet with her warriors, who had apparently already assembled elsewhere.

"Stay here," she said to us both. "I will not be too long," she promised. And with that, she was gone again.

It was quite late that night when Ndalla finally returned to the clearing. She excused Yolana, and Ndalla and I settled down for the evening. I knew I was tired, which meant that she had to be exhausted.

But rather than settle down to sleep, Ndalla sat down opposite me, clearly prepared to talk.

"What is it?" I asked.

"I would like to prepare you for what will happen tomorrow," she said.

The next day, at mid-day, as she'd said we would, we made our way back to the same place where the Ceremony of Welcome had occurred. By the time we arrived, the people were already assembled.

As she had on the day of the Ceremony of Welcome, Ndalla stood before her people. Only this time, the mood was solemn. Word had already spread about what had taken place.

She addressed the crowd calmly, assuring them that the immediate threat had been taken care of. "But," she said, "this is not the end of this matter. The Daeika, it is clear now, have been preparing themselves for war against the Ndalla. I do not know for how long. But I believe the battle will happen soon."

way to live her life, and so she knew what she must prepare herself to do.

"And so, she prepared to leave on her journey, not knowing if she would ever return to see her world again."

He seemed to end his tale as he sat there looking at me.

"But what wisdom did she gain by making her journey?" I wondered aloud. "What did she bring back with her that she did not already have before?

The old man laughed out loud.

"It is the obvious that so often escapes us, is it not?"

Then he looked at me and saw that I still did not understand.

"Why, she brought back you!"

"Me? I'm certainly no source of wisdom, I assure you. And as for this business of war, I know nothing of war. I can be of no help at all to the queen."

His voice became quite solemn then.

"None of us can know what help we can be to another, traveler. Just as we cannot know what harm we can inflict on another, sometimes without even intending any harm at all. That is one of the Great Mysteries of Life. The queen knows this and respects it. You would do well to know it, too, traveler."

The solemnity in his voice, as much as the content of his words, disarmed me.

I excused myself from the storyteller's presence shortly after that. I needed to be alone to consider his words as I became aware of a certain heaviness sinking into my heart that I had not been aware of before.

That night I considered trying to consult with the Forces again as I was sure Ndalla would not return before morning, but I felt almost afraid to.

The storyteller's words stayed with me all afternoon and evening, and by the time I crawled into bed, I was tired of trying to understand things that felt so far beyond any level of understanding I might achieve. Instead, I pulled the covers up around my shoulders, determined to get a good night's rest before Ndalla returned in the morning.

But I could not sleep, no matter what I tried. I tossed and turned for what felt like hours. And for the first time since coming to Ndalla's world, I found myself actually wishing for a television set, if only to numb my mind long enough to let me fall asleep, unthinking. I was just about to get up in total frustration and head outside for a walk when I looked up and saw Ndalla stepping into our dwelling.

"I did not expect you so soon," I said, grateful and relieved to see her standing there.

But she misread my tone. "I am sorry," she said, turning as if ready to leave again. "You wanted to be alone?"

"No!" I nearly shouted at her.

She seemed confused. And I realized that she was probably registering my own state of confusion.

"No," I said, as calmly as I could. "I do not want you to leave. That is the last thing I want," I added, more to myself than to her.

"Are you all right? You seem—" But she seemed unable to finish the sentence. "What is it, Julia?"

I read the concern in her face, and somehow knowing that she was concerned triggered an even deeper level of concern and sadness within me. It was as if a wall broke somewhere inside of me, and a river of tears started flowing from some place I didn't even know existed. And I could not stop the flood once it began. Nor could I have told her what I was crying about or for, had she asked. But she did not ask. She only took me in her arms and held me until the waves of sadness finally subsided of their own accord. And the whole time, she rocked me in her arms as though I were just a child.

"It is all right," I heard her say at last, over and over again.

CHAPTER 11

Preparing for Battle

The next morning, I awoke to a series of gentle caresses, followed by other actions on Ndalla's part that transported me to another world, where the tears of the night before became a distant memory to be forgotten. She did not ask me about my tears, and I was glad to let go of the memory of them.

Yolana brought us breakfast once Ndalla had called to her to let her know that we were ready. And once again, Ndalla asked Yolana to stay and eat with us.

"I wish to share with you both what happened at the war council last night."

Ndalla shared with us that the council had decided to take the war to the Daeika.

"We have warriors watching their people now to see if they have already decided to move against us. But we have heard of no movement. And so, we will prepare ourselves to bring war upon them."

"Are you sure—" I got that far with my question, and then

I decided to stop.

"This is what my people have decided, Julia," she said simply, firmly.

And then she added, more softly, "Our preparations will include much more consultation with the Forces. Before we take such a terrible step, we will be sure that this is what we are being called upon to do."

But I could tell by the way that she spoke the last sentence that she already knew that the "time of testing" that her visions had spoken of had begun and that the war that loomed ahead of us was an important part of that test.

Then she shared with the two of us more of what would happen over the next two weeks. And I learned that there is much to do when a peaceful people prepare for war.

She explained that the young, the elders, and most of the women, all those not involved in the battle itself, would need to be kept safe. And she made it clear that she was relying on the two of us to play a major role in that part of the preparations. "When the time comes," she said, "you two will stay with those we leave behind."

I could see the unspoken protest in Yolana's eyes and could feel it in my own heart. Neither of us liked the idea of her heading off without one or the other of us there to care for her.

As if in answer to what she knew we were both not speaking, she added these words: "You both know that it is the wisdom held by the old and the young that we, who are in mid-life, fight to protect. To keep these individuals safe, I must rely on those I trust."

Yolana was clearly satisfied, and even I had to grudgingly admit that I too was swayed. Besides, I knew that I could be of no use to her in battle.

***

fallen to us to engage in this battle." She paused a moment. "Some would say this battle has been coming for a long time." A low murmur rose up from the people.

"The timing of this battle," she went on to say, "portends a time of profound change, coming as it does when the length of the day and the length of the night take up the sky evenly."

And I realized with a jolt that she was referring to the equinox, which made sense. She'd arrived in my world three months ago, just as the summer solstice approached there, but here in her world, it was the winter solstice that had been approaching when she traveled to my world.

When she spoke again, her tone had changed slightly. "We cannot know what kind of change is in store for us. Even so, we engage in this battle willingly. And as with all that we do, we embrace our role in the events that make up the Great Unfolding of Time and ask only the wisdom to see clearly as far as we need to see to be able do what we do with honor and in the spirit of both humility and pride that befits the Ndalla."

Then she concluded with the words, "Let us each consider carefully tonight our place in the Great Scheme of Life and ask for the strength to do well that which it is our place to do."

That night we went again to the clearing where we had passed so many joyful days and nights, this time to pass what we both well knew could be our last night together. I feared for her life and wasted no time telling her that.

"I too fear that this, my first battle, might just be the last I fight in this life."

It was not exactly the comforting response that I was looking for, but it left no doubt that this would be a night of honesty between us.

"Surely you have led your warriors into fights before this." And I thought of the last fight she'd been in, with those who had betrayed her own people.

"Fights, yes, but never a battle of this size." And she paused a moment before saying, "The Daeika are a noble people. I know that. They and we, the Ndalla, were once one."

"The storyteller told me this, but he would not say what happened, so many years ago, to pull you apart. Do you know?"

She shook her head. "Not really."

"The storyteller told me that different people believe different stories," I said.

She put her head down, apparently uncertain whether to share with me what she was thinking.

I gently tilted her head up so that I could look her in the eye. "Please tell me."

"Some say it was a matter of love, a very powerful love that two men had for the same woman, and so they fought. When the one man had killed the other, the friends of the dead man attacked the man who had won the fight, and his friends then came to defend him. It was a fight no one saw coming, the size of which had never been seen before. When it was over, the man who had won the original fight took the woman, along with those who wanted to come with him, to start a new village, our village. We called ourselves the Ndalla, to signify our triumph and also our intention to live our lives in peace, with joy and celebration. And so we have ... until now."

And then I heard her say, so softly I almost couldn't hear her, "It will be a fight unlike any that my warriors or I have known." I took her in my arms and felt her tremble. Then she pulled back, moving away from me slightly as she did so, and her hand went to her forehead.

"What is it?" I asked.

"I cannot see things related to this battle as clearly as I would like, Julia." Then she removed her hand from her forehead, and her eyes held mine for a moment before she

CHAPTER 12

Recovering the Queen's Body

The three of us stumbled with practically every step as we made our way as quickly as we could over the rough terrain that surrounded the caves, trying to keep up with the sure-footed warrior. I ran faster and farther—and with more fear in my heart—than I thought my body ever could. And despite her advanced years, the healer did the same, as did Yolana.

As for Bakka, he did not seem to hold back on account of the three women who followed him. He paused only a handful of times, just long enough to make sure that we could keep pace with him before taking off again at what seemed like his normal speed. He seemed in as much of a genuine hurry to get to his queen as I knew the three of us were.

As we neared the village, Bakka broke off in a direction that I was all too familiar with, and I knew we were headed for Ndalla's beloved clearing.

The healer called to him as she broke pace. "I must get some things from the village. Yolana, come with me." And the two women headed off in the direction of the village. I didn't stop to wait for her explanation. I just kept running toward the clearing.

Just as I got there, Bakka managed to position himself between me and what appeared to be Ndalla's lifeless body. I felt my body running toward where she lay on the ground.

"No!" I heard a voice wailing before realizing that it was my own voice that I heard.

Bakka managed to block my way, just before I would've fallen on the ground beside her.

"Step back," he said firmly, his strong hands on my shoulders.

"The queen lives," he said quietly. And then, taking another couple steps away from where Ndalla lay, still not moving, he said, "But much of the Life Energy has left her body. You must calm yourself, or you will frighten away what little energy remains in her."

I nodded, unable to speak.

He let me pass only when he was satisfied that I had gained control of myself.

I dropped to my knees beside where she lay. I remember taking in the fact that her hair had been shorn and at the same time wondering why that mattered. I wanted to touch her, to somehow let her know that I was there. But I could not find even a square inch of her that was not covered with blood or discolored from bruising or raised with swelling.

Then it occurred to me that Bakka had either lied to me on purpose or else been mistaken.

I saw no sign of life.

And with that recognition, I felt an anger rising inside of me.

... At Bakka for lying to me.

... At the Daeika, whom I had never even known, for doing this to the woman I loved.

Once the open wounds had been tended to, the healer turned her attention to the bruises and the many places of swelling that covered the queen's body. The healer carefully positioned warm, moist pouches with God-knows-what inside of them that she carefully prepared, one at a time, dipping them in water from the river that had been just slightly warmed over the fire.

"These will provide some relief," she said, speaking out loud for only the second time since I had returned from the riverbank.

At one point, she paused in her ministrations and handed me something that looked like a tea-bag, a small pouch filled with something, tied up with a string.

"Put this inside her mouth so that she can get some nourishment. But hold onto the string so that she does not choke on it."

I did as she said.

"For how long?" I asked, holding onto the string as she had said to.

"Until I say so," said the old woman, not mincing words or worrying about tone.

I watched as the healer continued to pack her mysterious poultices around what seemed Ndalla's entire body, and then when she had done what she could, the healer covered Ndalla with a light blanket.

"To guard against the night cold," she said, apparently to no one in particular.

Then she turned to me. "Remove the pouch from her mouth, and try once again to offer her some water, as you did before."

I did as I was told and was encouraged to see Ndalla respond more quickly to the feel of water on her lips.

"Carefully, soothe her forehead and cheeks with this cloth dipped in the water from the river," the healer said. "It will feel refreshing to her now and provide a sense of assurance to her that you are here."

The healer was right. Ndalla did respond to the feel of the cool water on her face.

"You may stroke her ... carefully," the healer said to me. "And offer her water to drink, as you have been, as often as you can. We will leave you with her, alone now, for a time. We will not be far."

I did not sleep at all that night. I talked to Ndalla all night, telling her over and over again that she was safe now and offering her water as often as it seemed she would take it.

And I stroked her short-cropped hair and gently touched those parts of her face that I thought I could touch without adding to her pain.

She seemed to rest through the night, comfortably I thought, and for that I was grateful. Her only movements all night were in response to the feel of water on her lips or the cool cloth on her face. When I spoke, she lay there unmoving, but her breathing seemed to grow steady as the night went on.

By morning, I began to register my own exhaustion, both physical and emotional.

The healer returned with Yolana at her side and said simply, "You have done well, traveler. But you must rest now, to be able to help her again later. Yolana and I will be with her."

I was too tired to protest, and we both knew it.

It was probably mid-day when I awoke from my few hours' sleep and looked over to where Ndalla lay. I had not wanted to be far from her as I slept.

I was surprised to see Yolana supporting Ndalla's head as the healer held a cup and was urging her to try to drink. I hurried over to see if I could help.

CHAPTER 13

The Queen's Physical Recovery

When I awoke the next morning, I found that I was the last of the group to rise. Even Ndalla had apparently awakened before me. I looked over from where I lay to see that Yolana and the healer had propped up her head to make it easier for her to drink out of a cup that Yolana was offering her. But even from where I lay, I could see that she was not interested in whatever she was being offered.

I got up quickly to go over to join the three of them, to see if I could help, only to find myself forced to sit back down again to regain my balance. My head pounded; at the time, I had no idea why, but neither had I the patience to even think about it.

I got up again and made my way carefully across the few yards that separated us, holding my head as I walked.

"Ah, traveler, come and sit," said the healer as she jumped up to give me a hand. "And see for yourself how much better the queen looks this morning."

But I couldn't see anything at first as I waited for the blood to return to my head.

And then I registered Ndalla's voice, a little raw but beautiful to my ears, and I knew for certain that she had come back to us. "Julia," I heard her say. "Come." And I could just make out that she was raising her bruised left arm to invite me to take my place beside her. "Lie down next to me a moment and regain yourself."

Gladly, I thought to myself. But I hesitated to lay my head on her shoulder as she seemed to be indicating she wanted me to, for fear that I would cause her pain. "I am not that fragile, my friend," she said softly, as if she could read my concern and intended her words for my comfort and for my ears only.

Although I could still see nothing clearly, I heard the smile in her voice, and I registered a comforting sense of relief.

After just a moment beside her, the blood returned to my head, and I sat up to take in the sight of her. The swelling that had been so apparent the day before seemed to have gone down, but the bruises and cuts still covered her body. And I could see that her right arm, which looked lifeless, was propped up on some blankets beside her. But her eyes were clear as they met mine.

"Julia," she said when she could see that my head had cleared. And that was all she said. It was all she had to say, for the fact that she was sitting up, even just a little, with her eyes open and clear, smiling that beautiful smile of hers, was enough.

It was the healer who spoke, doing her best to sound stern despite her obvious relief at the sight of her patient so miraculously transformed this morning from how she had looked when we first saw her, just a day and a half earlier.

"Here, traveler," she said, handing me the cup that Yolana had been trying to get Ndalla to try to drink out of. "Perhaps you will have more success than we have had with our queen this morning. She should drink this now—and more as the sun ery," said the healer, smiling.

But Ndalla, as if in answer to her friend, paused, and I saw her hand move up to her head a moment before she spoke, and I thought I heard a note of concern in her voice as she said, "But I cannot seem to recall much of what happened after the battle began."

Then it seemed to me that the healer's attitude changed subtly, in a way I couldn't quite put my finger on. "Don't worry about recalling anything from the battle right now," I heard the healer say. "You must stay focused on matters at hand. Your lack of recall is only temporary, so that you can keep your energies focused on matters of healing. It is as it should be."

Ndalla seemed hesitant to let the matter go for a moment, and then Yolana arrived with supper, and the matter was dropped.

Ndalla made it clear that she wanted both the healer and Yolana to join us for the meal. And so the four of us shared a meal together that night, the three of us very much encouraged by Ndalla's ability to get down at least a little solid food. She still could not eat much. But the fact that she was sitting up with less apparent pain, that she was alert and in good spirits, and that she was able to eat and drink anything at all in so short a time after having been returned to us in the shape she was in, relieved us all.

That night, after Yolana and the healer left, Ndalla asked me to help her up to relieve herself. She was still weak, but it clearly did her good to feel her legs under her again as she walked the few steps required. And then, as I settled her back down to rest, she asked me to lie down beside her.

Ndalla had been clear-headed enough to ask the healer, before dismissing her earlier, to bind her right arm to her side so that the weight of it, which in itself seemed to cause her pain, especially when she tried to sit up, let alone when she tried to stand and walk, would not further aggravate her shoulder, which seemed to have borne the brunt of whatever had happened in the battle. With her right arm bound to her, she was now able to turn onto her left side enough to give her back some relief.

I lay down beside her, and I felt her curl up beside me and take comfort in the feel of human contact once again. I slipped my own arm under her head so that I could cradle her as much as her wounds would allow. And I stroked her gently until I could feel her breathing growing more steady and slow. And when I knew she was asleep, I slipped my arm out from under her and let myself fall asleep as well, beside her.

Over the next several days, the queen surprised us all by insisting on getting up and walking about the clearing more than any of us thought she was yet ready to. But as queen, she was used to getting her way. And, in addition to that, it soon became apparent that the walking did her more good than any amount of simply lying about would have done.

By the third day of walking, she even made her way, with my assistance, all the way down to the river. Of course, at the pace that she was able to move and with the number of rests that she had to take along the way, it was late afternoon by the time we arrived there. She didn't seem to mind, though. She simply suggested that we make our bed there for the night, on the riverbank. And so, we did.

It wasn't until we were lying there, looking up at the night sky, that I realized how full the moon had grown in the week since Ndalla's recovery began.

Of course. She and her warriors had left just about a week after Ndalla and I had been together on the night of the last full moon; they were gone then about two weeks, and another week had passed while Ndalla recovered from her wounds.

She reached over and held my hand.

"Happy anniversary," I said. Then I felt her cuddle up against me, and we fell asleep.

something to ask you. I need your help, my friend."

"How can I help you, my queen?" The healer sounded relaxed and happy.

"By doing whatever you can to help me restore my recall of events." I thought I noticed the healer stiffen a little at these words. But Ndalla continued, not having noticed a thing. "Ever since my journey back, I cannot seem to recall the details of the battle or anything that occurred after the battle, and I feel I must find a way to recall these things."

"But—" The healer, it seemed to me, paused to choose her next words carefully, a little too carefully, I remember thinking at the time. "Surely, you realize that you lost consciousness at some point in the fighting. You cannot recall what you were not even conscious of at the time."

"I do not believe that I was unconscious for that much of the battle, though." And then, after thinking a little more, Ndalla added, "When I try to recall, it is almost as though I can recall. I start to bring back the images that I am reaching for, and then they suddenly become unavailable to me. It is like nothing I have ever experienced. I thought you could perhaps help me."

The healer's eyes fell at that point, and she seemed either unable or unwilling to speak.

"What is it, healer?" The question was spoken with concern.

But when the healer did not answer, Ndalla's voice sharpened.

"Healer, what is it?"

The woman jumped at the tone in her queen's voice.

"I can restore your memory of the events of the battle," she said, with almost no emotion whatsoever in her voice that I could discern.

The queen brightened. "This is good news! But what troubles you so, healer?"

"It is I who made your memories unavailable to you shortly after you were brought back to the clearing by your warriors."

"You?"

"Yes, my queen."

"But why?"

Again, the healer kept her silence.

"Healer, what is this? Since when do you keep things from me?"

For the first time since she had lowered her eyes, the healer raised them now to meet her queen's eyes as she said, "After I realized you had given up on life and after I then talked to one of your warriors and found out why."

It was Ndalla who now found herself without words. She looked as though she had received a physical blow. It was sometime before she was able to speak.

"I do not understand you at all tonight, healer," she said at last.

Then she surprised us all by abruptly getting to her feet.

I jumped up myself to offer her assistance, which she quickly dismissed, although not rudely. And the healer and Yolana rose to their feet, too, out of deference.

"What conditions do you require, healer, to do what you say you can do?"

"I would give you something to help you rest, and then while you sleep, I would recall your memories back to you. They would flood back in while you slept, and when you awoke, you would remember them, just as they occurred in the physical realm."

Ndalla nodded in response, wordlessly. Then, after a moment, she spoke.

"You three stay and eat, if you wish. I will walk a while."

Then, turning to me, she said, "I will head back in the direction of the clearing. When you have finished eating, Julia, no idea what the evening ahead had in store for her.

The healer instructed Bakka and myself to move a short distance away. Then, turning to the warrior, she said, "Tonight, as the queen sleeps, you must tell the traveler the story of the battle. The full story. Try to leave nothing out, especially as it concerns the queen."

Bakka seemed willing to do as he was told. But before we removed ourselves, the healer turned to me.

"Find a place far enough away that Bakka's words will not be heard by the queen but a place that will allow you to see the queen as you listen to what Bakka shares with you tonight, traveler. Know that she will be reliving the same story you are hearing told to you." She paused a moment before continuing. "Tonight will be difficult for you, traveler. You will find it hard to hear what Bakka has to tell you. And you will find it difficult to not want to wake the queen as you witness her reliving all that you are hearing about. But you must let Yolana and myself attend to the queen. I will call you if we need your help. But if I do not call you, you must be strong and let us help the queen the only way she can be helped, the way she herself has chosen to be helped tonight."

"I understand."

"Do you, traveler?" And our eyes met and held each other a moment before she spoke again. "For the queen's sake, I hope you do."

Once we were settled, Bakka wasted no time beginning his story. The journey to the land of the Daeika, he said, passed quickly enough. When they arrived outside the Daeika village, they spent several days and several nights just watching these people, to see if, in fact, a war was necessary. He said the queen wanted to find some way to avoid such a battle if she could. And so they waited until the queen had satisfied herself that there was no other way to proceed.

"She consulted with the Forces every morning as the sun came up and again in the evening as the sun went down. And as she did so, we watched their warriors preparing for battle, just as we had prepared ourselves before making our journey to their land," said Bakka.

"And we saw too that the Daeika sent their elders and their young ones somewhere to be safe while they prepared themselves for battle, just as we had."

He described for me then how, one night, the queen had led her warriors right up to the edge of the camp where the Daeika warriors slept, just outside their village.

"It would have been easy enough to kill many of them in their sleep before they knew that we were upon them. But that was not an honorable way to fight, the queen said, not the Ndalla way. And so she stood in the middle of their camp and called to the Daeika to awake.

"When they did so, they were too stunned to move. And the queen took advantage of their surprise to address them.

"She told them that the Ndalla did not want war with the Daeika. But if it was war that the Daeika wanted, the Ndalla were prepared to defend themselves and their way of life.

"She asked if there was one who would speak for their people. And one stepped forward. A very big, very angry-looking man. But the queen was not afraid.

"She asked him if the two of them could talk. She wanted to know why the Daeika were choosing to start a war with the Ndalla, who were not a threat to the Daeika people or the Daeika way of life.

"But the man laughed at her words. And then he said, 'The Ndalla need to understand that their time has come. They will be great no more. It is time now for the Daeika to triumph. Too long have we lived in the shadow of the defeat we suffered at the hands of the Ndalla, in the last great battle between our

"Without really thinking through what I was about to do," Bakka continued, "I quickly exchanged looks with some of the Ndalla warriors closest to me, and then I lunged at the Daeika warrior who held his knife to my queen's throat. I moved quickly, while the Daeika were focused on congratulating each other over their great victory.

"I drove my own knife into his neck as he had threatened to drive his knife into my queen's. Not only once, either. I stabbed him again and again.

"And as I did so, the Ndalla warriors closest to me defended the queen's body from any other Daeika warriors who tried to move on her.

"And so, the battle resumed.

"In the confusion that followed, a group of us were able to carry the queen's body safely away from the battlefield and move her to a place where we could better protect her.

"The fighting continued well into the night and did not end until sometime close to the time the sun would rise again in the sky.

"Our warriors showed the Daeika no mercy once we had our queen back among us. We did not want any of them to live. Before the last of them were killed, we found out where their young and old were hiding.

"And we went there to kill them too, taking with us the queen's body, still unmoving but still alive, so that she too could witness, if only from the spirit realm, the actions we would take to avenge the wrongs that had been done to her.

"But when we arrived and were ready to start the killing, the queen called out of wherever her spirit had gone. It was an unearthly sound that she made.

"And it was clear from that sound that we heard that she had already traveled far on her journey to the other side. We took her cry of warning to mean that she would not approve, especially as she had to travel so far back from the spirit realm to make herself heard among the living. Out of respect for her, then, we stopped what we were so ready to do.

"Instead of slaughtering them, as we intended to, we showed them what their warriors had done to our queen, and we told them that all their warriors had died in the great battle.

"And we told them that it was only the queen's mercy that saved them from our wrath, that if we'd had our way, they too would be killed in payment for what their warriors had done to our queen.

"We left them then and began our journey back here. We knew that the queen was already making her journey to the other side, and we knew too that she would rather pass over here, in her beloved clearing, than anywhere else." He looked around him as he said this. "And so, we came as quickly as we could, to arrive here before her spirit left her body altogether. We tried to keep her as comfortable as we could on the journey, but we knew too that we had to hurry. There was already so little of the Life Energy left in her body when we set out."

He paused before adding, "You know the rest, for I came to the caves to get you at the same time that the queen's body was brought here to the clearing."

I thanked Bakka for sharing his story with me. I watched him leave the clearing, and then I got up and went over to join Yolana and the healer in their vigil at the queen's side.

It was like watching someone struggle with a hideous nightmare, only it was worse, as we could not offer her any relief by simply shaking her awake.

"If this is too hard for you to witness, traveler, you can wait down by the river."

"No. I will stay here, by her side," I said to the healer.

"You can be of no help to her now," said the old woman. "This is a burden she must bear herself. But you can save your uncertain whether to continue on her way or come back. Your words to her in the spirit realm removed all uncertainty."

We had reached the riverbank by this time, and I sat down on a rock while the healer filled the containers that she had carried with her. When they were full, she came and sat down beside me before beginning the journey back to the clearing.

"I do not know what unfinished work on the part of the queen your words referred to, traveler. Nor does the queen. But with her memories restored, she will soon discover what work awaits her."

She seemed to be waiting for me to speak, but I had no words.

"You have performed a great service for the people of Ndalla by bringing our queen back to us. No one else could have done what you did, traveler."

She paused yet again, but I felt empty. In that moment, it felt as if no words would ever find their way back to me.

"Your courage and wisdom, and your great love for our queen, have earned you a special place in the hearts of the Ndalla. You must know that, traveler."

And then, perhaps seeing that I was unable to move just yet, she said, "Rest here a while. Yolana and I will be with the queen if she needs anything. And she will not awake until morning. Rest a while, if you can, so that you can be there for her when she awakes tomorrow morning. She will need you then."

The old woman then put her hand on my shoulder before speaking again.

"You have acted honorably in all of this, traveler. Know that. We have all done what was in our power to do, to help our queen in any way we could. That is as it should be. Surely, she has done the same for her people. All her life she has been willing to do the same: whatever was in her power to help her people. And by bringing her back to us, you have made it possible for her to go on doing that."

And then I heard her say, "On behalf of the queen and her people, I thank you, traveler."

I stayed at the riverbank most of that night, my mind uncomfortably full of events I knew I could not understand and questions I knew I could not find answers to.

Finally, even though I knew I wouldn't sleep, I lay down by the river and let myself rest as long as I could. It was hours later before I rejoined Yolana and the healer at Ndalla's side. I could tell it was still a few hours until sunrise.

"The queen's sleep is fitful," said the healer, bringing me back to myself. "But even so, she will not wake up for a while yet. It will be sometime after the sun rises, I am sure. Try to rest here beside her for a while, traveler. I will wake you before she awakes fully. I promise."

And so I lay down and let myself fall asleep at last, my mind still full of such thoughts as had filled it earlier, but my body too tired now to give me access to any of those thoughts.

words surprised me completely.

It was all that she said, all that she seemed to want to say. She was not yet ready to engage in conversation, I knew that. And so I smiled and gave her hand a slight squeeze by way of response and was encouraged to feel her return the squeeze ... although it would be sometime before I would see that smile of hers again. I knew that, and I knew I could wait. I would give her all the time she needed to find her way back again after what she had been through. All I wanted was to be there to help in some small way if I could.

We made our way down to the riverbank, and it was much later in the afternoon then, after Ndalla came out of the water and stretched herself out on the blanket I'd spread out for us, that she even let herself fall into a light doze there on the riverbank.

Only then did I spot Yolana at some distance away, trying to get my attention but not the queen's. I got up as carefully as I could and went over to the woman, only to discover that she'd brought us an evening meal to enjoy by the river.

"The healer," she said, "is happy that the queen allowed you to stay with her. Does she need anything?"

"No. Only time," I said. "More time alone, I think." And then, more to myself than to Yolana, I continued. "Even though I am with her, she is still far away from here and just needs time to find her way back, I think." Then, looking at Yolana, I said, "I will let you know when she is ready to share a meal, the four of us, like old times. Until then—"

"I will make sure there is enough food and water back at the clearing," said Yolana. "But I will not come again."

"Thank you, Yolana."

And she quickly disappeared.

When I returned to where Ndalla lay, she appeared to be still sleeping. So I quietly spread out the food Yolana had brought and prepared myself to wait until she awoke. I hadn't waited even a minute when I heard Ndalla's voice.

"She is not afraid to come to me, is she?" I looked over to find that her eyes were still closed. Only when she felt my eyes on her did she open her eyes.

"No," I said. "It's just that she didn't want to disturb your rest." And then, unsure of what she might really have been asking me, I offered, "I can call her back if you want."

"No. Please don't," she said. "I just did not want to think she was afraid of me," she said, sitting up.

"No," I assured her again.

I smiled, and I saw her attempt a weak smile in return before she turned away.

"Will you eat a little something now?" She seemed to be considering her answer. "For Yolana's sake?" I ventured. "After all, she took the trouble to bring this good food all this way just so that you might eat something. You have not eaten anything since mid-day yesterday."

"For Yolana's sake, you say?" I thought I heard the hint of a smile in her voice.

"And for mine. After all, I, for one, am starved. I have not eaten all day. But even so, I cannot eat now if you will not."

And still she seemed to be considering her answer.

"All right," she said at last. "Let us eat."

She tried, but again her stomach, going so long without food, had shrunk on her again, and she could not eat much before she felt the need to stop and rest a bit. Her thoughts seemed to keep taking her far away from where we sat. And I found myself feeling very alone throughout that brief meal.

When at last it was clear that she would eat no more, I started to clean up.

Her voice, coming out of the long silence, surprised me. "Have you had enough to eat, Julia?" And she put her hand on my arm, as she spoke, as if to stop me from cleaning things up before the meal was really over.

if I was helping or hurting.

"But ... what if ... I cannot recover?"

It was clear that just to voice the question had been nearly impossible for her.

"You can," I said. "I know you can."

"How do you know?"

"Because I know you," I said. "I know your strength. And I know that what drives you is your love of your people. And I know that unless you find the strength to recover from this, you will never be in a position to help your people recover from what they have experienced."

"But my people know what happened."

I couldn't tell if she was making a statement or asking me a question.

"Yes, they know. And that is why they need your strength now, to help them find a way through their own confusion about what has happened."

"But if they know what happened, then they cannot—"

"There is nothing that will ever cause them to lose faith in their queen, save the queen's losing faith in herself."

"But—"

"No but. The Daeika did not take anything away from the people of Ndalla. Not yet."

She raised her head then and looked right at me.

"Unless," I continued, "they succeeded in breaking the queen's spirit. Then, and only then, will they have achieved any kind of victory over the Ndalla. For in doing so, they will have robbed the Ndalla of their beloved queen."

I saw her eyes fall as she considered this, and I felt her wavering.

"Do not give them that victory, my love. They do not deserve it."

It seemed to me that a part of her just wanted to fall into my arms and sob.

But another part of her seemed to be just beginning to feel the edge of an understandable sense of anger that I thought might still be frightening to her. And I wanted to help her reach that anger if I could, so that she could use it to fight her way back to me and to her people. But I also feared that such anger would have the power to pull her apart, so vulnerable did she seem to me at that moment.

"Remember what they did to you."

Her eyes flashed at me, and I feared for a moment that I would only succeed in making her angry at myself.

"What do you feel?" I asked.

She turned away from me, her chest starting to heave in anger. It was so clear what she felt, but it was clear too that she didn't know what to do with such strong, negative feelings.

"Look at me. What do you feel?"

But she only turned farther away from me, withdrawing from me, as I'd feared she would if I mishandled the moment.

"Ndalla," and I reached for her.

But she pushed me away.

"What do you feel?"

She started to get to her feet, and I feared I'd lost her.

"Ndalla, do not run away. Turn and face me. Tell me what you feel."

As she almost managed to get to her feet, I pulled at the only thing within my reach: her right arm. And I heard her let out such a scream. I realized then that I had a way to trigger her anger. It took everything within me to do it, but I said a silent prayer that she would forgive me, and then I yanked her arm, only much harder this time.

Again, I heard her scream.

Only then did she finally take action, it seemed to me without thinking. In her pain and anger and confusion, she turned and lashed out at me, pummeling me with her left fist,

Part Four:
The Spirit Realm

her voice.

"You are not so heavy, especially now. You are only now starting to eat again."

She looked down at her body as if to challenge my assessment of her weight. I realized then that she had no idea how slight she had become during the last two weeks of her recovery, not counting however many more days it took for her warriors to get her body back here to us.

"I can walk," she said at last.

But before she could think, I had her in my arms.

"Julia!" she gasped.

And I heard that beautiful laugh of hers once again.

"I will tell you when I am tired," I said. "And then, and only then, you can walk."

She looked at me a moment, considering my offer. "All right," she said, apparently happy with the compromise we had reached.

She was light enough that it required no effort at all to carry her all the way to the river. Even so, I allowed her to marvel at how strong she thought I had become during the past several weeks in her world. "Living in my world agrees with you, Julia."

"Yes, it does," I said, but not in reference to my increased physical strength.

Once we had the riverbank in sight, she insisted that I set her down, and when I did so, she took off in a race to the water's edge and jumped in without hesitation.

"Come on," she called back to me.

But she knew that I was not one for jumping into cold water.

"I'll wait here," I hollered to her.

She stayed out there for a while, and when she'd had enough, she came and lay down beside me, looking up at the stars.

"Do you want to sleep here tonight, or back at the clearing?" I asked.

"Back at the clearing," she answered without hesitation. "Give me a chance to catch my breath, though, before we walk back."

"You're not walking anywhere," I corrected her.

"Julia." And I could tell by her tone that she thought I was joking.

"I'm serious. Only those who walk to the river are allowed to walk back to the clearing. If you were carried here, that's how you must get back."

"But—"

"No but. That's the rule."

"Julia," she said, her tone conveying the message that she'd had enough teasing.

But I did not back down. And so she let me carry her back, after we'd stayed at the river a while longer.

I laid her down carefully when we got back to the clearing, and I felt myself remain over her a moment longer than I really needed to after I'd already released her.

I started to pull back, afraid that it was too soon for such intimacy, but before I could pull away, she reached up and held me there with her left hand around my neck. I felt frozen, unable to move. Her eyes seemed to hold mine. Unsure whether or not to act, I did nothing.

She pulled herself up and met my lips with her own. Then I heard her whisper, "Be with me tonight, Julia." And all uncertainty left me as I felt my body move in response to hers.

It was much later that night, after we'd said all that we could to one another without words, that we lay beside each other, somewhere between wakefulness and sleep.

"Julia," I heard her say at last. "Are you still awake?"

She sounded more awake than I felt at that moment, so I

in love, Julia." And with that, her lips once again met mine, and once again our bodies began to move as one.

"I love you, Julia," I heard her say again. "Deeply." And then I lost track of the trees and everything else around us as I happily gave myself completely to her, once again.

CHAPTER 17

Encountering a Great Emptiness

Over the days that followed, Ndalla got stronger as she let her body recover fully ... at an amazing pace. Other than our being joined by Yolana and the healer every afternoon for a shared meal, those days reminded me of my first week in Ndalla's world, when the two of us enjoyed so much time to ourselves in the clearing, before the affairs of her people took over our lives.

One morning, after Ndalla and I had spent several hours giving each other pleasure and saying what could not be said in words, I lay back at last and listened to the light breeze playing in the trees' uppermost branches. I closed my eyes and felt Ndalla's gentle touch on my skin as she unthinkingly stroked my side. I could tell that she too was listening to the trees.

"I don't know that I can hear any kind of message from them," I said at last. "But I can certainly feel something."

She sat up then, clearly excited by the possibility that I

But now I found myself filled with doubt: was such a gesture somehow dishonoring Ndalla's own strength?

And I thought too of certain things she'd said, ways she'd acted in the past couple days. I recalled her apologies, both to me and to the healer, apologies that I knew she was unaccustomed to giving. I had even witnessed the healer's uncomfortable reaction to the queen's apology, as if I needed further evidence of how uncharacteristic such an act was. At the time, Ndalla's apology seemed appropriate enough. But now, what struck me was the fact that it was so unusual for her to offer such words.

And I recalled too Ndalla's having second-guessed herself the day she'd first thought that it was time to be among her people once again, the way she changed her mind once I convinced her to reconsider. Such second-guessing herself, I knew, had never been her way.

I had not seen it before now, but Ndalla had softened in the time I knew her. But then I dismissed such an assessment as soon as it entered my head.

Certainly, she was weaker now, but only because she was still convalescing. Surely, I thought to myself, she was just as strong today as she was when I first met her. But then I recalled incidents that reminded me just how proud and strong she'd been when I first met her.

I recalled how easily her pride had been hurt when, back in my world, Makei had been offered employment and she had not. Such a simple slight had thrown her world upside down.

And I thought too of how, on the night of the Great Welcoming Ceremony, she had left me and gone to the bedside of a young girl and taken her life. Mercifully, yes. But nevertheless. What strength had such an act required of her? Had she such strength now, I wondered? If called upon to act in that way again, would she? Could she? Or had the queen softened during our time together in ways that were not good for her?

And then I found myself wondering just how long it was that we had been together. With no calendars in Ndalla's world and no references to time—no appointments, no clocks, not even a reliable way to talk about the passing of weeks in her world since everything was related to the longer "moon cycle," I realized just how difficult it was becoming for me to try to keep track of the passing of time, something that had once been so central to my life. My old life, that is. And then the obvious occurred to me: Ndalla was not the only one who had been changed by our life together. I smiled to myself as I realized that there had been a time when I could not have sat so, without pen and paper at hand, and just let the thoughts that filled my mind move through me, consider them briefly, and then let them go again. I used to have to capture such thoughts on paper, so afraid I was of losing their truth if I did not actively reach out and "catch" them for myself in words. My thoughts now did not always appear to me in words. I knew that.

And I thought of Ndalla's way of listening to the trees and realized that if I really chose to let myself, before long I could hear them as clearly as she herself did. If I only let myself.

And once again, the obvious made itself known to me.

I took a deep breath and recognized in myself the desire to help my mind clear itself. No more words, I thought. Let the images come and go. Become a space within which to feel life moving through me, unbidden, unchecked. Life in all its grandness. Feel it. Know it.

I have no idea how long I sat like that, feeling my mind empty itself. At some point, I recognized the welcome sensation of that emptiness growing within me, and then I felt myself let go of even that awareness, as my mind became emptier still. I did not reach for a vision of any kind. All I wanted to achieve was that total emptiness.

me. I was wrong. I didn't know." I could hear in her voice the pain that my thoughts had inflicted. Or was it confusion she felt? I didn't know. All I knew was that she had turned away from me and seemed to want to be left to her own thoughts right now.

I felt the silence between us lengthen. But I hesitated to even try to speak for fear of making what seemed to me a bad situation, even worse.

"Sometimes," she said at last, "when I am reminded of the tremendous differences between our worlds, I feel a terrible sadness within me." I went over to where she sat then, knowing she would not mind my taking her in my arms.

"Oh, Julia," she said, as she gave into the comfort of feeling my arms around her. "I do not know what will come of our having brought our two worlds together like this. I only know that it has felt like the right thing to do. And yet there are times—"

"Like tonight?"

"Yes, when I just feel such a sadness. And I do not know what it means."

Nor did I, but I hardly felt the need to say that.

"Twice now since coming to your world," I said, both times after having talked with the storyteller, I thought to myself, but did not think that point worth mentioning at the time, "I have been visited by a tremendous heaviness in my heart."

"Really?" She sat up then and looked at me.

"Yes. The first time was that night that you met with the war council. Do you recall?"

"I came back and found you in tears. You could not stop crying. Yes, I remember."

"And then again today."

"But why, I wonder. What could have made you sad today? Or that day? Are you not happy here?"

"I am very happy here." And I pulled her to me and held

255

her a moment to convince her.

"Perhaps," I ventured, "it is that very happiness that is tied up somehow with the sadness I feel at times." And having spoken those words, I felt something "shift." I know how ridiculous that must sound, but I cannot think how else to describe it.

"Yes," she said, sitting up suddenly and looking at me again, apparently not bothered at all by the contradiction I had just heard in my words. In fact, the way she sat up and looked at me suggested that my words had offered her a key to the puzzle of her own confused emotions.

"Yes," she said again, giving me a hug as she did so.

And then she said, "You are wiser than I think you know, Julia."

"Uh, was that a compliment or an insult?"

And with that, she let out her beautiful laugh.

"It was both," she said at last.

I took her in my arms, happy to see such happiness within her again.

For a while, I was content to just hold her, knowing that her heart had somehow been made lighter. But finally, my curiosity got the better of me. "What is it that has brought such happiness back into your heart?" I asked her at last.

"Shall I tell you?"

"By all means!"

Then she sat up and looked at me and became, it seemed to me, unnecessarily solemn.

"I think—" but then she paused again. "Are you sure you want me to say this?"

"Yes!"

"Up until now, I had been seeing only half of why the Forces had brought us together. I had been seeing only what a difference your presence has made in my life."

"Has it made a good difference?"

night, with the Forces?"

"Yes," she said, lowering both her eyes and her voice. "As I told you yesterday, there is much I would understand, if I can, before I meet with the elders this evening."

I felt an anger growing inside me, despite myself. How did she hope to fully recover her strength if she did not take care of herself?

"Do not be angry, Julia."

Are you reading my thoughts? But she did not answer, nor did she give any sign that she had heard my question, so I spoke it out loud.

"No," she said, and I thought I heard a sadness in her voice as she spoke. "The Forces have made it clear to me that since you have not the power to block your thoughts from me, it is not proper for me to do so."

I felt so many conflicting emotions at that moment. Anger with the Forces for chastising her. Anger with her for not resting as she should have. Anger with myself for getting angry with her when all I wanted to do was get back to the closeness I had felt with her just last night. And tenderness for her, as I sensed that she was struggling with something this morning, something I could not help her with.

Finally, I just spoke the truth. "You seem so far away from me this morning, especially after I felt so close to you last night. I'm sorry if I seem angry. I have no right to be."

She reached over then and put her hand on mine. It was not, in all honesty, what I had hoped for, but it was something at least. "Julia. It is I who should apologize, not you."

And then I felt her pull her hand back again, and I saw it go up to her forehead, a gesture I recognized all too well, and I felt something unwelcome in the pit of my stomach.

"I too felt close to you last night," she said after a moment, and I heard a tenderness in her voice that bridged the distance between us, just like that.

Again, she touched her hand to mine. "When you fell into such a peaceful sleep after our time of togetherness, I heard the Forces call me." And as she said this, I felt her hand withdraw from mine as it made its way back up to her forehead.

"I did not know I would be with them all night," she said. "I thought perhaps they would show me something that concerned the two of us, something that had to do with the conversation we'd had with each other. I went willingly. I did not know I would be gone so long."

"Did they show you anything that had to do with us?" I asked.

She looked up at me then and tried to smile, but it was clear that her heart was not in it. "Only that it is not proper for me to read the thoughts of someone who has not yet developed the power to block those thoughts, should she choose to do so. I should have known this myself."

"I never minded your reading my thoughts," I said, trying to make my voice sound as tender as I felt.

"Still, it was not right. I am sorry."

"Don't be."

But I could tell that my words, even as I spoke them, offered her little comfort, whether because she felt herself chastised by Forces far greater than my forgiveness could ever hope to outweigh or because of other, more important, messages they'd had for her, I couldn't know.

I searched my mind for a way to get her mind back on the food before us. She had a long day ahead of her, between first the meeting with the elders after dinner and then the meeting after that with her warriors. She needed to keep her strength up. I knew all too well that she was not one to be cajoled into eating when her mind was distracted, and I could see that it was.

"Let us speak no more of the Forces until after we have

eaten," I said. "And then only if you want to. Instead, tell me about your morning swim. Wasn't the water cold?"

"Freezing," she said, with just a hint of a laugh as she recalled her time in the water.

"How do you do it? Jump into water that cold, I mean. I can't do it."

"You could if you wanted to, Julia."

"I've tried. And I can't. Someday," I said, passing her a basket of fruit, "you'll have to teach me your secret."

Taking the basket, she said with a smile, "I think you know all my secrets already, Julia."

After breakfast, I got her to lie down beside me, and I intentionally kept the conversation light, hoping that she would let herself fall into a much-needed sleep.

Only twice did I see her hand make its way up to her forehead while we talked, and I quickly brought up something—anything—to distract her so that she would not focus on whatever it was that hovered at the edge of her mind, threatening—or so it felt to me—to intrude on the time of rest that I felt she needed so badly right now.

When at last she fell asleep, I stayed at her side, intent on warding off any visions that would try to make their way into her sleep. But she rested peacefully, and for that I was grateful.

She awoke not too long after the sun had reached its zenith, and I knew we had hours yet before Yolana and the healer would join us for a late-afternoon meal.

I dreaded what I thought would be her agenda for the afternoon, and then I thought rather than avoid the subject, I would hit it straight on. "Will you spend your time this afternoon with the Forces again?" I asked her as she was still waking up.

"No, Julia. If it's okay with you, I will spend the afternoon here with you."

It was more than okay with me. I was delighted. And I

watched as she stretched herself fully awake.

"Perhaps," she said, "we can talk."

Talk? That wasn't exactly the first thing on my mind, but it would do. "Certainly," I said. "What will we talk about?"

And then I saw that playful smile of hers as she said, "I never got a chance to finish my thought last night. Have you forgotten?"

"Oh, that's right," I said. And I allowed myself to enjoy for a moment a replay in my mind's eye of how that train of thought had gotten derailed the night before. "Let's see," I said, smiling. "That's going back rather a long way. I'm not sure I can recall the first part of that conversation."

"I can," she said simply. "We were talking about a compliment that I had paid to you that was also an insult, do you remember? I said that I thought you are wiser than I think you know."

"Ah, yes. I remember that," I said, making a face. "And somehow, that was tied to your feeling much better after having been sad earlier in the evening."

And as soon as I spoke the words, I regretted having brought up her sadness the night before, but then I was happy to see that my mentioning it didn't seem to make her sad at all now.

"I recall," I said.

"I was trying to tell you—" She stopped then. "It is so hard to put into words, though."

"Try," I said. "I want very much to know what it was that seemed to bring you such happiness last night in the face of such sadness.

"That's it," she said. "You had just said something like that. You had just said something about how perhaps your happiness here is tied up with the sadness that you seem to feel at times. Do you remember saying that?"

"Yes, but—"

"Well, that was it. That was when I said that you are wiser than I think you know."

I waited, clearly still missing something.

"Since we came here to my world, I have been so caught up in the affairs of my people."

And I saw her hand begin to make its way up to her forehead again.

I took her hand in mine and held it as I spoke. "You have had rather a lot going on, it seems to me," I said by way of tremendous understatement.

"Yes," she said, and I was happy to see that her hand stayed in mine. "But I should have been a better host. After all, you left your world to join me here."

"What do you mean? You have been a wonderful host!"

"Not good enough," she said simply.

"How could you have been a better host? What have you not done for me?"

"That's what struck me last night, so clearly, Julia."

"What?" I was clearly still missing something here.

"At first, when I read your thoughts about the Forces last night—and I know now that I should not have done that—I felt such a tremendous sadness." I wanted to reassure her, but I did not dare interrupt her train of thought.

"What I read in your thoughts," she said, "reminded me of the tremendous distance between your world and mine and also the distance that can separate the two of us at times. And I felt such a heaviness in my heart." And I recalled the times when I too had felt such a heaviness as she had just described, each time after a conversation I'd tried to have with the storyteller.

"But then," she continued, "you spoke of the connection between your happiness and your sadness. And that brought me out of my sadness as I was reminded of your wisdom, Julia. You have a wisdom that you do not know you have, Julia. And

I believe you also have powers that you have not yet discovered as well." And then her eyes and voice fell. "Your visit to me in the spirit realm is evidence of that."

Then she looked up again and held me with her eyes as she said, "I think perhaps part of the reason the Forces have brought you here is to discover your own power, your own wisdom." I hardly knew what to say in the face of that. And I found myself wishing at that moment that she would allow herself to read my thoughts again so that I would not have to search for any words. Her eyes fell then as she said softly, "I heard that request, Julia." Then she looked at me again. "But I think it is not proper for me to do so anymore."

But what if I invite you into my thoughts? Surely the Forces cannot say that is wrong.

"Please, Julia, do not invite me into your thoughts until you have the power to block those thoughts you would from me."

"But how can I learn such a thing?" I asked out loud, aware that my merely thinking my half of our conversation was making her uncomfortable.

"I can teach you." Her eyes glistened with excitement as she spoke.

"When can we begin?"

"Right now," she said.

And so, we spent the afternoon, until Yolana and the healer joined us, engaged in our first lesson in how to block my thoughts from a woman I had no desire to block my thoughts from.

Over dinner that evening, the healer took in just how much better the queen looked.

"You have always shown remarkable powers of recovery, my queen, but you have outdone yourself this time."

Ndalla smiled, obviously comfortable with the compliment.

"I have had much help this time." And she looked at all three of us as she spoke. "I have enjoyed the benefit of not only your own powerful medicines, my friend, and Yolana's delicious meals, but this time I have also had Julia's assistance. All three ingredients deserve credit."

"Do not forget the queen's own resolve," said the healer. "You are a strong woman. We, your people, are fortunate to have you as queen."

"Thank-you, my friend." She took a moment to allow her gratitude to be heard before changing the course of the conversation. "Now, let us talk about tonight. Can you tell me what the mood of the elders is, or shall I wait and discover that myself?"

"They are eager to see you," said the healer. "They have heard the stories that the warriors have told and have seen the warriors' injuries for themselves. They know what a serious battle it was. They will be relieved to see you so recovered from your wounds."

"I appreciate their concern for the queen's person, but I was curious to know of their mood beyond that. Can you tell me that, healer, or should I wait and see for myself?"

The healer's eyes fell then. "I think you should be prepared to encounter much anger, even among the elders," she said after hesitating a moment. "There are those who feel the matter with the Daeika is not yet finished. They feel that the Daeika have not yet paid dearly enough for what they did to you."

"Even after almost a full moon cycle has passed?" asked Ndalla.

"Many moon cycles can pass, and still there will be much anger, I think."

Ndalla seemed to consider this a moment, and then I saw her hand travel to her forehead.

"Thank you, my friend," she said after a moment.

And then, whether to change the subject or simply because she had heard all she needed to, she said, "Let us all walk this evening, by the river, when we have finished eating."

And for the remainder of the meal, she kept the conversation light.

As we walked by the river that night, Ndalla took my hand and slowed her pace a little, indicating that Yolana and the healer should walk ahead. "We will catch up in a moment."

Then she turned to me and said, "I need to ask your permission to do something tonight."

"What is it?"

"I would like you to accompany me to the meeting of the elders."

I was flattered but a little at a loss. "Is such a thing done?"

"I will have to ask their permission, but I think they will allow it. I did not want to even ask them, though, until I had asked you first."

A part of me wanted to ask, "Why?" But another part of me knew that the answer to that question didn't really matter. If she wanted me there, then I wanted to be there for her.

"Yes," I said. "If you want me to attend the meeting, I'd be happy to."

"Thank-you, Julia."

Then we rejoined the others and followed the river back to the village, where Yolana went one way, and the three of us headed to the meeting of the elders.

When we reached the Circle of Elders, the queen took the time to approach each elder in turn. She kept me by her side as she did so, introducing me to those I had not had the occasion to meet on my own.

It was clear by the way they greeted her that they felt a great tenderness for their young queen and that they were relieved to see her so recovered and amazed at her remarkable powers of recovery.

After she had made her way around the circle and the elders had taken their seats, she spoke up and requested permission to have me stay at her side throughout the meeting that was about to begin.

A few quick glances told me that this was an unusual request. But as she had predicted, they had no problem granting her request.

And then, even though the request had already been granted, she continued. "Julia has proven herself to be a valuable companion. I have come to rely on her wisdom this past moon cycle, as I have tried to find my way back from where it was that my spirit traveled to after the battle." And then she took my hand in hers as she said, "Were it not for Julia, I do not think I would be standing before you now. We, the Ndalla, owe her much."

The elders made it clear that I was welcome and invited us both to sit.

I had no idea what to expect when Ndalla invited me to attend the meeting with her. But whatever I had, at some level, expected, that was not what I encountered.

Ndalla listened much more than she spoke. And as she did so, I realized that she had come to the meeting to receive the counsel of the elders, not to tell them what she thought. When she did speak, it was almost always in answer to their questions or to ask them a question. Rarely did she offer her own opinion, I noticed. And even when asked her opinion, she surprised me by deferring to them, making it clear that she was still in the process of forming her own opinion on the matter of the Daeika and what action should be taken next.

The entire meeting was unlike any I had ever attended. Everyone listened to the people around them and considered their thoughts carefully before offering any ideas for consideration.

We definitely heard from those who bore the anger to

which the healer had referred earlier in the evening. And I noticed that the queen listened patiently to those who felt such anger as well as to those who felt the anger was misplaced.

At one point, she was asked directly what the Forces had shared with her concerning the matter of the Daeika. I watched as her hand moved to her forehead, and she made that gesture that had become so familiar to me, as she appeared to attempt to physically force the thoughts, apparently still unclear to her, out of her mind to share with the elders.

"I have only recently regained the strength to consult with Them," she said. "Their messages are not yet clear to me."

"We must continue to meet until they do become clear. Can you tell us anything yet?"

I could see the agitation growing within her as she struggled to satisfy their need to know what she herself was clearly unable to see yet. "No," she said at last.

"Let us plan on meeting again ... when the moon has reached its fullness. By then, you will be able to tell us something." I felt my own reaction to their presumptuousness, assuming that she had the power to will such things to become clear to her on their timetable.

But the queen did not object. She simply nodded as if obeying what she took to be their command.

I waited as she took the time, once again, to make her way around the circle and thank each elder individually for taking the time to meet with her tonight. "Your wisdom is valued," I heard her say more than once.

And when at last the affair was over, I took her aside. I could see how tired she was, and I knew that her evening was, by no means, over.

"Must you meet with the warriors tonight?"

"Yes. They are waiting for me now."

"But you are tired."

She smiled. "Dear Julia. Sometimes I think my recovery

has been harder on you than it has been on me. You worry so. I will be fine."

"Do you want to sleep in the clearing tonight or here in the village?"

"Yolana is preparing our dwelling here in the village for us tonight," she said.

And so, whether it was simply because her dwelling in the village was closer, and she really was as tired as she looked, or because she wanted to be among her people once again, I realized that our time in the clearing had, once again, come to an end.

CHAPTER 19

The Queen's New Symptoms

It was not until the next morning that I saw Ndalla again. She hadn't awakened me when she returned from her meeting with the warriors. I awoke and found her sleeping peacefully next to me.

Resisting the urge I felt to wake her, I opted instead to let her catch up on her sleep while I went and found Yolana, and got her assistance in putting together what I thought would make a fine breakfast. It was a little later in the morning then that I finally gave in to my temptation and woke Ndalla up gently.

"You have slept long this morning," I observed.

"And I could sleep longer still if you would let me," she said sleepily.

"Shall I?"

I watched as she tried, without success, to rouse herself.

"Just a little longer, Julia," I heard her say at last, falling back asleep almost before the words were out.

It was sometime after mid-day when I saw her start to stir again.

I waited this time to see if she was ready to be helped awake. And when I could see that she was, I happily helped her. "Good afternoon, sleepy one," I said as I kissed her awake.

My words had the desired effect as she tried to sit up. "Is it after mid-day already?"

"Yes, I think so. You have slept the morning away. Your meeting with the warriors must've gone late last night." I could see her trying to bring back to mind the events of the night before. "You must have slept heavily," I observed. She was not usually one to take any time at all to come to herself in the morning. I helped her sit up, and still I could see that her body longed only to lie flat once again. "Here," I said, climbing around behind her. "Let me hold you a while and let you wake up."

"Why am I so tired this morning, Julia?"

"I don't know. Perhaps you were more anxious about your meetings last night than you realized. After all, you have kept largely to yourself these past weeks."

"Yes. Perhaps that is it."

All of a sudden, it occurred to me that she might have spent another night sitting up with the Forces. "You did come to sleep last night after you met with the warriors, did you not?"

"Yes," she said, putting her hand on my arm to reassure me.

"Did the meeting go long?"

"Not that long."

"Well, then, it is probably just that it was your first time being among so many of your people again. The two meetings probably took more out of you than you realized they would."

I could see a half-hearted smile make its way across her face as she did her best to accept my word for something that

I could see still troubled her.

"How about something to eat? You should be starving by now."

But I saw her hand go to her stomach in response to the idea of food. "Not just yet, Julia. I would like some tea, though."

Tea? Where did that come from? "Certainly," I said, wondering, for just a moment, where I might get some tea. And then I recalled that the people in the village seemed to have it on to boil endlessly. "I'll be right back."

But when I returned, she was lying down again, and I feared she had fallen back asleep. I set the container of tea down as carefully as possible and considered getting the healer.

But before I could act, I heard her ask, "Is that tea?" She sat up again, a little more steadily this time, but not much. "Thank-you," she said, taking the cup from my hand.

After some minutes and several sips of tea, she even found the energy to resettle herself enough that she could lean back against the flat rock that served as our headboard, and after a little while, she seemed to feel a little better.

"I've only known you to drink tea when you're not feeling well, usually because the healer is giving it to you, saying, 'Drink this'," I said with a smile, making my voice sound as gruff as I could. Then, too, I recalled her asking me for some tea, on the very first day we met, back in my old world, when she was fighting off the effects of the traveling sickness.

"I have felt better," she admitted.

"Shall I go and get the healer?"

"No. I think you are right. I am just overtired this morning. It will pass. I am feeling better already. Let us see what you fixed for us to eat."

I brought over to the bed the breakfast I had fixed for us hours earlier. She did her best to show interest in the meal, out of politeness, I thought. I could tell that the idea of food still made her feel a little queasy. After some more time had passed and some more tea had made its way into her, she was able at last to eat something, but it was not much.

"I will take it easy today, here, among my people," she said, perhaps in answer to the look of concern on my face.

"They will be glad to have their queen here with them," I said.

"It will do me good, too. Being with them will help this tremendous tiredness pass."

And that's exactly how she passed her day, growing stronger, it seemed to me, as the day went on. In fact, as I watched her interact with her people, a curious dynamic began to become clear to me: the more freely she gave of her time and energy to her people, the stronger she seemed to feel.

It was late in the afternoon, then, when Yolana and the healer approached, and the four of us went inside to share our evening meal, as had become our custom by then.

As whatever it was that had afflicted Ndalla earlier seemed to have passed as the day went on, I decided not to say anything to the healer about her extreme tiredness that morning. But I kept a careful eye on Ndalla, something that it seemed to me the healer had decided to do that evening as well.

At one point, the healer asked the queen how her meeting with the warriors had gone the evening before, and I listened as Ndalla expressed some concern over the extreme anger that the warriors had expressed at their meeting.

"It is understandable. It was, after all, a fierce battle," said the healer.

"I know that," said Ndalla, rubbing her forehead. "But we cannot hope to move forward from here if the Ndalla hold on to such anger toward the Daeika." After considering the matter some more, she said, "The Daeika do not deserve such anger. They are a people who lost their way. Now their warriors have all been killed. And I find myself wondering how their young and their elders are getting along since we left them." She continued rubbing her forehead until I wanted to take her hand in mine to make her stop. "I feel we must move past this anger that so many of my people are holding onto if we are to do what we must be willing to do," she said at last.

"How would you have them release such anger?" asked the healer.

Then Ndalla looked at me and smiled. And I was relieved to see her hand finally leave her forehead as she said to the group, "Perhaps Julia has some ideas."

"Me?"

"You certainly helped me release mine, as I recall."

"How, traveler?" The healer was serious, apparently believing—or at least hoping—that I had some cure for anger that could be applied at the group level.

"With the queen, it was relatively easy." I looked over at Ndalla to see if she minded my continuing. I read only amusement on her face, and so I continued. "With the queen, all I had to do was aggravate her bad arm."

Yolana gasped.

"You what?" the healer exclaimed.

"I pulled on her bad arm until it hurt so badly and she got so angry that she started hitting me. And then I simply let her keep hitting me while she yelled at the Daeika."

The healer didn't know how to respond.

Ndalla, on the other hand, was clearly amused by my telling of the story, delivered so matter-of-factly. "It is true," she said. "That is exactly what she did."

The healer tried her best to compose herself in the face of her queen's confirmation of the truth of my words.

"Of course, there was a little more to it than that," said Ndalla, assuming some level of seriousness. "Thanks to Julia's actions, I was then able to spend some time the next day in the company of the Forces, who were able to help me see how much more help to my people I could be if I were able to let go of the rest of the anger that Julia had helped me release some of the night before." And then she looked at me and smiled before adding, "I hardly think, however, that we can set up such a situation for each of my warriors."

"Probably not," I said.

It was not too long after that part of the conversation that our evening ended, the healer having made the observation that the queen seemed tired.

"Yes, my friend. I do feel tired already tonight."

Yolana quickly cleaned up the remnants of the evening meal as the healer made her way to the queen's side. She held the queen's hand and seemed to be studying her appearance closely for a moment or two.

When she became aware of the healer's close and continued attention, Ndalla dismissed the healer's attempts to assess her state of health. "Do not be concerned, healer. It is only a little tiredness. It will pass." And then, looking at both the healer and myself as she spoke, she added, "Certainly with everything that has happened, I have earned the right to be a little tired without everyone overreacting."

The healer then looked at me, and I knew she would want to know more once we were out of the queen's presence.

"Yes, my queen," said the healer. "You have earned the right to rest."

As I walked the two women out, the healer turned to me.

Allowing there to be no uncertainty about what she was about to say, she looked me in the eye and said in a low voice, "I will talk with you tomorrow, traveler. Away from the queen."

The next morning, Ndalla once again slept late. And when she awoke, again she seemed unready to entertain even the idea of food and asked, once again, for just some tea.

I was worried about her. But instead, I said, "The healer is concerned about you, you know. Last night when she left, she made it clear that she wanted to talk with me today. I think she wants to know how you are really feeling."

"She knows how I am feeling: a little tired. That is all," she said as she forced her tired body to sit up.

"That is not all," I challenged her.

The flash of anger, which I fully expected to see, made its way across her face. But then I saw her soften, almost immediately. "You are right," she said.

"Why would you keep the fact that you do not feel well from the healer? She only wants to help."

"I know," she said. I could not read her tone.

"What is it?" I asked.

But she seemed unwilling still to talk, so I offered to go and get her some tea, as she had requested, to give her time to compose herself.

When I returned, I found her doubled over, a wave of nausea apparently having come over her.

I rushed to her side. "That's it," I heard myself say. "I'm going for the healer."

"No, Julia," she called to me just as I reached the entrance to the hut.

It was something I heard in her voice, rather than the words themselves, that stopped me.

I turned and saw her trying to sit up, reaching for me. I went to her and held her in my arms.

"Stay with me."

"I'm not going anywhere," I said, gently stroking her hair, offering her what comfort I could.

"Stay with me today," I heard her say.

"But—" I started to say.

"Please, Julia." Her voice was weak. "Do as I ask." Then I

heard her say, "Just today."

"All right," I said at last, not really understanding what it was that I was agreeing to.

She slept again for several more hours after that. True to my word, I stayed by her side. Not only did I not want her to awake and find herself alone, but I knew too that if I did venture outside, the healer would find me for sure.

It was Yolana's arrival with a meal at mid-day that finally caused Ndalla to stir.

"I'm sorry," she said when she realized that she had awakened the queen from her sleep.

"No, it is all right, Yolana," said Ndalla, attempting a smile. "Come here," she said softly, before speaking quietly with the woman.

After Yolana left, I went over to where Ndalla lay, looking much weaker than I wanted to admit. "You seem to have a way of losing again the strength your body has such an amazing way of regaining."

She looked at me, clearly having had some trouble following my words. But then I had to admit, I was not exactly sure just what it was that I was trying to say either.

"It's just that your body has such amazing powers of recovery, but then when you stop eating, as you have done now on a couple of occasions, your body has nothing to fall back on. And I worry about you then."

"I am all right, Julia. You must trust me."

"But you are not all right. I can see what I can see."

"And for me to see what I can see, I must do what I must do."

I'm sure my face expressed the confusion I felt at that moment. I had no words.

"I have told Yolana to let the healer know that we will not be sharing our evening meal tonight—or the next several nights."

I could well imagine the healer's response to that news.

"I need you to do something for me, Julia."

"Anything," I said without thinking.

"I need you to take me back to the clearing tonight, after darkness falls. I am not strong enough to walk there on my own. I need you to carry me. Will you do that?" But even before I could answer, I saw her smile as she said, "As once you carried me to the river and back."

"Yes," I said.

"And I will need your help to do what I must do there tonight."

"But what must you do?"

"Trust me, Julia. Now I must rest."

And with that, she fell into a sleep that held her until well after dark.

It must have been past midnight when at last Ndalla awakened and called me to her side. "Let us leave for the clearing now," she said.

I knew better than to suggest that she should eat something first, but I did offer her some tea, which she surprised me by taking the time to drink.

"Thank-you, Julia," she said as she let the first sip go down. "It tastes good to me."

I did not let myself speak, so full was my mind with questions and concerns. I knew I would not be able to offer anything that she would want to hear right now, so I kept my silence, hoping she would choose to share more of what she had in mind to do.

But she seemed content to keep her own counsel. As she drank the tea, she seemed to go increasingly inside herself, as though preparing herself somehow to become even more distant from me.

When she had finished her tea, I took her in my arms, and we headed for the clearing. I registered the fact that she felt even lighter to me now than she had the night I carried her down to the river, but I said nothing.

When we arrived at the clearing, she directed me to the same private spot I had found her in only one time before, when she was trying to come to terms with her recalled memories. I had not intruded then, and even now there was something about this spot that felt different.

"This is, for me, a sacred spot, Julia." And I could not tell if it was the sacredness of the spot or the fact that she was so weak that made her voice so hard to hear. "Come and sit with me a while, Julia. I need your strength for what I am about to do."

It took every ounce of self-restraint to resist the urge to ask what that was. I took my place beside her, and then she turned and fell back into my arms.

Her eyes were closed when she said, "Just hold me now, Julia." Then she opened her eyes and held mine a moment before adding, "Whatever happens, do not leave me." I remember thinking that would be the last thing that it would ever occur to me to do.

As she settled back in my arms then and closed her eyes, I tried to prepare myself for whatever was about to happen. By the time I opened my mouth to ask her if there was anything I could do to help, whatever it was that she had come to do had begun.

It is hard for me, even now, to find the words to describe what happened that night. It was more than a vision. It was as if she and I were physically "picked up" by some tremendous force and carried through time and space to another dimension, another world, another space. It was a world in which nothing appeared to me as I had known it to be in the world we came from or even in the world I had known before coming to know Ndalla's world. It was a world in which the senses I had come to rely on to tell me what was going on were of no use to me whatsoever.

It was a world in which I could not see, hear, smell, taste, or feel anything in the physical world around me. All I could do was feel the emotions inside me. And the one emotion I felt more than anything else at first was tremendous fear. And then I "felt" Ndalla's presence, so close to me that it almost felt as though she were within me, and I felt the fear subside.

And then I felt more than Ndalla's presence; I felt an assurance of some kind from her, and I knew, with more certainty than I could ever recall feeling in my life, that we would be all right, that we were, both of us, safe. I felt a kind of safety, security, a feeling of being protected, that I cannot adequately describe. Never had I felt so safe. Even though I could still see nothing outside myself, I was struck by the image of a baby in the womb, and I felt the rightness of that image.

That is how safe I felt, like a babe in the womb, unseeing still, unborn to the world outside, as safe and protected as one can be. And connected. I remember still the profound sense of connectedness I felt.

I felt like that babe whose image I saw, that babe who—connected by an umbilical cord to all that it needs to nourish and sustain it—has the power to simply *be* ... without the burden of any cares or concerns.

Never could I recall having felt such a welcome combination of safety and protection, on the one hand, and profound freedom and limitless possibility, on the other. I bathed in the warmth and security of that sensation, feeling it wash over me again and again, until I felt reborn in some way I know I will never be able to describe in words.

And then I awoke. Ndalla lay in my arms, her eyes closed. And although I could not believe it, the sun was already high in the sky. I didn't know what to do at first. I tried to wake her, but she did not seem to be able to hear me calling her or feel me shaking her.

I felt for a pulse and found one. And then I could see her still breathing, but it seemed to me that her breathing had gotten very shallow. Then I recalled her last words to me. "Whatever happens, do not leave me."

I got to my feet, still holding her in my arms and began to walk out into the clearing. Surely, she would not want me to keep her from the ministrations of the healer now. I hadn't gone but a few steps when I saw the healer and Yolana too. They were headed straight for me.

I don't know who was hurrying faster: they to me, or I to them. But when we met, I dropped to my knees, and the healer bent over Ndalla. It seemed to me that she was doing what I had just done: trying to see if the queen still lived.

By the time the healer reached for it, Yolana had poured something into a cup, which she then handed to the healer. But rather than offer it to the queen herself, as I fully expected her to, the healer handed me the cup and said, "You must get her to drink this. Quickly."

The two women held Ndalla's head up just enough that I could put the cup to her lips. But still, she did not respond.

"Quickly, traveler. There is not much time."

Silently I called out to Ndalla, as I felt a fear growing inside myself that I would not be able to reach her spirit in time. I did not know where her spirit was. All I knew was that it was not there with us in the clearing.

"You must find her, traveler."

But how? I thought to myself in a panic.

"By talking to me, as you are now," I heard Ndalla's voice say, calmly.

I nearly dropped the cup I still held in my hands.

I looked down at Ndalla's body, still unmoving, her eyes

still closed.

And then I realized that neither Yolana nor the healer had given any indication that they'd heard the voice that I'd just heard.

Can you hear me? I asked the question in my head, as I had done so often when I knew she was reading my thoughts.

"Yes," I heard her say.

How can I help?

"Keep talking to me."

Where are you?

"I am making my way back, but it is not easy. Try to get some of the healer's medicine in my body, Julia. And I will do what I can to help."

I did as I heard her voice tell me to do. And I saw her lips move as she tried to take in the drink I offered to her. And I looked to the healer, whose face confirmed what I had just seen.

"You have found her, traveler," I heard the healer say. "Now, bring her back to us."

Can you still hear me?

"Yes, I can hear you."

And again, I tried to get the drink past her lips, and again her lips responded to the feel of the cup that I pressed against them.

"You are doing well, traveler," said the healer. "Do not stop."

I love you.

I said the words, over and over in my mind, and all the while, I could feel my own sense of Ndalla's spirit growing stronger all around me. And then her body took in a deep breath, and like that, she was back with us again. Her eyes were still closed, but her breathing was definitely growing stronger.

And I heard Ndalla's voice say, "Thank-you, Julia," although I do not think the words were heard anywhere but in my own head.

And then all went black.

When next I awoke, it was already late in the day.

The healer was bent over me, telling me to drink what she held before me. It smelled awful. "This will give you strength and help ward off the dizziness you will no doubt feel as you try to sit up." She was right about the dizziness. I felt it as soon as I raised my head to try to drink the terrible-tasting concoction.

"Is this what you give your queen to drink? It's a wonder she can stomach it," I said, and then I thought to myself but did not say aloud, *especially now when her stomach seems to turn at the very thought of food.*

"You have done well, traveler. You must rest now."

"But—"

But before I could voice my concern, the healer said, "The queen rests well. You have brought her back to us again. She will rest comfortably now through the night, as must you. Take your rest when you can. She will need you tomorrow, I think."

It did not take much to convince me to lie back down, with my head beginning to pound the way it was. And so, I slept.

The next morning, I was surprised to find all ill effects of the night before gone, as I sat up and registered nothing but concern for Ndalla. I went over to her and found her asleep.

"You see, she rests well, as I told you." It was the healer, kneeling beside me, looking as relieved as I felt. "Here, this is just tea. It will taste good to you this morning, though, I think."

And it did. For someone who has never really appreciated the taste of tea, I found this cup to be delicious.

Perhaps in answer to the surprised look on my face, the healer said, "Participating in such journeys to the spirit realm has certain after-effects that I have become familiar with."

"Because you have made many such journeys?"

"Not so many as you would think, traveler," the old woman said with a smile. "Some healers have such powers that allow them to make many such journeys. In fact, for some healers, making such journeys is their major contribution. My powers lie elsewhere. Among our people, it is the queen who has been gifted with such powers, more so than any other member of our people. It is in helping her recover from such journeys that I have become familiar with their after-effects."

"I see."

"Do you, traveler?"

"Excuse me?"

"I believe you see much more than you perhaps understand."

And suddenly I thought of Ndalla's own words to me just days earlier.

"The queen said something like that to me not too long ago. If I can recall her words, they were, 'You are wiser than I think you know.'"

The healer smiled as she considered her queen's own wisdom.

"Yes," she said at last. "It does not surprise me that the queen herself is wise enough to see this."

Just then, Ndalla started to awake, and we both turned our attention to her.

"Julia," she said as her eyes settled on me and brought me into focus.

And then she took in the healer's presence, and then she saw Yolana, who had—I am certain—been waiting silently by the queen's side the entire night, just in case she would wake up and need anything. Ndalla's beautiful smile conveyed her appreciation for being surrounded by so much concern.

"And so, the four of us gather once again in my beloved

clearing, which we cannot seem to get enough of these days," she said, in a weak voice. Then she looked at each of us in turn as she said, "Thank-you, Yolana, for bringing the healer here. And thank-you, healer, for coming so quickly." And then, turning to me, she said simply, "And thank-you, Julia."

I took her hand in mine and gently stroked her hair as I said, "You look much better this morning than you have looked lately."

I could see all too well how weak she still looked, but there was a renewed clarity in her eyes and a sense that her spirit really was with us that I found heartening. "Does this mean that whatever it was that was troubling you has passed?" I asked, aware of the hope I felt as I voiced the question.

"Dear Julia. There is much that must go on troubling me if I am to be queen. You must learn to accept this."

She could read the disappointment in my face, I think, and so she added, "But yes, what has been so very troubling and unclear to me lately has become clear to me at last."

Then she looked at all three of us as she spoke her next words.

"We must focus our energies now on helping me regain my strength, for I can see now what it is that we must do. The four of us," she said, "are going on a journey."

CHAPTER 20

Sharing a Vision with the Elders

We spent the next week and a half or so at the clearing, and Ndalla amazed us all, once again, with her amazing powers of physical recovery. When she put her mind to it, she seemed to have the power to will her body to do things that I'd never known anyone else to be able to do.

Only her arm seemed to trouble her still. And she was not so stubborn that she couldn't let herself see that whatever she was trying to do to make it stronger was only aggravating it, and so one afternoon she gave in to the healer's suggestion that she let the healer bind it once more in an effort to keep it still.

The healer even took advantage of her queen's somewhat rare moment of acquiescence to construct a binding this time that was much more involved and restrictive.

It was clear that Ndalla was not happy with the contraption as it effectively made it impossible for her to do anything at all with that hand or arm. "And how long would you have me wear this thing?" she asked, her exasperation showing.

"Until I say so," was the healer's abrupt reply. And then, enjoying her own rare moment of having the upper hand with the queen, she added, "You will remove it only when you go in the river to swim. Other than that, you will wear it until I say so." And much to the surprise of all three of us, I think, the queen said nothing in reply. She only took in a deep breath and let out an equally deep sigh, and then seemed to let the matter go.

Ndalla still seemed unusually tired, as she had been back in the village, but in my mind, that was to be expected now, after all she'd put herself through. And she was still uninterested in eating the first thing in the morning, something I also attributed to her extreme exhaustion and the fact that she was at least listening to her body and trying to give it the rest it needed. It was not until I was talking with the healer one afternoon while Ndalla slept that it occurred to me that the queen's symptoms might be the sign of something I hadn't thought of.

"Tell me, traveler," said the healer, "did the queen ever share with you the significance of the spot we found you two emerging from the day you brought her back to us?"

The significance of the spot? I had no idea what she meant. Ndalla and I had not spoken of what had happened that night. I assumed she would bring it up when she was ready.

"No."

The healer was busy with her medicines at the time and did not seem to pick up on the silence in the conversation, so I asked the obvious.

"Will you share its significance with me?"

The healer put down the container in her hands and looked over to where her queen slept.

"I think such a sharing would be all right," she said, turning back to me, after considering the matter for a moment. "It is where her mother's spirit passed out of the physical realm," she said at last, "and entered into the spirit realm for the last time."

I recalled then the storyteller's having told me that the queen's mother had died while giving birth to Ndalla. "Then it is also the spot where the queen's own spirit first entered the physical realm," I said.

The healer's eyebrows shot up. She could not have known that I'd heard the story of the queen's birth from the storyteller. And it was only a small bit of hubris on my part that led me to remain silent and let her wonder at the source of my small bit of wisdom.

It took the old woman a moment to find her voice. "As such," she said at last, "it is a very sacred place, for all of us, but especially for the queen herself."

"She shared with me that it was sacred," I said, "but not why it was so."

I realized then why the healer had hesitated to speak of such a thing without the queen's express permission. "I thank you, healer, for sharing such information with me."

And then, perhaps because I'd taken the time to thank her for her sharing, she surprised me by choosing to share more. "The queen's mother also had the power that the queen herself has, to journey into the spirit realm and back. Many believe that the queen came back here so often when she was a child because she could feel her mother's presence so strongly here."

"That is why the clearing is so dear to her then?"

The healer merely nodded. "Some believe that it was her mother's spirit calling to her that helped her learn so well how to enter the spirit realm while her own spirit was so young and ready to learn such a power. Others believe that the power to travel between realms was simply passed on, from mother to daughter."

"Which belief do you hold?"

The healer merely smiled at my question. "I believe that the queen was born with the power to travel between realms that her mother possessed ... and that her mother helped her develop that power, partly in an effort to maintain a connection with her daughter that, as a mother, she knew was severed much too early in the young queen's life."

"So you believe that both views are true," I said with a little laugh.

"I believe what I believe, traveler. It is that simple," she said with a shrug. "If my belief satisfies those who believe differently, it is not my concern."

I considered then the vision—if that's what it had been—that I'd seen the night that I held Ndalla in my arms in that sacred spot. Was the significance of the vision in some way tied to the sacredness of the spot? Did the image of the babe in the womb simply appear because that is where Ndalla's own spirit entered the physical realm? I wondered.

And then I stopped wondering when I heard the healer say, "I believe the queen will pass the same power on to her own children when she has them."

I looked over at Ndalla at that moment and was surprised to find her awake. I went over to her and helped her sit up.

"Did you sleep well?"

"Yes, Julia." Her eyes were clear, and it looked as though she really did feel better upon waking than she had for some time. The healer, I noticed, had left us alone.

I considered bringing up the matter that the healer and I had just been discussing but then thought better. I knew that my thoughts concerning the vision that I assumed we had shared were still too muddled, and I hesitated to speak of such things before my thoughts became clearer.

"Shall we walk a while before it is time to share the evening meal?" Ndalla's words brought me back to myself.

"Yes," I said. "Perhaps you would even enjoy a swim."

"Yes," she said, her face effectively conveying her feelings about the idea of removing the healer's contraption from her arm, even if only for a brief time. "Let us go to the river."

When we arrived at the riverbank this time, I was surprised to find that we were not alone. Always before, the river that ran by the clearing had been ours to share in privacy.

In answer to the surprised look on my face, Ndalla said simply, "I asked Yolana to let the people know that I needed no more privacy. They have been very generous to give me so much. But I would like now to swim in their company again."

She could not get the contraption off her arm quickly enough before making a dash for the water. Once there, she joined her people, playing games with the young and racing those who were brave enough to take her on. Even from the riverbank, I could see that her injured arm kept her from winning many races, although she didn't seem to mind that at all. When she'd had enough, she came out of the water and lay down beside me on the riverbank.

We lay there a while in comfortable silence, enjoying both the feel of the sun on our bodies and the sounds of her people yelling to each other and playing various games, clearly making the most of their time in their queen's presence. She seemed content. I didn't want to intrude on her thoughts, so I simply enjoyed the sights and sounds surrounding me.

I was glad she'd thought to invite her people to join us. It gave me a chance to see once again what I'd seen often enough that I no longer found it surprising: the symbiotic relationship that Ndalla shared with her people. I didn't know which party basked in the presence of the other more.

"You will accompany me to the next meeting of elders, will you not?" Ndalla's voice surprised me. I looked at her then as she lay there and realized that she'd been thinking only of her responsibilities, and a wave of tenderness washed over me.

"Of course, if that is your wish," I said before turning away to regain my composure.

After a moment, I could feel her eyes on me. I turned to meet her gaze. She looked at me a moment longer. "I will speak with the elders of what became clear to me the night you brought me back here to the clearing." Again she paused. "You have not asked me to speak of that night, Julia. This surprises me."

"I knew you would speak of it when you were ready," I said simply.

She smiled, perhaps in appreciation of the space I'd granted her to consider carefully what she'd encountered in the vision before even trying to put it into words. I sensed something else too, I thought—a hint of tenderness on her part that I was just trying to figure out how I might respond to, especially with so many of her people present, when I heard the healer's voice.

"Let me help you with that, my queen."

We both turned to see the healer approaching, her eyes falling disapprovingly on the binding for the queen's arm that lay, abandoned on the ground, at Ndalla's side.

"Thank-you, my friend," said Ndalla, her face betraying her disappointment, whether at the simple idea of the binding being replaced or at the interruption in our conversation, I could not tell.

As the days went on and her meeting with the elders approached, Ndalla continued to regain even more of her physical strength and stamina at a pace that amazed me.

I knew she was not merely putting on an act or trying to fool anyone by pretending to be in better health, better spirits, than she actually was. Rather, and I knew this now in a way I could not have known before coming to Ndalla's world: the very act of spending time with her people gave her the motivation to take the very best care of her physical self so that she would have the strength necessary to be able to focus her entire attention on them and their needs. But then, at other times, especially when she felt the Forces calling her away from her people so that she could get a clearer sense of how to help them here in the physical realm, her own physical body and its needs seemed the last thing on her mind and, as such, merited little or none of her attention. It was a fascinating dynamic to watch, or it would've been, were it not for the fact that the one person about whom I cared so much was at the center of it. Given how I felt about her, I could not help but worry about the tremendous toll that the whole dynamic had to be taking on her physical body.

And then I wondered too about the thought that had crossed my mind that afternoon when the healer and I talked, when the healer had mentioned the prospect of the queen's own children, and my mind had begun to see the vision of the babe in the womb in a whole different light. Could it be that Ndalla was carrying new life inside of her, life born of the violation at the hands of Daeika? And if she were, did she know it? And if so, how did she feel about it?

And then the question that hurt the most: If she did know she was carrying life within her, why had she chosen not to talk about such an important thing with me? Was she afraid to talk with me about it? And if so, why? I knew that she trusted me. And yet ....

And then another thought occurred to me suddenly: Did she think I already knew? Was she perhaps operating under the misapprehension that I'd understood the vision we'd shared in a way that I did not? And then I wondered: Was she waiting for me to bring up the subject?

I thought then of our aborted conversation at the river-bank a few days earlier and the look of disappointment that had crossed her face when the healer had joined us, and our conversation was abruptly ended. At the time, I assumed her look of disappointment had more to do with the healer's insistence on replacing the binding on her arm, a restriction I knew she detested. And yet, even at the time of that look, the thought had crossed my mind that her disappointment was about something else.

Had she been hoping to have the chance to talk with me that afternoon about the whole matter? Was that why she'd brought up the subject of the shared vision, within the context of her speaking about the next meeting with the elders? But that made no sense. If she'd wanted to talk about it, she certainly would've brought the matter up again, even after the aborted conversation. She was not, after all, one to hold back when she wanted to talk about things. I knew that.

And so, my thoughts became more jumbled as the days went on, one question colliding with the next. Between the extra rest that I knew Ndalla was trying to get as her meeting with the elders approached, and the time she seemed to want to spend increasingly with her people, the two of us didn't end up having too many extended moments alone. And even on those occasions when we were alone, she seemed content, more often than not, to enjoy the comfortable silence that fell between us.

The truth is—and I am ashamed to admit this—I began to feel over the course of the week, a little neglected in the scheme of things, an awareness which, when I recognized it, only made me angry with myself. With all that she was trying to deal with right now, did I really think it unfair that she didn't have more time and attention to give to me?

Come on now, Julia, I scolded myself with more than a little impatience.

I think I was actually smiling to myself in response to this last thought one afternoon when I became aware that Ndalla was calling to me. I looked around but could not see her anywhere. And then I realized that I'd heard her voice only in my mind.

I closed my eyes and thought of her and called back to her

in my mind.

"Where are you?" I heard coming back to me, again only in my mind.

And so I told her.

"Wait there. I will come to you," I heard.

And sure enough, I saw Ndalla approaching several minutes later.

"You have certainly found a secluded spot," she said out loud as she arrived and sat down next to me. "Would you rather be alone right now? I did not mean to intrude." And she appeared to be genuinely ready to get to her feet again.

"No, I would rather have you here with me," I answered honestly.

And then I felt her hand on my face, tenderly stroking it, as I heard her ask, "What is it that troubles you so?"

I looked down, unable to meet those direct eyes of hers. And then I felt her hand under my chin as she raised my face to meet her gaze.

"I sensed that you have been troubled for days now," she said. "And I have tried not to intrude." And then I saw her eyes fall before she said, "It is selfish of me to come to you now."

"Selfish? How can you call your own concern for me selfish?"

Her eyes stayed downcast as she explained. "My meeting with the elders is tonight." She hesitated. "And it is hard to focus on that meeting when—"

"I'm sorry," I said, registering a little hurt. "I did not mean to be a distraction."

"Do not be sorry, Julia," she said, putting her hand gently on my lips. "It is I who should be sorry. I think perhaps now I should have come to you sooner. But I wanted to give you ... space," she said, using the same word she had heard me use to describe those times of silence I had tried to honor, times of silence that I knew she valued. "It is what you are always willing to give me when you know things are not yet clear enough to me to try to put into words."

And then I realized just how selfish it was of me to have felt hurt. She was only trying to help, and I knew that. I, on the other hand, was the one who didn't seem to know what I needed. How could I blame her? I took her in my arms then, unsure what to say or do next.

"I don't know what to say," I said at last. "I know I have missed you as I have felt you called to spend more time with your people and also to spend more time just resting in an effort to regain your strength. These are things I want to see you do. I have just missed you, that's all."

For a while, she just let me hold her. But then, after a time, she pulled away and looked me in the eye before speaking.

"I do not think this is all."

"Excuse me?" Was she accusing me of lying now?

"Perhaps these are the only things you will let yourself see, or perhaps the only things you feel ready to talk about," she said softly. "But they are not all that is troubling you, I think."

Was she really challenging me about what I was feeling right now? I decided to answer her with a challenge of my own. "If you know of more, then say it."

She turned away then at the sound of my voice, which conveyed an anger that surprised even me.

"I'm sorry," I said, reaching out to her.

But I felt her recoil, a response that left me feeling sick to my stomach.

"Please," I said. "I'm sorry. I didn't mean to sound so angry. I don't even know who or what I am angry with. I am just so confused right now. I don't know what to think."

"Confused about what?" she asked, turning back to me. And I heard genuine concern in her voice.

"About you, for one thing," I answered honestly.

"Me?" She seemed genuinely surprised. "What about me?"

Once again, I felt something inside me snap. "C'mon, you must know. Surely, you've been able to read my thoughts. Surely you can read them now."

And once again, the anger in my voice caused her to turn away.

"You know I will not do that again until you have learned to block your thoughts." Her voice sounded weak and far away as she spoke the words.

"But just now, you were in my head as you called to me to find out where I was."

She turned to face me, and her voice had an edge to it as she said, "I called to you, yes. But I was not 'in your head,' Julia. Had you not answered, that would have been the end of it. As it was, I heard only those thoughts you intentionally sent my way. Nothing else."

She stood then before adding, "If you cannot trust me to keep my word about such a thing, then—"

But she seemed unable to find the end of the sentence. She did not seem angry, only hurt. Very badly hurt, it seemed to me, as she stood there, her back to me.

I reached up then and held her hand just as she would have tried to walk off.

After a moment of silence between us, I heard her say, "I cannot have this conversation now. I was wrong to come."

"No," I said. "I was wrong to give in to such anger. I am not angry with you. And I do trust you. That's not it." I waited, but she seemed unwilling to try to speak. "Please stay," I said.

Still she did not move, though. She stood there, her back to me, her left hand still held by mine. But she gave no sign that she was open to trying again to reconnect.

"Please," I said again, as gently as I could.

"I do not think this is the time to have this conversation," she said at last.

"I'm asking you to have it now." I wanted her to be able to

clear her head of this matter before her meeting later in the evening with the elders. She did not need to have our unfinished conversation lingering in her mind as she tried to concentrate on more important matters.

"Julia," was all I heard her say.

Never had I heard her speak my name with such sadness in her voice, a voice so weak and so soft that I could barely make out my name as she spoke it. I felt my heart would break.

I was just about to stand up and take her in my arms when she sank to the ground. She kept her back to me, though. I listened but could not hear her cry, and yet it felt to me as though she were crying. And so I took her in my arms, determined to find some way to make everything between us right again.

At first, I could feel her body refusing to relax into mine. But as I sat there, stroking her hair gently, I could feel her muscles begin to loosen a little.

"I'm sorry," I said at last. "I'm very sorry. I should've come to you sooner to try to talk about what was in my head and heart. But I was so muddled. And I didn't want to bother you."

She sat up and looked at me. "Bother me? Is that what you thought I would think of your sharing your thoughts with me? That they were a bother to me?" And it was clear that it hurt her that I might think this.

"It's just that I knew you had more important matters to attend to right now. That's all."

She smiled then and said, "Do you not know how important you are to me, then?"

I was flattered, I admit. And yet, I didn't seem to be making myself clear.

"I guess you are not the only one struggling to find a balance right now," I said.

She looked at me, then, not necessarily sure that she understood what I meant, but sure, I think, that I was saying something that would help her find a way "in" at last.

"I'm not sure I always know," I began, "how to give you the space I feel you need to be the queen you are, on the one hand, and at the same time, hold you close as the beautiful woman with whom I find myself so deeply in love."

And then I saw that beautiful smile make its way across her entire face before she buried her head in my neck and squeezed me with her left arm as hard as she could.

"We must try to help each other find the balance that we each seek from now on," she said. I couldn't agree with her more. "If you want to share with me some of your confusion now, Julia, I am ready to listen."

I wanted her to know that I believed her and appreciated her readiness to hear me now, but at the same time, I thought it better to switch gears if we could. I couldn't speak for her, but this conversation had already gotten as heavy as I wanted it to get, especially as there was so little time before her meeting with the elders.

"I can feel your readiness," I said. "And I appreciate it. But I would rather wait to have this conversation until sometime after your meeting with the elders is behind you."

She seemed uncertain that it was best to wait, as she now understood that I definitely had something on my mind and that it had something to do with her, and so I added, "You need not worry about what is on my mind. I know now that we can talk anything through. Later tonight or even tomorrow is soon enough for me. My thoughts are not as heavy now as they were before you came to me. The talk we have had has already helped lighten my mood."

"Are you sure this is what you want, Julia? To wait until later to talk?"

"I am sure ... although that is not all that I want."

She seemed surprised by the second half of my response. Until, that is, she felt me pull her close to me and hold her in my arms. I felt her body relax completely into mine this time, without any hesitation whatsoever. And so, we enjoyed the seclusion of that spot where I'd initially gone that afternoon to ruminate and where she had then come to let me know that she was there to listen to my thoughts if I wanted to share them. We had not been intimate since the night before the last meeting of the elders. Little did I know when I chose that spot, in which to think on matters earlier that day, that we would be intimate again before the next meeting of the Circle of Elders that evening.

That night, when we arrived at the meeting place, Ndalla once again took the time to speak with each member of the Circle and thank them personally for taking the time to meet with her. Much concern was voiced over her appearance, and I realized that the last time we'd met with the elders, her arm had not been bound. Both she and the healer assured the elders that it was merely a precaution that the healer insisted on to help the arm regain its strength.

Once again, Ndalla asked permission of the elders to have me stay, and once again the Circle granted it. But unlike at the last meeting, at which she was prepared to listen above all, Ndalla had come to this meeting to make known what it was that she had decided to do.

That became clear when she opened the meeting with the words, "Certain things have become clear to me since we last met."

As she spoke, I noticed that her left hand came up and rested on her abdomen, just below where her right arm was bound, and I saw again the vision we'd shared. And like that, I knew three things with absolute certainty: that she was indeed pregnant, that she knew she was, and that she thought I knew because of the vision we'd shared. Never had such certainty come to me so suddenly. It took me a moment to regain myself so that I could hear the words she spoke.

"One thing that has become clear to me is that we must do all that we can to help our people understand how much the Daeika have lost in this battle with the Ndalla." She waited for that idea to sink in before moving to her next statement. "Because our warriors won the battle so decisively, the Ndalla now have an obligation to the Daeika, an obligation I plan to honor and one that I will have my people honor as well."

At this point, Ndalla paused for a longer time, to see if any would choose to question her on this. And she looked directly at those in the Circle who had expressed anger at the Daeika at the previous meeting, just two weeks earlier.

Finally, one of them spoke. "What obligation is it that you believe the Ndalla have to the Daeika, who brought this battle on themselves and who—some of us believe—must now be left to suffer the consequences of their actions?"

Ndalla seemed pleased to have the question out in the open so early in the meeting, a sentiment she made clear in her carefully worded response.

"I thank you for voicing a question that many in our village will have on their lips when they hear me speak of such an obligation. And I thank you too for sharing the belief that guides a good many of our people, I think: the belief that the Daeika deserve to suffer now for what they have done to the Ndalla."

She paused here before launching into what I'm sure many thought would be her attack on the wrongness of that belief. But she surprised us all, I think, when she put a question to the elder who had voiced the question.

"I too felt such anger at the Daeika that I too held this belief for a brief time. But then I had trouble understanding something that perhaps you can help me understand. Can you help me see just how the Ndalla will benefit by sitting back and watching the Daeika suffer?"

The elder who had spoken was clearly not ready to be questioned about the rightness of a belief that he held so firmly that he had apparently not felt the need to question it himself.

"It is our right," he said at last. "Their suffering will ensure that they will never again presume to question the superiority of the Ndalla."

"But how are the Ndalla superior if they act no better than the Daeika would have acted had they won the battle?" Ndalla asked simply. "It seems to me that we have an opportunity and an obligation to demonstrate now what it is that makes the Ndalla the noble people they are."

She paused before adding, "Such an opportunity as this does not come along very often. This is the very opportunity that the Forces have helped me to see clearly since our last meeting."

One of the other elders spoke then. "What is it that you propose we do now?"

"My warriors and I will make another journey back to the Daeika."

She waited for the reaction to subside before continuing. "We must check on them and see how they are doing. The Daeika young and old have no protection now that their warriors have all been killed in battle. Our obligation is to ensure the safety of those that the Daeika warriors died to protect."

"But we were no threat to the Daeika young or to their elders. You misrepresent what the battle was fought for." It was the elder who had initially questioned the queen, finding his voice.

A dead silence followed this challenge to the queen's authority.

And then I heard in her voice something I had never heard before. "I was in the battle."

The restrained force in the queen's voice said more than her words did. "Perhaps," she said, "you have not listened well enough to the warriors who are willing to talk about the battle. Perhaps you have not heard how our warriors, after the battle was over, sought out the Daeika young and old and would have killed them too, for what—" And here she faltered as she tried to speak of something that was still too hard for her to speak of.

"—for what happened in the course of the battle," she said once she regained herself.

"Do not tell me we were no threat to the Daeika," she said. "Had I the strength after the battle was over that some of my warriors still had, I cannot say what I might have done to the Daeika myself." She paused once more. "Do not speak to me of misrepresenting the battle that the Ndalla fought. No battle is noble. It seems to me that what proves a people's nobility is how they deal with those they have fought in battle ... after the battle is over. Now is the time when the nobility of the Ndalla will be tested. This is now the time of testing that was foreseen."

And then there was a real commotion around the Circle.

Ndalla's reference to what she herself had foreseen as "the time of testing"—and what she had apparently discussed with the elders back before she had ever come to my world—threw everything that was now being discussed into a whole new light.

"You know this? Does this knowledge come from your time with the Forces?"

"My knowledge comes from many sources. I take responsibility for how I interpret what the Forces share with me. When I say that we are now in the time of testing that was foreseen, I am sharing with you what I believe. It is a belief based on many things: what the Forces have shown me, what I hear from you, my valued elders, as well as what I hear from my warriors and the people I meet with in the village."

"What you say makes sense. Share with us more of what it is that you propose to do," said one of the elders who had not yet spoken.

"With your consent, I will meet with my warriors tomorrow night and share with them what I have shared with you tonight. I will ask a number of my warriors and their families to make the journey with me, back to the Daeika village. I cannot tell you what we will do there, as I do not know what we will find there. But it will be our goal, upon arriving there, to make sure that the Daeika who are left understand the obligation that we feel to offer them protection and to extend to them our hand in friendship."

"Will you allow some of us to make the journey with you as well?"

"Of course," said Ndalla.

"How soon will you leave?"

"I will send word to you tomorrow night, following my meeting with the warriors. Unless they need more time than I anticipate, I would like to leave very soon after that."

"Very well."

As the meeting ended, once again, Ndalla took the time to go around the Circle and talk privately with each elder in turn. I noticed that she spent the longest time with the elder who had challenged her, and when they parted, it seemed to me that they did so as friends.

CHAPTER 21

The Queen's Hope

That night, we returned to the queen's dwelling in the village. The two of us were just starting to enjoy a light snack that Yolana had been thoughtful enough to leave for us, when I stopped eating and allowed myself, instead, the pleasure of simply enjoying the sight of Ndalla, knowing now what I felt I knew.

She seemed positively radiant to me that evening. And I knew that part of what I was seeing was a sense of relief that her meeting with the elders had gone so well, and part of it—I hoped, at least—was a result of the afternoon's time of closeness. But another part of it seemed to me to be tied to the fact that new life now grew within her. Now that I was certain of that fact, I wanted to speak of it, but I hadn't a clue how to bring the matter up.

And then she stopped what she was doing and what she was saying. She looked at me, and I knew she could tell what I was thinking. Not because she was reading my thoughts. I knew she would not do that again until I had learned what she was still in the process of teaching me. No, it was something simpler than that. She could tell what I was thinking, just as I could tell right now what she was thinking. It was a connection that had nothing to do with words.

It seemed to me that she didn't know what to say any more than I did at that moment. I took her in my arms then and just held her. "You did well tonight," I heard myself say, knowing full well that's not what was on both our minds. But it was an opening at least.

I waited, but she said nothing.

"I understand things now about which I was still confused earlier today," I said.

And still she did not speak.

"I know now what I only suspected earlier today: that you carry new life within you."

She sat up, moving away from me slightly so that she could face me.

I could not read what I saw when I looked into her eyes.

"I could not speak of it with you, Julia," she said as she lowered her eyes. But then she stopped herself abruptly.

"It's all right," I said. "There is no need to explain yourself. I only wanted you to know that I know now."

Then I took her in my arms again. I wanted to speak words of comfort to her, for I felt that she needed comfort right then even though I didn't understand the cause of her discomfort. And so I maintained my silence.

"I have such conflicting emotions inside of me," I heard her say at last.

I smiled, knowing she could not see my smile.

"How could you not?" I asked simply. "You have been through so much already. And you can see so much that lies ahead of you yet. You are concerned for your people and how they will handle the test that you feel still awaits them, concerned for the new life within you and how it will be received, concerned for the Daeika and how they will receive the visit by the Ndalla, and concerned even for me, I think. I do not know how you hold inside of you all that you do!"

I heard what I thought was a laugh, and then I heard that there were tears in it as well.

"Come," I said. "Are you finished eating?" I asked, knowing full well that she would eat no more tonight, now that her attention had shifted away from the meal, which remained largely untouched before us.

She only nodded wordlessly.

"Then come," I said, getting to my feet and lifting her up easily in my arms. She did not protest in the least.

I laid her down on the bed and slipped in beside her and took her in my arms again. I could feel her tears from where her head rested on my neck and shoulder.

"Everything is all right, you know," I said at last. I don't know what prompted me to say that, but I know I believed it at the time I said it. I felt her then roll out of my arms and over onto her back beside me.

I propped myself up on my elbow so that I could look at her. And I saw then that she had fallen asleep already, exhausted. I pulled a light cover up over her, lay down beside her again, and tried to let myself fall asleep as well, something that my body seemed unwilling to do until much, much later that night.

When I awoke the next morning, Ndalla still slept. I was not surprised. I knew now how tired she must feel, between the drain of new life within her and the uncertainty that surrounded the lives of her people, to which I knew her to be so sensitive.

When Yolana arrived, I asked her to clear away the light supper we had not eaten the night before and to bring us a light breakfast and lots of hot tea.

It was not too long after she had done so that Ndalla started to wake up. She smiled when she saw me propped up on my elbow beside her, just enjoying the sight of her as she opened her eyes and took in the world around her.

"I hope you have not spent the night so, or you too will need to have your arm bound."

I leaned over then and kissed her and felt her body become more fully awake in my arms. It was sometime later, then, that I got up and brought her a cup of tea.

She accepted it gratefully, even as I saw her take in the breakfast that Yolana had so thoughtfully laid out for us.

"Perhaps you will feel like eating," I said, "after you have had some tea first."

"Perhaps," she agreed. And then she leaned back to enjoy her tea more comfortably.

"You seem rested this morning," I offered by way of observation. "Did you sleep well?"

"Yes," she said with a smile that confirmed her response.

"You were exhausted last night," I said. And it seemed to me that only then did she recall for the first time this morning, our brief conversation the night before, or what she could of it.

"I am sorry if I fell asleep in the middle of—"

"Don't be. You were clearly in need of rest."

"But I think perhaps you were ready to speak of things that we had not spoken of before." And then, as if the conversation were coming back to her as she spoke of it, she said, "You spoke last night of—"

I waited to see what she would say next. She leaned forward then and set down the cup of tea that she'd held. Then I saw her hand once again move instinctively to where that life grew, as it had at the meeting last night. And then, only because she seemed to be trying still to recall the conversation,

I offered, "You said only that you could not speak of it with me before now."

She looked at me then in a way I could not read.

"I could not," she said simply. "You shared the same vision." I didn't know whether she was asking me for confirmation that I had, in fact, shared the vision or making the statement by way of explanation for her subsequent silence on the matter.

"I had the vision of the babe in the womb," I said at last. "But I didn't know what to make of it at the time. It was only several days later that even the possibility of your carrying life within you occurred to me, but I was not sure. And then last night, as you spoke to the elders, I saw your hand move to where that life grows, and when I saw that gesture, I felt certain."

I saw tears in her eyes, and I could not tell if they were tears of sadness or joy. I still felt that I understood so little of what there was to understand in all of this. I went over to her then and took her once again in my arms to offer her the comfort I knew I could not offer in words. I felt her curl up willingly in my arms, and I could hear her crying softly. "It's all right," I said.

And as I said the words over and over, I rocked her gently in my arms, aware as I did so that I had no right to speak such words, understanding as little as I did about any of what I sensed happening around me.

After a light breakfast, Ndalla made it clear that she planned to spend the day among her people. "I must get word to my warriors that I want to meet with them this evening, and I want to spend time with their families today as well, to prepare them for the journey that I will talk about further with my warriors tonight."

"I understand," I said.

And then coming over to me, she said, "I know there is

Ndalla's World

much that we still need to talk about."

"It can wait," I said.

She looked at me a moment longer. "I may not be able to get back here until tonight then, after the meeting with my warriors."

"Whenever you get back here, I'll be here. Go now."

I knew that even though it would be a long day for her, it would be a day that would strengthen her in that mysterious way that time spent with her people always had a way of doing. And I could sense that she needed the strength right now that only her people could give her.

As for me, I chose to seek out the storyteller. We had not talked for a while, he and I. Even though my talks with him always seemed to end with my encountering a heaviness of heart, I had to admit that his words to me had always been on target, and I felt in need of what back in my world I would've referred to as a "reality check."

When at last I found him, I saw that he was with the healer. I started to walk away, but the healer called to me. "Come, join us, traveler."

"I do not want to intrude," I said as I approached them with some hesitation.

"You are not intruding. We are happy to have you join us," said the old man, and it seemed to me that his pleasure in seeing me was genuine. "We were talking of last night's meeting. How is the queen this morning?"

I studied both their faces as I said, somewhat cautiously, "She is well. She is spending the day with her people, to start sharing with them the news of the journey that she has planned."

"I do not think she has planned this journey so much as it has been planned for us all."

The healer nodded in agreement with the storyteller's words.

"I think you're right," I said, acknowledging the subtle difference in wording.

"She is a brave woman, the queen," said the old man. "It is very possible that the Daeika will not welcome such a visit."

"Very likely too that some of her own people will not welcome the idea of such a visit either," added the healer.

"I am sure both possibilities have occurred to her," I said.

"Yes," they both agreed.

"There is not much that concerns her people that the queen does not foresee," said the storyteller. And a comfortable silence seemed to fall between the three of us then.

It was after some time that the storyteller spoke again. "Tell us, traveler, are you at all concerned about the queen's extreme tiredness that so many of us have taken notice of lately?"

"She has much reason to be tired," I said. "She has been through a great deal."

"Yes, you are right. She has been through much," he agreed and seemed to let the matter rest for a moment.

"And yet, this tiredness, together with her inability to eat much, speaks of something else," said the healer.

I looked at the two of them, aware of a sense of irritation growing within me. Had the queen no privacy, then?

"You speak of something that it is not my place to speak of in the queen's absence," I said simply, hoping that would be the end of it.

"Then you have noticed the symptoms too," said the healer.

"If you have concerns about the queen's health, healer, you should speak with her about those concerns and no one else, I think."

"Come," said the old man, his hand reaching out and touching my shoulder gently. "We intended no disrespect to the queen, nor did we intend to anger you. You cannot blame us for being concerned about her. There are things about which the queen herself is not free to speak, about which you, on the other hand, can speak."

"What do you mean?"

"It would not be proper for her to speak of the possibility of new life growing within her." His words, in both their accuracy and their boldness, stunned me. I could not speak.

The two waited patiently for me to find my voice.

"If such were the case," I began, emphasizing the "if" as much as possible, "why would it not be proper for her to speak of such a thing? It would seem more proper for her to speak of it than anyone else."

"A woman with child does not speak of such a thing in our world, traveler," said the old man. "It is too private a matter. To speak of such a thing herself would be to say to the Forces that she does not honor the sacredness of what they have allowed to happen to her."

"And as such," the healer added, "the act of speaking of it would tempt the Forces to take that life away again before it has a chance to make its way into the world."

"I didn't know," I said stupidly.

"If it is not this way in your world, traveler," said the old man, "then you must not be hard on yourself for not knowing how it is in our world. That, after all, is why you have come to our world—to learn. Is it not?"

I looked at the storyteller then and studied his face hard for a moment before speaking my next words.

"Let us be clear: I did not come here to learn about your world. I came because I could not bear to see the queen leave my own. I could not imagine my life without her."

Neither of them spoke again for some time, and I could not blame them. This whole conversation with them, coming as it did on the heels of so much still left unspoken between Ndalla and myself, had tapped into something deep within me.

Finally, the storyteller said, "Traveler, we hear your words. And we know how deep are your feelings for the queen. Were they not as deep as they are, you would not have been able to call her back to us from the spirit realm as you have, more than once now. And you must know how grateful the people are that the queen found you on her journey and brought you back with her. We acknowledge your great love for each other and are grateful for it."

His words did much to calm my emotions. "But you must know too," he said, "that the Forces would not have allowed the queen to bring you back here were there not a willing-ness—no, a hunger—within you to learn things about Life that your own world could not have taught you. Whether you admit this to yourself or not, you are here to learn about our world, and in so doing, to learn those Life lessons that are yours to learn. Your being here is not all about the queen, as you sometimes seem to think."

Hours later, the storyteller's words were still replaying them-selves in my mind. I could not get them to stop. Once again, his words had left a heaviness in my heart as I tried to sort out what they really meant to me. Was there a hunger in me to know things that my own world could not teach me? And if so, what were those things? And was I doing all that I could to learn them?

His words threw me back on myself, and I did not know how to find my way.

And then I heard Ndalla's voice ... much earlier than I thought I would.

And as I heard that voice, something inside of me, deep inside, knew that everything was all right. And like that, I knew that I didn't have to keep trying to figure any of it out, for I knew that everything would become clear to me in its own time.

"Julia?"

And I realized with a start that her voice was not in my head. She was sitting beside me. And then I realized that I didn't have any idea how long she'd been sitting there, nor did I have any idea where I was.

"Are you all right?"

I struggled for a moment to get my bearings.

"Yes," I said at last, although not too convincingly.

"No, I don't think you are. Come. Let me hold you for a change." And she took me in her arms. Never had I so welcomed the feel of another person's arms around me.

"You are shaking," she said. "What is it that you are afraid of?"

But I couldn't speak.

"Shhhh," I heard her say. "It is all right. Whatever it is, I assure you, it is all right."

And I let her go on holding me for I don't know how long.

When at last I could regain myself, she held me at arm's length so as to be able to look at my face.

"You must rest now," she said, gently pushing me back on the ground. "Wait here for just a minute. I need to find Yolana. I will be right back."

I hadn't the energy or the mental clarity to question, let alone disagree, with her.

When she returned, she took me in her arms again. It was only then that I noticed that her right arm was not bound. Without words, she read my expression of surprise and said, simply, "I have removed the binding for just a little while. It is all right. Rest easy in my arms."

I closed my eyes then and gave in to the soothing feel of her gentle touch.

"Will you eat something?" I heard her ask.

I opened my eyes then and found Yolana standing there, ready to hear what it was that I wanted, if anything. But I could not think of food. I heard Ndalla speak softly to Yolana, but I could not make out the words, nor did I care to. I felt myself drifting off into a light doze, and I welcomed the sensation of forgetfulness, especially as I knew I rested safely in Ndalla's arms.

It must have been hours later that I awoke. The sun had begun to set, and the most beautiful dusk was making a show of itself in the western sky. I sat up and realized that Ndalla, while keeping a close eye on me, had also been caught by the beauty of the setting sun.

"Come, Julia, and watch it with me," she said.

And so we sat there, silently, watching as the sun set and the night sky began to work its way through its repertoire of blues, first light, then dark, then darker. And finally, the darkness that bore no blue in it whatsoever.

"Come," she said at last. "And see what Yolana has fixed for us. You have not eaten all day. Am I right?"

"Have you?" I asked, turning her question back on herself.

"Yes," she said. "I have. But you, I think, have not. Come now, and eat. I insist."

I smiled to myself at the sound of her regal tone of voice, which she seemed to be able to call on without even being aware of it.

"How can I not follow so imperial a command?" I asked.

She studied my face only a moment before we both burst into a much-needed laugh.

"You must be feeling better if you have found your sense of humor, Julia. You had me worried earlier. You seemed so troubled. Are you all right?"

"I am all right now that you are here," I said simply.

"I would have stayed with you this morning had I known you were so troubled. But I did not sense anything then."

"No. It was later that my heaviness of heart set in."

"The same sadness that you spoke of to me before?"

"Yes."

"I am sorry I was not here when it first set in. How long were you sitting here before I joined you?"

"I really have no idea," I answered honestly.

"Do you know what caused it?"

And I thought of the storyteller's words. "Yes. But I would rather not speak of it just now if that is all right."

She hesitated only a moment. "Certainly, it is all right."

Perhaps it was just me, but the silence that followed her words felt uneasy, and so I said, "Should we not rebind your arm before you aggravate it?"

I could tell, by the extended silence before she answered me, that my sudden change of subject did not go unnoticed.

"No," she said at last. "My arm is fine."

She tried to busy herself with the food that Yolana had left for us, but it did not work. I saw her stop and look at me, not knowing what to say or do to help. "If you will not speak to me of what caused the heaviness in your heart today, I do not know how I can help," she said at last.

"I know." And yet I knew I was unwilling, or unable, to speak of it. "Do you not have a meeting to go to tonight?" I asked, suddenly recalling her scheduled meeting with her warriors.

"I have asked Yolana to let the warriors know that I cannot meet with them tonight, after all. I will meet with them tomorrow."

"But you spent all day today setting up the meeting tonight, did you not?"

"I spent today talking with my people. And it was time well spent," she said, sounding almost defensive as she did so. "My warriors will not mind having an extra evening in which to discuss with their families all that we will then talk about at our meeting tomorrow."

"I did not mean to cause you any trouble."

"You have not caused me any trouble, Julia." And her voice was tender. "Come," she said. "If you like, I will just hold you all night long. I would rather that you talk to me, but I cannot force you to talk of what you wish to remain silent about."

"I don't know," I said as I fell happily back into her arms. "I suspect you could force anyone to do anything if you put your mind to it," I said jokingly.

"Why would you say such a thing, Julia?" The sound of her voice made me feel that she was genuinely hurt by my words.

"I only meant that you are a very strong woman."

She said nothing in response, and I was left to wonder if I had, in fact, hurt her feelings, albeit unintentionally. Perhaps because of that uncertainty, I tried to bridge the gap I felt between us by talking about what had happened that day. "I paid a visit today to the storyteller and ended up visiting with him and the healer."

I waited but heard nothing in response. I took in a deep breath and then let it out again.

"Such a deep sigh. Was it your visit with them that left your heart feeling so heavy?"

"I suppose it was, although it was certainly not their intention to cause me any sadness."

"I cannot imagine that it was," she said simply. "Even so, if their words made you sad, I apologize."

"You? What in the world have you got to apologize for?"

"They are my people. I am responsible for them."

"You cannot possibly bear responsibility for all that your people say and do!"

"But I am their queen."

"Even so," I said, echoing her own words. By now, I was sitting up and had turned to face her. I tried to read her expression but could not. It seemed to me to speak of confusion and frustration and growing irritation. "Please," I said. "I didn't mean to anger you."

She turned away then, clearly at a loss as to how to help me without further encouraging me to say things that only seemed to hurt or anger her.

Not knowing what else to say, I blurted out, "They asked me about your health, and we spoke of your carrying new life within you."

It took her a moment, but finally she found her voice. "And it was this conversation that left you feeling sad?"

"Well, no. It was more than that." She waited, apparently unwilling to say or ask me anything else that might backfire on her.

"The storyteller ended up speaking of what it was that he thought brought me to your world," I said at last. And still she refused to speak, apparently until she heard something she could understand. I knew she was still waiting to hear what possibly could've been said to leave me feeling so sad, and I began to feel that I might never be able to make myself clear.

I tried to unravel the tangle of thoughts in my head. "He spoke of what he called my 'hunger' to learn things here that I could not learn in my own world."

"Yes," she said, apparently hearing something that she herself agreed with. "He is right." And again she waited, assuming that there was something still forthcoming to explain the onset of such sadness.

"It's just that I'm not sure I recognize this 'hunger' that he spoke of and that you too seem to recognize in me. And if I cannot even recognize this hunger, how in the world can I know what to feed it with?"

And I watched as the frustration and confusion and concern on her face were all washed away by that beautiful smile of hers as she took in the meaning of my words.

"Oh, Julia. Is that what you are troubled by?"

"Yes."

"Then surely everything is all right."

But I was not so easily won over. "What do you mean?"

She looked at me a moment, considering her next words carefully. "Have you never once eaten and satisfied your hunger without first consciously recognizing your hunger?"

"I suppose I have."

"One need not always consciously recognize one's hunger in order to satisfy it. Some hungers are recognized and fed at a level below the conscious mind's awareness. That does not make the hunger any less real or the satisfying of it any less ... satisfying!"

But she could see I was still not ready to give in.

"I sense that hunger too," she said, "although I would not have talked about it in such a way as to leave you with a heavy heart. You do want to understand things, Julia. You are open to learning new things. Do not doubt this. But do not fret about it either. You would not have made the journey with me here, to my world, if you were not open to learning new things. The fact that you made the journey is proof enough of the truth of what the storyteller spoke of."

She made it sound so simple. And I knew I wanted it to be that simple. And yet a part of me knew it was not that simple.

The storyteller's words had a way of awakening in me something that seemed to sleep when he was not prodding it awake. There was something more that I was here for, something I had not yet stumbled upon. His words had convinced me of that. And yet, at the same time, his words left me with no clue as to what that something might be or how I might find it.

"Julia?"

"I am here," I assured her.

"There is more in your heart, but I sense that it is something that you are not yet ready to speak of. Am I right?"

"You are always right when it comes to knowing my heart," I said with a smile.

And I could read the relief on her face that my heart really did feel lighter finally.

"Then let us eat. I am starved," she said.

"There is one more thing that I would speak with you about first, though," I said.

"What?" she asked, even as she was preparing some food to hand to me.

"I understand now why you could not speak of the new life that grows within you. The storyteller and the healer helped me understand why it was not something you were free to speak of with me. I did not know."

She put down the food, as I knew she would. And she kept her eyes cast down as she spoke. "I knew that you could not know, and yet I didn't know how—"

"You need not speak of it now either," I said, gently placing my fingers on her lips. "Know now that I know and that apparently your people have also begun to at least suspect."

I tried to read her expression, but once again I found myself unable, especially as she refused to raise her head to look at me.

"I need you to tell me only one thing," I said. "Is it all right for me to speak of your condition when I am asked about it by your people?"

She nodded wordlessly, not bearing to look at me as she did so.

"There then. We will not speak of it again. And, in fact, you have not spoken of it at all."

But still, she did not look at me. And I could see now that my having brought up the subject had been a mistake, for she seemed unable to regain her lighter mood now that the subject had been broached.

And then the thought occurred to me for the first time:

maybe she didn't want the life she carried within her. But then I thought if that were the case, and the Ndalla really did believe as I'd been told, then surely, she would have spoken of the life she carried so as to tempt the Forces to take it away from her.

Or maybe not. Maybe she could not bring herself to do that, but perhaps she still had some reservations about bringing a life born of such sadness and violence into the world. How could I hope to know? How could I ask her to speak of such things? I could not. Not if she believed it was improper for her to speak of such things. And yet, now that the thought had occurred to me, I felt I had to know how she felt about the child she carried. How else could I know how to help her through what was bound to be such a trying pregnancy?

"I must know one more thing." I took a breath before I continued. "Do you want this child?"

I saw her chest rise before she turned to look at me, anger in her face. Anger at me for asking such a stupid question? At the Daeika for the violation? At the Forces themselves for having given her this new life? At her situation, which prohibited her from even answering the question I had just posed to her? I didn't know.

"Yes," she nearly spat at me. And for a moment I heard her "yes" to be an answer to all the questions that had just been running through my mind. And then I realized that she must've meant it to be an answer to the only question I had voiced.

She got up quickly then to leave. But I moved just as quickly and caught her. "I'm sorry. I had to know. I understand that you can speak no more about it. Please forgive me."

But my question had apparently tapped into something deep within her, something she couldn't stop now. And her tears flowed freely as she pushed against me, either out of anger or sadness; I couldn't tell. It was a long time before I could feel her start to calm herself down, and then only because I think she had worn herself out. I didn't know whether she wanted to talk more or whether she felt she had already said more than was proper for her to say. I didn't know whether to ask her questions, to try to get her to talk, or to maintain my silence, and to try to help her regain her composure. All I knew to do was to hold her for what began to feel like an eternity of silence between us. And then, finally, I heard her voice, sounding very weak and far away.

"In my world, Julia, women who believe they are carrying life within them do not speak of such a thing."

I started to assure her that I knew that now, but I was afraid to interrupt her. So I listened as she continued. "I thought that when we shared the vision, you would under-stand it to mean what I thought it to mean. Even so, I should have spoken of it with you."

Again, I stopped myself from interrupting her. "I sensed your confusion," she said. "I should have known what I did not let myself know. I was so focused on regaining my strength and preparing my thoughts for the meeting with the elders."

I wanted to assure her that I understood all of this now, but I feared that even a minor interruption would cause her to stop talking altogether, so weak was her voice still.

Then she turned around in my arms to face me, and I thought my heart would break. I saw such sadness in her face.

"Let me finish," she said when she saw that I would speak. "I now believe that the Forces would have understood my choosing to speak of these things under the circumstances. But I did not think it then. Then I could think only of what I grew up believing all my life. And so I did not let myself speak."

She paused here, and I watched helplessly as tears welled up in her eyes.

"I will speak now, and I will ask the Forces to understand why I do so and to not take the new life that grows within from me."

And I could see how hard it was for her to speak of this, and I almost asked her to stop, but I did not feel I had the right.

"You ask me if I want this child. Yes, Julia, I want this life that grows within me to be born, for it will be life born of Daeika blood and Ndalla blood. It is a life conceived in violence, yes, but it will be a life that will grow up and know peace if I have anything to do with it. You joked earlier this evening that you thought I could force anyone to do anything if I put my mind to it. But that is not so. I cannot force my people to open their hearts to the Daeika. But I dare to hope that my child can help them to do that, just by being who he or she is. This is what I feel when you ask me if I want this child. This is what I mean when I say 'yes' to your question."

Part Five:
A Time of Testing

CHAPTER 22

Sharing the Queen's Hope

The next morning, Ndalla's exhaustion, which was a result of our emotional conversation the night before, as well as of her not having eaten anything at the end of such a long day during which she'd been so actively engaged with her people—got the better of her, and she was unable to rouse herself, even after several attempts. At one point there was a knock at the entrance to the small hut, and when Ndalla saw that it was the healer, she gestured that the woman should come in.

The healer's face conveyed her concern at seeing the queen so weakened. Then the healer flashed a look my way before asking, "My queen, shall I get—"

But before the question was out, Ndalla had gestured that the healer should go and get whatever medicine she wanted. "I will take whatever you offer me this morning, my friend."

As I waited with Ndalla, I took in just how weak she was. "I should not have asked you to speak of ... things last night," I said, certain that's what had taken so much out of her.

"Do not say that. It was time that we spoke of such things."

But at what cost to you? I thought to myself.

"Now that you know my feelings," she said, "you should know that there are those who will ask you to share what you know."

I looked at her. "Should I? I mean, do you want me to share what you shared with me?"

She tried to smile but hadn't the strength. "I shared with you what I did because you asked me how I felt. I did not share it with you for any other reason. What you do with what you now know is your concern. I only wanted you to not be ... caught off guard," she said, using what was now a familiar expression between the two of us.

Again, she tried to smile. And then, perhaps seeing that I still hadn't gotten the answer I was looking for, she added, "If you feel yourself inclined to share what I have shared with you, know that it is all right. I do not keep secrets from my people."

When the healer returned, the queen drank what was offered to her. Then she lay back and asked that only Yolana stay with her and that she be allowed to rest.

As I stepped outside with the healer, I prepared myself for a barrage of questions. But the healer didn't seem to know where to begin. And so I found myself starting the conversation once we had found someplace private in which to sit and talk.

"The queen and I spoke of much last night."

"She is greatly changed from how she looked when I saw her earlier yesterday."

"Part of that is due to the fact that she never ate supper last night," I confessed. "And I know what an exhausting day she had."

"You must get her to eat her evening meal, traveler. Between having no appetite in the morning and then going all day, she must eat her evening meal. It is the only time she has to get the Life energy in her that her body needs right now."

"I know, healer," I said, putting my head down.

"But her state this morning is due to more than her not eating," said the healer. "I think that something else happened last night."

I took a deep breath. "We spoke last night of the life she carries within her."

"You spoke of it, you mean."

"No. I mean, I asked her to speak of it."

The healer could not hide her alarm and her disappointment in me at hearing this news. "Traveler, did you not understand what you heard when we were with the storyteller yesterday?"

"Yes, I understood."

"Then you had to know that she could not speak of what you asked her to speak of."

"And yet she did."

The healer turned away from me then and got up. She seemed unable to take in what she was hearing.

"She would not have put the life of the child that she carries at such risk. She would not have," said the healer.

"And yet she did."

"Why are you telling me this, traveler?"

"Because what she shared with me was important enough to her to take such a risk." The healer turned to face me. I considered only a moment before saying, "I believe what she shared with me is important enough to share with the Circle of Elders. Can such a thing be arranged?"

"Today?"

"As soon as possible."

The healer thought for only a moment. "You must wait right here, traveler."

"I will wait."

"Are you sure this is what you want?" And then, before I could answer, she asked, "Are you sure the queen would approve of your sharing this in such a way?"

"I am sure this is what I want. And as for the queen, I have her permission to share what she had the courage to share with me last night."

"Very well, traveler. You must be here when I come back to get you."

"I'll be here."

I waited then, and the healer returned within what I judged to be about an hour.

"The Circle has gathered and is awaiting you. Are you still sure this is what you want?"

I merely nodded.

"Then let us go, traveler."

It was only when I arrived at the Circle and saw the elders all gathered before me that I had second thoughts about what I had asked to be allowed to do. I realized, all of a sudden, that without the queen there, I had no idea how to address such a group. And yet it seemed to me that they should know what she felt was important enough to share with me at such risk to herself and her unborn child.

"The healer tells us, traveler, that you have something you feel is important to share with us today in the queen's absence," said one of the elders without ceremony.

"Yes," I said simply, hoping my voice would not fail me.

"We understand that the queen is not well this morning. Our thoughts are with her. Will she be well enough to make the journey of which she spoke to us when last we met?"

"I think she is only overly tired this morning," I said. "Once she has had a chance to rest, it is still her intention to make the journey she spoke of, and soon, I think. She does not want any more time to pass than must before making the journey of which she spoke."

In the silence that followed, I realized that they were waiting for me to continue. "In fact, I believe I now understand a little better why such a journey is so important to the queen."

"I think she was clear when she was last here," said one of the elders, "about what she hopes to accomplish with such a journey. But if you think you understand something now that we did not understand then, we appreciate your sharing it with us."

I glanced over at the healer, who seemed to be sending me a sign that it was all right and I should continue.

"Last night the queen spoke with me of the life that she carries within her."

I waited a moment, partly for the group to quiet itself, partly for the information I had just shared to finish sinking in, and partly to think to myself just how to proceed from here.

"I know she did so at great risk, both to the life she carries within her and to herself. I have no doubt that it was her speaking last night of such things that has taken such a toll on her."

"What she shared with you, traveler, must have been important for her to risk so much."

"As she shared with you when she met with you," I continued, "the queen believes that the real time of testing of her people is happening now, that the battle itself was only part of the test or perhaps just a precursor to the real time of testing. It is clear that she sees the child she carries as being involved in that test."

I paused, again unsure how to explain myself. "The queen knows that the life that she carries within her has within it both Daeika blood and the blood of the Ndalla," I said. "And while she knows that the life within her was born of an act of terrible violence and confusion, it is the queen's hope that the child she carries will know a life of peace between the two peoples whose blood he or she carries."

I paused again, but only briefly. "This is the hope that the queen had the courage to speak of with me last night. At first, she would not speak of such a life, fearing that to do so would put the child's life at risk. But she knows that I am a traveler from a world where things are not as they are here. And out of respect for that fact, she asked that the Forces understand her need to speak of such things. She asked that the Forces not take the life from her, the life that she feels will help her people open their hearts to the Daeika when we make the journey that she feels it is so important for the people of Ndalla to make." The silence, when I was finished, extended itself for some time as the elders let the full weight of the words they had just heard sink in.

"We thank you, traveler, for sharing with us what the queen shared with you last night. For many of us sitting around the Circle, I believe what you have shared with us only confirms what we already believed our queen felt about the life that many in the village had started to believe she carried within her. But it is good to hear it confirmed by what you say are the queen's own words. For some of us, this news will perhaps invite some rethinking of what our position has been up until now. You will leave us now while we talk over what you have shared with us."

I nodded and prepared to leave.

"But before you go, traveler, tell us: did the queen herself ask you to share this with us?"

"No. It was difficult enough for her to share it with me, I think."

"So you took it upon yourself to share with us the queen's thoughts that were shared with you in private?"

"The queen told me this morning that there would be those who would ask me to share her thoughts with them. And when I asked her whether or not I should do so, she indicated that would be my decision to make, mine alone."

"I see."

"She did, however, take care to remind me that she keeps no secrets from her people."

The old man who spoke for the group smiled at me then.

"You have done well, traveler. The Circle appreciates your giving us this glimpse into the heart of our queen. If you choose to share with her that you have spoken with us, and I think you will, please extend to her our concerns for her health and our wishes for a quick recovery of the Life energy she chose to spend last night in sharing these important thoughts with you."

And with that, I left the Circle of Elders to talk among themselves.

When I returned to see how the queen rested, I found her still asleep, Yolana at her side.

"Does she rest comfortably?"

"Yes," said Yolana, speaking softly so as not to wake her queen. "She awoke once and took some more of the medicine that the healer left for her. I do not think she will awake again now until perhaps this evening."

It was only then that I remembered the meeting with her warriors that she was to have had last night but that she rescheduled when she found me and knew that she wanted to spend the evening helping me with whatever had been troubling me. How long ago that felt to me now.

"I will be back," I said to Yolana.

I hurried out to see if I could find Bakka, but when I arrived at his dwelling and talked with his family, I found that he was not there. Apparently, he had just been called to meet with the Circle of Elders.

And I realized that from here on out, I should leave matters in the hands of the elders. I had done what I could. The rest was out of my hands.

While I was out, I decided to go for a walk down to the

river before heading back to check on Ndalla. Yolana was with her if she needed anything, and I did not know if I could sit quietly enough for as long as I knew she really needed to be allowed to rest today. I went to the river directly from the village and then followed the riverbank to the spot that I knew was just a short walk from Ndalla's beloved clearing.

All along the riverbank, I could see and hear her people enjoying themselves, some of them swimming, some of them playing with their children in the water, some of them just sitting on the riverbank, some engaged in various projects and/or conversations with one another. They all acknowledged me as I passed. And as they had done before, many gave me gifts to pass along to the queen to let her know that she was in their thoughts.

As I turned away from the river and headed to the clearing, the noise along the riverbank fell away, and I found myself in the presence of a grand and glorious silence. Was it any wonder Ndalla loved this spot so? None of her people seemed to come here unless invited by their queen. They seemed to honor it as the queen's space, sacred to her, and so, off-limits to others except by invitation.

I stayed there the rest of the day. Somehow being there allowed me to feel closer to her spirit than I thought I would feel sitting next to her sleeping body back in the dwelling. I even found myself wondering if, as she slept, she perhaps came here in spirit. This was such a restful place, after all. I thought briefly of trying to contact her spirit, but then thought better of it. For one thing, I knew she needed her rest more than anything else right now. And for another, I knew I should not *play* at things I did not yet fully understand. And yet her spirit felt so close to me as I sat there.

As dusk approached, I headed back to the village. Before I arrived at the queen's dwelling, however, I was met by the healer.

"Traveler, where have you been all day?"

"Why? Did something happen?"

"No, do not be alarmed. The queen has rested well all day. She has only now awakened and was just asking for you." Without thinking or speaking, I started to leave. "Wait a moment, traveler. Collect yourself. The queen is fine. She is not in any danger. But if you go in to see her with that look on your face, you will frighten her."

I stopped then to collect myself, as the healer had suggested.

"I was looking for you earlier, traveler. You did well today when you addressed the Circle of Elders."

"Thank-you, healer. Your look of encouragement helped me greatly."

"You should know that after you left, the Circle had a chance to consider carefully what you shared. The elders then called for Bakka to come and meet with them. They decided that the elders themselves will meet tonight with the warriors."

"Does the queen know this?"

"No. That is why I am telling you this, traveler, so that you can tell her," the healer said, almost matter-of-factly.

"Me?"

"I think it would be best."

"I think she is liable to resist the idea of the elders taking over what she sees as being her job to do," I said.

"Then I trust you will help her to see the wisdom of the elders' decision," the healer said simply. "It is their wish that she use what strength she has now to prepare herself for the journey. They have taken it upon themselves to help prepare the warriors and their families for the same journey."

"You make it sound like such an easy thing to explain to her."

But the healer totally ignored my concern over how the queen would take being told all of this. "You can tell her that

Bakka will come to her to find out how soon she will be ready to leave. She will be the one to decide when the people will begin their journey," she offered.

"But—"

"I will leave you now, traveler. You have much to discuss with the queen."

And with that, the healer left me standing in front of the queen's dwelling, wondering how in the world to begin the conversation it seemed that Ndalla and I were about to have.

When I entered, I was pleasantly surprised to see Ndalla propped up enough that she could hold a cup in her hands and drink out of it unassisted.

"My, you look as though you feel a lot better already," I observed.

"I do," she said, and even her voice sounded stronger to me.

"You could barely open your eyes this morning, let alone sit up as you are now."

"Come, Julia," she said, patting a spot beside her. "Sit here and tell me how you spent your day."

"Well, I spent a good part of this afternoon in your beloved clearing," I said by way of openers. She surprised me with her response.

"I thought so." I waited for her to explain. "I thought I felt your presence. My spirit went there to rest while my body slept."

"I felt your spirit's presence as I sat there," I said, amazed. "In fact, I almost called out to you in my mind."

"You should have, Julia. I would have heard you. While I did not have the strength to initiate a conversation with you in the spirit realm, I would have been able to answer you."

"I didn't know."

She reached out then and put her hand on mine. "There is much I can teach you of these things if you want to learn."

"I want to learn anything that helps me feel closer to you."

And for the first time in a long time, I saw that beautiful blush of hers spread up her neck and color her cheeks.

"I think your reason to learn of things in the spirit realm should be based on motivations that are more noble than that, Julia," she said at last, smiling.

"You are right," I admitted to her. "And I do want to learn. But let us not worry about such things until you have regained your strength." Just then, Yolana came in, carrying supper.

"Ah, food," said Ndalla, apparently having regained her appetite. "Thank-you, Yolana."

It was only after Yolana had left us and we had started to eat that Ndalla spoke again.

"I must meet with my warriors tonight," she said, apparently remembering only then the appointment that had slipped her mind until this point.

"Let us not speak of such things now," I said, determined to keep anything heavy from creeping into the conversation until after she had eaten her fill. "Tell me instead," I said, happy to have found something with which to redirect the conversation, "how it is that you managed to convince the healer to leave your arm unbound this evening. I thought for sure I would walk in this afternoon and find it bound again."

Ndalla laughed then. "I simply told her that as long as I was resting, it had earned the right to rest, too." She seemed to take a moment to think further before saying, "Actually, she surprised me by backing down so easily. That is not at all like her, you know."

"She can be quite insistent," I agreed.

She looked at me then before she spoke.

"Was she too hard on you today? I was afraid she would blame my feeling so weak today on you somehow."

"No," I said, still determined to keep the conversation as light as possible. "I think she understands that your strength is still not fully recovered and that it does not take much to use up what Life energy you have in you. I told her that you did not eat your supper last night, and for that she chastised me. I assured her that I would make sure that you eat your supper tonight, and every night from now on."

"You are not my nursemaid, Julia. She has no right to place such a responsibility on your shoulders. I will tell her so."

"Ah, but the responsibility to see that you eat your supper every night is one that I gladly take on."

"Why in the world is that?"

"It assures me that at least once every day, I can tell you what to do," I said with a smile.

"I would hope," she said with a smile of her own, "that I listen to what you tell me to do more than just once a day, Julia."

"Listen to me? Yes. But actually do as I say? Now that's another matter."

She seemed to catch my smile before she said, "Surely you are not calling the queen headstrong, are you?"

"I would not dare." And we both burst out laughing. And so I managed to keep the conversation light throughout the rest of the meal.

When it was clear that she had eaten all she could, I moved the remains of the meal aside and lay down beside her and took her in my arms.

"Are you quite content?" I asked her once I knew she was comfortable.

"Quite," she said, and I could hear the smile in her voice. "I even feel a little sleepy. If I am not careful, I will doze off and miss my meeting with the warriors tonight. You will not let me do that, will you?"

"About that meeting—"

"Hmmm?" Her voice sounded even sleepier already.

And I debated saying anything to her at all, just letting her doze off. But that would just be putting off the inevitable, and I preferred being as honest and up-front with her as I could.

"You don't need to worry about that meeting tonight."

And I could feel the energy surge through her body even before I could see the look of concern on her face as she sat up suddenly to face me.

"What do you mean?"

"I mean that the elders have themselves decided to meet with the warriors tonight to discuss with them the upcoming journey. They wanted you to rest tonight instead."

"How do you know this?"

"I got word just before I came in to see you this evening. I was asked to let you know."

"And yet you said nothing until now?"

"I did not want anything to interfere with your eating your supper tonight."

She sat back then, although not back in my arms, to consider this.

"I do not know that I like the elders using you as some sort of messenger."

"I did not mind their asking me to share this message with you. Please don't let that trouble you. I was happy to share such welcome news. I wanted you to be free to rest tonight."

I took her in my arms again, registering the tension that I now felt in her body, where before there had been none. "How can I get you to relax again, as you were just moments ago?"

"Was there more that you were asked to share with me that you have not yet?" she asked, sitting up again to face me.

"Only that Bakka would come to you in the next day or so to find out when you want to begin the journey, and that you will be the one to decide when the journey will be under-taken."

"That is all?"

"That is all I was asked to share with you," I said honestly, knowing full well that I had more to share with her: namely, news of my meeting that morning with the elders, if I chose to share it. "I did not think you would mind their asking me to pass along such good news. I'm sorry if my doing so has upset you."

And then, as she registered the apology she heard, I could feel her mood change. I could even feel the difference in her body, as I felt the tension I'd felt only moments earlier replaced by tenderness.

"No," she said. "I am not upset. Only surprised. I was ... caught off guard," she said with that beautiful smile of hers. "That is all."

"Are you sure?" I asked her, taking her in my arms again.

"Yes, Julia. I assure you I am not upset." And then as if to convince me, she took me in her arms, and I felt her lips touch mine, gently at first, and then more urgently as I felt a new kind of tension take hold of her body, a tension that moved her body in accord with my own.

And if I had thoughts of any further conversation with her that night, such thoughts dissipated quickly.

CHAPTER 23

The Journey to Daeika

It did my heart good to see how rested and relaxed Ndalla obviously felt the next morning as I watched her stretch herself to full wakefulness.

"Good morning," she said as she saw me watching her.

"What a difference a day makes," I observed. "You look totally recovered already."

"I was only overly tired yesterday, Julia. It was really nothing more serious than that."

And then, before I knew it, I'd asked the question that had been running through my mind while waiting for her to wake up. "Can we spend some time together in the clearing today? There is much I'd like to learn from you."

She smiled. "Of course, we can. That would be a wonderful way to spend the day."

And then I thought. "Unless you had planned to spend the day with your people today."

"Let us go to the clearing. We can go down to the river to

be with them when we take a break for the mid-day meal and again for the evening meal. I would like to teach you more about how we can connect with one another in the spirit realm. I sense in you a ready learner."

"All right then."

We heard then a knock at the door and saw the healer when she entered, her face showing the relief she surely felt at seeing her patient so clear-eyed and awake so early this morning.

Ndalla invited the healer and Yolana to share a light breakfast with us. And after breakfast, before she left us, the healer insisted on replacing the binding on the queen's arm.

"If you want it to heal properly, you will have to show it more patience, my queen."

"Yes, my friend. I know. It is just that—"

"Just that you have no patience for it, I know."

"I will go for a swim this afternoon," said Ndalla, a reference to the fact that she planned to remove it when she went into the water.

"Then I will re-bind your arm again when I come to see you later this evening."

"Then join us for our evening meal, my friend, and you can re-bind it then. We will eat at the riverbank, by the clearing. Yolana, will you bring us a light lunch there as well?"

Yolana nodded. And then, speaking to both women, Ndalla announced, "Julia and I will spend the day in the clearing."

We left for the clearing soon after that and spent an enjoyable morning there. Ndalla was a patient teacher, and she was right: I was ready to learn.

In fact, much of what we spent the morning doing, I had already "felt" my way toward, during the time I had spent in Ndalla's world. I could feel my own improved ability to calm my thoughts and clear my mind when it was time to. And I knew, too, how to "hear" her voice when it was in my head and how to "send" my own voice back to her. There was nothing to it, really.

It was only when it came to learning how to "block" my thoughts from her that I started to struggle. Something about the very idea of keeping my thoughts and feelings from her made me balk. And yet, as she patiently explained to me, more than once, unless I could master that power, she had no right to enter my mind and read my thoughts. She would not. That alone gave me the incentive I needed to learn what she had to teach me.

We lunched down by the river, where many of her people made a point of stopping by to see for themselves how well the queen felt and to express their joy at her quick recovery and—much to Ndalla's surprise—to express their excitement about the upcoming journey that they understood many of them would be making with her. Throughout the meal, which was constantly interrupted by her people coming up to her and wanting to talk to her—a fact she did not seem to mind in the least—she kept looking my way as she listened to her people saying things she had apparently not heard them say just two days earlier, when she'd spent the entire day with them.

After lunch, we headed back to the clearing, and I braced myself for her questions. I had not yet shared with her anything about my meeting with the elders the day before. But she asked me no questions, and so I decided to maintain my silence … for now.

When we got back to the clearing, we picked up where our morning lessons had left off. It was later in the afternoon, then, that I felt I'd learned what she was trying to teach me as well as I could learn it and told her so.

She surprised me by suggesting then that I concentrate for a moment on a thought that, for whatever reason, I wanted to keep from her. "At least for now," she added with a smile. "It might be something that you would share with me sometime in the future, just not yet perhaps."

And then, no doubt in response to the surprised look on my face, she said, "It is time to test your ability to block me from reading those thoughts you would not have me read. If you pass this test, I will be convinced. And if not—"

She let her words trail off. I knew the end: she would not let herself read my thoughts again, not until I had proven to her that I could block from her those thoughts that I was not yet ready to share with her.

As I searched my mind for a thought to keep from her, the only thought that filled my mind, of course, was that of my meeting yesterday with the elders. I was not yet ready to share that with her, not now. And yet I wasn't sure enough of my own abilities to use such a thought for this test, either. But I could see no thought other than this one as I searched for something I wanted to keep from her.

"Are you ready?" she asked.

"What if I don't pass my test?"

"You know the answer to that, Julia: then I will not read your thoughts until you can block your thoughts from me."

"No, I mean, then you will know the thought that I have chosen to keep from you."

"Yes, I will."

"Does that not trouble you?"

"Not if you really are ready to be tested. If you are as ready as you say you are, then I will not be able to reach that thought."

She paused as she studied me a moment. "Would you rather not be tested now?"

"Let us practice a little longer first."

"Very well," she said patiently. She seemed in no hurry. And so I spent the rest of the afternoon practicing what I realized I now had a new-found incentive to learn. I smiled as

I thought to myself that she was perhaps a better teacher than I had given her credit for being.

That evening, we were joined at supper not only by the healer and Yolana but by many more people as well. Supper ended up being a kind of impromptu potluck to which every family brought some part of the grand and glorious meal.

It began innocently enough. When Ndalla and I arrived at the riverbank, following our afternoon of lessons, she quickly removed the binding from her arm and dashed into the water to enjoy a swim with her people before supper.

As I helped Yolana lay out the supper for four that she had brought, though, we began to notice that more and more families started to add their dishes to the food Yolana had brought. Without even being asked, they offered the explanation, "The queen said it was all right to join her this evening." Yolana and I exchanged surprised looks, but there seemed little left for us to say or do, other than to try to accommodate all those that the queen had apparently invited to join us.

The queen stayed in the water far longer than was her usual length of time for a swim. It was clear that she was in a mood to play in the water with her people as long as they wanted to extend the play. And when at last she did come out of the water to sit down to supper, ours was the only spread on the riverbank for as far as the eye could see.

She seemed positively delighted by how the dinner, originally planned for just four, had grown, taking the time to walk the length of the entire gathering before taking her seat.

The evening took on a very festive tone as it went on, and it went quite late.

At one point, I saw Bakka approach her, and she excused herself to step away and talk with him in private. They talked for some time. When she returned, I tried to gauge her mood, but it seemed unchanged from when she had left the group. She seemed totally relaxed and happy that night, as she enjoyed the company and goodwill of her people.

When at last it was time to call it a night, we all joined in the clean-up of the meal—even Ndalla herself. And she walked with her people along the riverbank as we all made our way back to the village.

Once again, many of her people, the children especially, came up to her with small gifts: often shells and smooth, white rocks they had just picked up along the shore. She gladly accepted all their gifts and took the time to exclaim what a find each and every one was as she accepted it.

I was afraid, when first we arrived back at her dwelling, that the moment she was out of sight of her people, I would see how tired she really was. She had to be. She had just hosted an impromptu party for what I estimated to be well over a hundred people!

But she seemed only pleasantly tired, not exhausted, as I was afraid she might be. Once again, spending time with her people had apparently only given her strength, not sapped her of it.

Over the next several days, the queen's strength and stamina continued to grow. Even the morning sickness that had been troubling her seemed to become a thing of the past as she started once again to eat a hearty breakfast each morning.

She seemed content to divide her time between being with her people, as they prepared for their journey to meet the people of the Daeika, and being with me, as I practiced the skills she tried to help me master in the clearing.

One afternoon, as we sat in the clearing talking of such things, she shared with me for the first time how much I had frightened her when, weeks earlier, I shared with her that I had cleared my mind completely but had not asked the Forces to show me anything within the void that I had so successfully created. I recalled the afternoon. It was the afternoon I'd gone to the riverbank following yet another unsettling conversation with the storyteller.

I recalled how I had sat there, doubting myself and my decision to come to Ndalla's world, doubting whether my presence had affected her life in any positive way. I recalled how I'd cleared my mind that afternoon and searched only for an awareness of the great emptiness I hoped to find there. I recalled too the look of concern on Ndalla's face when she'd found me later that evening. I recalled our conversation still later that evening, when she'd asked me how I could have cleared my mind so completely without having asked the Forces for their help to see what I could see then. And I recalled, finally, how she'd then stumbled unaware on thoughts that I tried too late, and without success, to block from her: my awareness of the profound difference between us when it came to her belief in the power of the Forces and my own lack of belief.

It was, I believe, the last time she allowed herself to read my thoughts.

"To encounter the Great Emptiness without first asking the Forces to help us find our way through it is not something that the people in my world would think very wise to do," she offered as tactfully as she could as we sat that afternoon in the safety of the clearing.

"I think I discovered that the hard way," I said with a smile.

She tried to return my smile but could not. "This is not a light matter, Julia." And I saw that she lowered her eyes as she spoke.

"I'm sorry."

"You need not be sorry, Julia. You did not know. It is I who should apologize. I can see now that I should have spoken with you earlier about the Great Emptiness. It just did not occur to me that you would encounter it so soon in your spirit travels."

"Can you tell me now?"

It took her a moment to prepare herself to speak of what was clearly a subject of some importance to her. "My people believe that the Great Emptiness that you encountered surrounds the Life that we live and the Forces that help us to find our way through it. We believe that Life offers us the opportunity to learn from the Forces here in the physical realm so that when our bodies die and our spirits pass, we will not get lost in the Great Emptiness. Those who get lost in the Great Emptiness, either while still here in the physical realm or while in the spirit realm, are doomed—or so my people believe—to lives of great unhappiness and emptiness."

She paused here before continuing. "It is my belief that some of the Daeika found their way into the Great Emptiness and could not find their way back out of it again. That is why, I believe, they thought they had to fight the Ndalla. Only by engaging in such a fight with such a noble people did they feel they could find, once again, a purpose in Life. For surely the worst part of encountering the Great Emptiness must be the loss of purpose that one encounters there."

"Have you ever encountered the Great Emptiness?" I asked her.

"Not without the help of the Forces to guide me."

"Have any of your people ever encountered it?"

"I think some must have, for they conspired with the Daeika to help them in their fight with the Ndalla."

And I recalled only then, the time she had gone out with a small group of her warriors to face those who had betrayed their own people.

"When I came upon you that evening, after you had encountered the Great Emptiness, I could see its aura surround you still."

And I recalled how she'd kept her eye on me the rest of

that evening. Only now could I really understand why.

And then I recalled how she had stumbled upon my unguarded thoughts about the Forces and how little they meant to me. No wonder she had pulled away from me.

"I have so much yet to learn, do I not?" I said at last.

"As do I," she said. "It is not a one-way street, you know," she said, using an expression I had never heard her use before.

"Where did you pick up that expression?"

"In your world. I just never had the opportunity to use it before now." And once again, I found myself gifted with that beautiful smile of hers that had a way of opening my heart to Life itself.

Ndalla called for a gathering of her people the evening before the journey to the Daeika village would begin, just as she had the night before they had left for the battle itself, two moon cycles earlier. And as the earlier ceremony had been, the ceremony on this evening was both solemn and brief.

"We will undertake tomorrow a journey back to the land of the Daeika, this time not in a spirit of war but in a spirit of peace. It is my hope that the Daeika will open themselves up to the spirit in which we come. But even as I voice such a hope," she said, "we must remain mindful of the possibility that the Daeika might not welcome the Ndalla, who will arrive so soon after such a decisive victory as our warriors won for us."

She paused then, perhaps to honor the curious juxtaposition of her words of peace and war.

"I never had the opportunity to thank our warriors for all that they gave in the battle with the Daeika. And while it may seem curious to honor our warriors for their courage in war as we prepare this evening to travel back to the Daeika, this time in the spirit of peace, it is nevertheless important that we do so. For it is only because of the warriors' courage and strength in battle that we are able to make this journey back to the Daeika in peace. Let us honor the great courage and strength of our warriors tonight."

And she paused while her people cheered for their warriors and the tremendous courage they had shown in battle. When the cheering had subsided, the queen spoke again, this time with a slightly softer tone of voice, I thought.

"And speaking now as a warrior myself and not the queen, I say publicly that I owe my fellow warriors a depth of gratitude for their quickness of action at a decisive point in the battle. Were it not for their courage and their ability to act as quickly as they did, I would not be here tonight. I know that." And again, she paused while her people cheered, this time both for the queen herself and for the warriors who had moved quickly in order to save the queen's life.

Then, her voice growing in strength, she said, "Nor would any of us, the Ndalla, be standing here as we are today, a free people, free to live our lives as we feel is right, guided by the Forces' wisdom and our own determination to live lives of meaning and purpose."

Once again, she paused as her people cheered for their warriors' courage as well as for themselves and what they knew guided their lives.

"And so we prepare to travel tomorrow to the land of the Daeika and extend to them the hand of peace and cooperation," she said, bringing back into focus again the primary message of this evening's ceremony.

And then I heard her close the ceremony with words that echoed in my mind what I had heard at the closing of the previous ceremony. "And as with all that we do, we embrace our role in the events that make up the Great Unfolding of Time and ask only the wisdom to see clearly as far as we need to see to be able to do our work well and in the spirit of both

ing. We need to move her to some place that will give her more privacy before nightfall."

"All right." But to myself, I thought, "Yeah, right." I knew that, if asked, Ndalla would not agree to such an arrangement.

Together, Yolana and the healer and Bakka and I found a place that would suffice, and after Ndalla fell asleep, after having eaten what supper she could stomach, I managed to carry her to the spot without waking her. That fact alone was enough to convince me that Yolana was right: the queen's vision would visit her before morning. And if I hadn't been already, I found myself grateful that Yolana had accompanied us on the journey, and I told her so.

She only smiled and went about seeing what she could do to make her queen more comfortable and to afford her as much privacy as possible.

It was sometime after midnight that the queen's vision began. It was one that involved more violence; that was clear. We did what we could to keep her from hurting herself as she thrashed about, but we were careful not to wake her. She seemed to keep raising her hands to ward off blows to her face, and I thought too I could see her taking blows to her stomach, her back, and her side.

At one point, as whatever violence she was living through continued, the thought occurred to me that perhaps she was merely reliving in her mind the violence that had already occurred to her at the hands of the Daeika, and not seeing any scene from the future at all.

I ventured to say as much to the healer sometime after the vision had ended as Yolana was doing what she could to soothe the queen, eyes still closed, to sleep.

The healer only shrugged her shoulders as she said, "Past. Future. They are one and the same, are they not?"

And I recalled then what Ndalla had told me, back in my world, about the way that she (and her people) viewed time:

not as a straight line with the past at one end and the future at the other, but rather as a circle, an enclosed sphere really: with the past and the future connected in some way we could not hope to understand from our vantage point, caught in the present as we are. And I wondered what this all meant. But Ndalla never opened her eyes following the vision, and I certainly wasn't about to wake her up to ask her.

Sometime after, when it seemed clear that Ndalla would probably sleep through the rest of the night, we all decided to settle down and get some sleep ourselves.

It must have been a few hours later, then, when I was awakened by a sudden movement. Ndalla had been lying next to me, sleeping. But when I opened my eyes, she was sitting straight up. I didn't know at first if she was awake or still asleep.

I sat up slowly so as not to startle her, and I put my hands gently on her shoulders.

I felt her jump at the feel of my touch. "It's all right," I said softly. She seemed somehow frozen, unmoving and unspeaking.

"It's all right," I said again. But still, she did not respond. And I wondered if she could even hear me. Then finally I felt her move. She doubled over then, although not as if in pain.

And then, after a moment she sat back up straight, and I saw her bring her left hand up to her forehead, but not to rub it in the gesture that had become so familiar to me whenever she felt a vision trying to make its way to her. This time I watched in amazement as she struck her own head, hard, with her hand. And she would have continued to do so, again and again, had I not reached up to stop her.

"Stop it. What are you doing?"

And still, she would not speak. She seemed inconsolable.

After what felt to me an agony of silence and no movement whatsoever on her part, I began at last to feel her body release the long, silent sobs that seemed to fill her whole being.

I took her in my arms and felt the waves of emotion move through her body, one by one.

But her crying remained largely silent, either out of concern for her people who slept nearby or simply because she hadn't the energy to make a sound. I knew not which.

I held her and held her, and she did not make a sound. I held her until I felt the sobbing subside, and then still I held her, hoping for her sake that she would simply let herself fall asleep and rest, hoping for my sake that she would be able to talk before she slept so that she could help me understand what was happening.

Finally, she sat up, moving out of my arms as she did so. I waited. But she did not turn to face me, nor did she make any movement to get up or to lie back down. Once again, she seemed frozen.

"Can I get you anything?" I waited, and finally she shook her head to indicate she wanted nothing.

I registered the relief I felt at finally getting some sort of response from her.

"What is it that has you so upset? Can you share it with me?"

I saw her eyes fall as she heard my question, and after a moment she turned her head but could not raise her eyes to look directly at me.

"I fear I have led my people into a trap."

CHAPTER 24

Having Second Thoughts

She said no more to me that night. She seemed unable to speak, so upset was she by what she'd seen in her vision. At last, she did lie back down. I'm not sure, though, that she ever closed her eyes again that night.

In the morning, as the sun rose, I looked over at her, and still she was awake. She'd not slept all night, I thought to myself. She would be too tired to walk that day. I was just wondering how we would stop her from wanting to try to walk with her people when she surprised me by turning to me and saying, "We will go no farther today. I must tell my people that we will take an extra day to rest here."

"I will tell them," I offered.

"Will you do that for me, Julia?"

"Yes. Do you want me to tell them anything more?"

"Tell them I will talk with them further this evening." And then, before I got up to go deliver her message, she put her hand on mine. "Thank-you, Julia."

I was happy to deliver her message. And her people, in turn, were happy to hear the news that their queen would take an extra day to rest.

They too had seen the signs over the past couple of days, perhaps even more clearly than I had. They knew there had been a vision making its way to their queen, and they knew too what a toll such visions could sometimes take on their queen. They also knew, I suspect, how stubborn the queen could be at times when it came to taking care of her physical self.

"Tell her that we appreciate the extra time she is giving us to rest," said one of the elders.

"I will tell her," I said and returned to find her sleeping at last.

"I have given her something to help her regain her strength," said the healer. And when the queen awoke at mid-day, she looked a little better. She had some tea and said she would eat after she had rested a little longer.

That evening, when she was ready to eat something, she asked me if I could arrange it so that we could eat in private.

"Of course," I said. I went and got some supper for the two of us and explained to the healer that the queen had requested to eat alone.

"You will be with her?"

"Yes," I said, not sure of the significance of her question.

"Good," said the healer. And that was that.

After Ndalla had eaten as much as it seemed her stomach would allow, she sat back with a cup of tea in her hands.

She hadn't talked at all, and I'd begun to wonder if perhaps she just wanted to be left entirely alone, after all, when she said, all at once, "Julia, I fear I have made a terrible mistake in bringing my people along with me on this journey. I sense much danger lies ahead for us. I have been considering sending back to the village all but the warriors I will take to

Daeika with me."

I took in all that she said and then sat there wondering what to do with it. Was she asking for my opinion? She looked at me, apparently waiting for some kind of response.

"Is this because of the vision you had last night?"

She turned away then as she recalled the images that had come to her.

"Yes," she said softly, after some time had passed in silence.

"Are you sure that what you saw was a vision of future events?"

She just looked at me then, in a way I could not understand.

"What do you mean?"

"Perhaps your mind was reliving the violence you have already encountered at the hands of the Daeika. Perhaps making the journey back here has merely triggered your memories of the past, not a vision of the future."

Again, she looked at me, unspeaking. I could not tell whether she was considering my words as being somehow useful to her or if she was wondering how in the world I could be so dense as to suggest such a thing!

"Is it possible," I asked, "that your mind has this time dredged up from the past, events as they already occurred?"

"But the Past and the Future are connected, Julia."

And then I thought of a way to get her to see the difference. "Did you see children and elders in your vision last night? Or did you see only warriors?" Her eyes drifted away from me as she searched her mind, making it impossible for me to study her face.

"There were children," she said at last.

"But were they participating in the violence that you felt, or merely watching it?"

She turned to look at me again. "I cannot be sure, Julia. It was, after all, a vision." But then, after considering further, she said, "The children were participating." And she looked away as she said this, her voice sad.

"Are you sure?"

"Yes," she said, contradicting the uncertainty in her earlier statement.

And then I heard her say, "I should send my people back." But I could hear that she did not want to do this, even as she felt it was the only logical decision to make in light of what she'd seen in the vision.

And then, as though to bolster her own faith in her own logic, she added, "I will not put my people in harm's way, just to serve my own dream of achieving peace and friendship with the Daeika."

"You could put the matter to your people and let them decide."

I saw her then turn and look at me, a small ray of hope appearing in her eyes at last.

"You could share with them what you think your vision last night meant and then leave it to them to choose what they think best: to continue on with you, or to return home while you and the warriors go on alone. You have certainly put such important matters to your people to decide before," I said, recalling her having left it to her people to decide whether they would take the war to the Daeika or whether they would wait for the Daeika to bring the war to them.

Apparently, it had not occurred to her to let them decide this. And then I realized she had probably felt too responsible for having influenced them to come in the first place, and so she was not thinking as clearly as I knew she could. That, and she was pretty tired right now, too.

"I think you can trust your people to make the right decision in this matter," I said.

I read tremendous relief then in her expression. "Then

that is what I will do, Julia. Once again, you have been a great help to me."

"If I have, it is only because you had the courage to share with me your uncertainty. Had you not spoken of your fear, I could not have even tried to help. I thank you for not shutting me out at such a critical time."

And I saw tears come to her eyes then as she set down her tea and came over to me and settled in my arms for a brief rest before she would go to meet with her people.

It was later that night, then, that Ndalla did as she said she would and put the matter to her people to decide.

She shared with them what she feared awaited them because of the vision she'd had the night before. "I am afraid," she said, "that the Daeika might not be as ready to receive an offer of peace and friendship as I would like to believe they are. And if they are not, then we may well be walking into a trap."

She waited, but when no one offered to speak, she continued. "I think it might be wiser for me to travel on alone with just my warriors. I think perhaps the rest of you should return to the village and wait there for us to return. I will send a handful of my warriors with you to see that you get back safely."

There was silence as they took in what she was saying and as they considered their own safety and that of the children and elders among us.

"Is it the queen's command that we return to the village?" one of the elders asked at last.

"No," she said. "It is merely what I think—"

But she did not finish this thought. Not, however, because she was interrupted. It was rather that she seemed to reconsider her response mid-sentence.

"No," she began again. "It is not my decision to make. You have all expressed great hope and faith in what I had hoped to accomplish with this journey. And for that, I thank you. I still believe that we are meant to make peace with the Daeika. I am just uncertain now of the timing. I fear, because of the vision I had last night, that now might not be the time to try to achieve this peace. And if I have misjudged the timing of our attempt, I realize I could be putting your lives at risk. I am not willing to do that."

"But you are leaving the decision to us?" asked the same elder.

"Yes. The decision is yours. I advise you to turn back now. But I do not command you to do so."

"May we have some time to talk among ourselves?"

"Certainly," said Ndalla.

"May we have until morning to decide?"

"Yes."

"Then we thank you for sharing with us your vision and for leaving this to us to decide."

And with that, Ndalla retired for the night.

The next morning, I awoke and was relieved to find Ndalla sleeping peacefully at last. With Yolana's help, I made sure that we had a nice breakfast, complete with a big pot of tea ready for her when she awoke.

"Julia," I heard her say upon waking.

We hadn't spoken last night following the meeting with her people. She'd seemed too tired. The sound of her voice this morning assured me that she had slept well. She sat up then and saw the meal spread before her. She turned to look at me, and I saw that she could tell I was trying to spoil her.

"You did not need to do this, this morning. I am much stronger now. I would have been happy to break the fast with my people." Then, perhaps reading the disappointment on my face, she said, "But come. Let us enjoy this grand breakfast together as long as you have gone to such trouble."

"You will eat then?"

"Yes," she said with a smile. "I will eat. What your world calls 'the morning sickness' has not returned. I was only affected the last couple days by the approach of the vision. Now that it has passed, my appetite has returned."

And she did eat a pretty good breakfast. And when she had finished, she wanted to go and find out what her people had decided. But before she could get to her feet to do so, Bakka approached and stood before us.

"My queen," he said. "The people have decided to continue on to the Daeika village with you, as we all originally intended."

"Come and sit, Bakka. Talk to me. Your family is a part of this group. You recognize the danger. You must."

"Yes, my queen."

"Then—"

"Your people have faith in you, that what you set out to do in the first place is the right thing to do."

"They should have more faith in the visions that are shown to me."

"With respect, the people have faith in your visions too. We all believe that your vision has warned us to proceed with great caution. And so, we will. I have already sent two warriors on ahead, to take an advance look at the Daeika village, to make sure that no surprises await us there."

"The people are all decided in this?"

"To a person," he said with certainty. Then he added, "If I may, my queen—"

"Go on."

"The people did not want to return to the village and, in so doing, add to the distrust that some back there already feel for the Daeika. They understand the risk they are taking. But to a person, it is a risk they are willing to take."

"But we have children with us, and elders."

"The people feel this will help the Daeika better understand our intention than they might if only warriors were to show up to offer them friendship and peace."

Ndalla could not argue with his logic, especially as it was originally her own when she'd asked the people to make the journey with her.

"Very well, then."

"The people ask to be allowed to rest here just one more day, though, before we travel on."

Before she could protest, he said, "This extra time should give one of the two warriors who traveled ahead the chance to report back to us what they have seen ahead of us."

Once again, she found herself unable to argue with her people's logic.

"Very well. But you will keep guards posted from now on."

"Yes, my queen. With your leave." And with that, he left us.

"I am glad for the delay," I said, "as this gives you an extra day to rest up."

"Hmmm," was her only response.

"Your people have clearly given the matter much careful thought. You are wise, both to have put the matter to them in the first place, and then to abide by their decision."

"Hmmm," was, again, all she said.

"They care for you a great deal," I said, more softly this time. "I urge you to trust in their wisdom, even as they trust in yours."

She looked at me then, this time saying nothing. I could see that she was concerned for their safety, and nothing I said was going to allay the fear that had made its way deep into her heart.

And then I thought of something. "As long as we're going to be here an extra day, would this be a good time for us to continue our lessons? Or would you rather be among your people today?"

She considered this for a moment.

"I would like to consult with the Forces today. Perhaps, if you are interested, you could help me in that."

"I am very interested. There is much I would like to learn about the Forces."

She studied me then, a little skeptically, I thought.

"I do not think I can teach you about the Forces. Your learning about the Forces is a matter of your allowing yourself to feel them, Julia. If you truly wish to learn about them, then you must teach yourself how to feel their presence in your life. I cannot help you in this."

"Very well. Then let me help you do what it is you want to do today," I said.

We found a secluded spot then and ended up spending our entire day together there. It would be hard for me to describe, though, exactly how we passed the time.

I remember our finding a spot that seemed to me to inspire a little of the same sense of extreme peace and tranquility that I felt whenever I spent time in Ndalla's beloved clearing.

We sat down then, opposite one another, and she didn't even need to say anything. I knew it was time to clear my mind of all extraneous thoughts. And as I did so and felt the now-familiar sense of emptiness fill my being, I thought only of the Forces themselves as Ndalla had first described Them to me. And I let myself feel the profound sense of trust in Them that her words always conveyed to me. I cannot recall one specific image that came to my mind that day, only a very calming sense that everything was all right. I don't know how else to describe it, even as I am aware of how ridiculous—or, at the very least, naïve—those words must sound. But that is as close as I can come to describing what I felt, as we sat there for what turned out to be the better part of the day.

When at last I opened my eyes, and I cannot recall what prompted me to do so, Ndalla was still sitting opposite me. Her eyes, however, were open, and she was smiling beautifully.

"I can see that you have let yourself feel the gentle power of the Forces today, Julia."

If that was the name for what I had experienced, then so be it. All I knew was that I could very easily become addicted to such a pleasant sensation.

"How long have we been here?" I asked at last. A part of me felt that I had only just begun to feel what I wanted to be able to continue feeling for the rest of the day.

"It is late in the day. We should be heading back soon for the evening meal, I think."

"It can't be." I didn't feel at all as though I'd been sitting all day.

"Time spent in such direct contact with the Forces tends to move very quickly."

"Why is that?" I asked as we both began to stretch ourselves out of the sitting positions we had apparently maintained all day long and get to our feet.

She laughed that beautiful laugh of hers that always made me think of the secure little child that clearly was very much alive within her. "I do not know why it is, Julia. It just is," she said simply. "Come, let us go back and join the others. I do not want them to worry, with our having been gone so long."

And so, we did. Once Ndalla had checked in with Bakka, to see if the warriors had yet returned to let us know what they had found when they scouted on ahead, she came back to me and indicated that she'd let the others know that we would be eating our meal alone tonight. "I would like to talk with you further about your experience today, if that is all right with you."

"Yes," I said, happy to have her all to myself for a little

while longer on this journey, a journey that I had begun to sense would somehow take her further from me as time went on.

After Yolana had brought us some supper and left us alone again, she asked me if I could describe to her any of what I'd felt that day.

"Only extreme peace and a sense that everything is all right somehow."

"I too felt that," she said with a smile that conveyed her obvious relief, especially in the face of the troubling vision that had visited her only the night before last.

"Are you aware of anything else that you feel tonight, though?"

"Like what?" I asked, not aware of anything else that I felt important enough to share.

"I feel," she began somewhat haltingly, "that this journey will pull me away from you somehow."

And then I thought of my own vague sense of that same feeling. Only my sense of it was so vague and so unclear that I had not wanted to speak of it.

"Yes," I said. "I felt something of that too this evening, but I did not want to speak of it."

"It is all right," she said, putting her hand gently on mine. And I didn't know at first if she meant that it was all right to feel such a thing or that it was all right to not want to speak of it.

"I too was reluctant to speak of it when I first became aware of it," she admitted. "But I think it would be better to speak of it, do you not?"

I registered only my own reluctance still.

"May I speak of it then?" she asked, in the face of my own silence on the subject.

"Of course."

"I feel that this journey back to the Daeika is filled with the potential for both great gain and great loss." She said these words very solemnly, her eyes lowered as she spoke them.

Then she raised her eyes and met mine as she continued. "I feel that the time of testing that I foresaw so long ago—long before you came into my life, Julia, and I into yours—involves not just a testing of the Ndalla but a testing of the people of Daeika as well. I feel that this is their test as much as it is ours, that we are somehow bound up together in this."

She paused then, and I found myself wondering if she'd gotten all of this today, during her time with the Forces, when all I'd experienced was a sense that everything was all right! I considered asking her, but I didn't want to interrupt what she seemed to be only in the middle of sharing with me.

"I sense too that this journey will only pull me further into myself somehow and therefore further away from you."

I felt myself turn away from her, despite myself. "Julia. Do not misunderstand me. I need you now, more than ever." But I still felt unable to face her.

And then she said something that made me feel what I've heard described as the shudder you experience when someone has walked on your grave. "You know how to call me back from the spirit world if I should get lost there."

I looked at her then and saw what I felt to be fear in her eyes. But fear of what?

"What are you talking about?" I asked, the fear I read on her face fueling my own.

"I told you before, Julia, that I believe that some of the Daeika got lost in the Great Emptiness. Some of those who got lost then, before the battle, are liable to still be lost there."

She studied my face a moment before continuing.

"I do not know what will happen when we arrive there," she admitted. "But I believe that our visit with the Daeika will involve those who ventured into the Great Emptiness who have yet to find their way back. I think this is the danger that my vision showed me the other night."

"But why would you get lost there?"

"I do not know that I will, Julia. I only know that if I hope to reach out to those who are lost, I myself will have to be willing to take some risks. I am willing to take these risks, both for the sake of my own people and for the sake of the Daeika. But I need you to understand what I am doing and why. And I need you to be ready to help me find my way back if I should—"

I took her in my arms, not letting her finish the sentence.

"I understand," I said as I held her.

She looked at me a moment, before saying, "Julia, I will not always be able to explain things to you the way I would like to. I must rely on what you can sense." She paused. "I know that there is still much about my world that you do not yet understand. I wish we had more time to spend together before we arrive in Daeika."

"But we do not," I said simply, aware of something within me rising to meet head-on the fear I'd registered and felt a little overwhelmed by only moments earlier. I even managed a small smile as I said, "Surely, the Forces know this. I do not think they would put us in this situation if we were not, at some level, ready for the challenges that await us. Do you?"

I could feel Ndalla shift her position in my arms. She sat up then and faced me.

"No," she said. "I do not think they would."

And I enjoyed seeing the surprise on her face that it was I—and not she—who had made this rather simple and, I thought, astute observation.

CHAPTER 25

Extending an Invitation

The next morning, one of the warriors who'd been sent ahead returned and let us know that he and his companion had found no surprises along the way. And so our party continued on toward the Daeika village, albeit much more cautiously than we'd been doing up until now.

And as Ndalla had foreseen, she drew increasingly inward, the closer we got to our destination. She still walked among her people, ate with them, and slept with them, but she seemed to me—and perhaps to others, too, I don't know—to become more withdrawn, more caught up in her inner world. She also had us stop for the night earlier than we had before now. And every night, she spent a few hours in consultation with the Forces.

When we arrived at the place where we would camp, out of sight of the Daeika but only a half day's journey to their village, Ndalla ordered the warriors to triple their guard. "We must be vigilant, so close now to their village," she said.

We camped there for a few days so that Ndalla herself could observe what the scout had been observing for days prior to our arrival: a peaceful village, its inhabitants going on about their business, with no apparent awareness of our presence.

On the morning after watching the Daeika for three full days, a small party headed off toward the village. We did it in the full light of day so that the Daeika would not misjudge our approach and think it to be some kind of surprise attack. The party consisted of a dozen warriors, hand-picked by Ndalla herself, along with the healer, Yolana, Ndalla, and myself.

As we emerged from the cover of the woods that surrounded the Daeika village and made our way across an open field, the villagers clearly caught sight of us. We heard shouts of alarm and saw people running in every direction. I watched as our warriors tried to position themselves between the village and the queen, but she would have none of it. Apparently, she wanted the people in the village to see her, not her warriors, as the party approached.

When Ndalla judged us to be within the right distance of the village—close enough to be seen and heard but not so close as to appear more threatening than I'm sure we already did— she had us stop, and she stepped forward alone several more steps.

"We are the Ndalla. We have come in peace. We do not wish to fight with the people of Daeika. I am queen of my people. And I have come to talk with the Daeika about the future of our people. It is my belief that we are meant to join our forces from here forward in time, not to use them against each other in battle."

She waited for her words to sink in, knowing that she had said much that many to whom she was speaking had not been prepared to hear.

"I would ask that you send out a small party of your

people, with one who can speak for the Daeika so that I can speak further. With your permission, my party will make camp out here in the open field and wait. I would ask that you send your party out well before the setting of the sun so that you can see that we mean your party no harm."

And with that, she bowed slightly in the direction of the village, a gesture that surprised me and, I think, a number of her warriors as well. Then, she turned her back on them, exposing herself to their weapons if they chose to use them at this distance, and gestured to the rest of us to follow her. To their credit, I thought, the warriors to the rear of our party did not let down their guard, though, and walked backwards the whole way, keeping an eye out for any surprise attacks from the village.

But no attacks came. We walked a distance out into the middle of the open field that lay before the village, set up an impromptu camp, and waited, as the queen had announced to the Daeika that we would. We waited several hours as we watched the sun begin to make its way toward the horizon. And just about the time I was ready to ask what we would do if they did not come, we saw the small party of just three leave the village and make its way in our direction.

As they got closer, I could make out that the group consisted of one elder, a young woman who appeared to be not yet twenty, and a young boy of no more than fifteen, I thought. The boy walked first, with the elder and the young woman flanked out on either side of him, walking a little distance behind him, perhaps out of deference to him, I thought even at the time.

Ndalla rose to her feet as she saw them approach. Quietly, she turned to Bakka and asked him to have his men retreat a distance so as to leave just Ndalla herself, Yolana, the healer, and myself there to meet the group of three. And just as quietly, Bakka gave the order, and his men gave ground.

Not surprisingly, it was the boy, whose very way of carrying himself conveyed his sense of his own importance, who spoke for both himself and his companions once they arrived.

"I am Daeikabah, leader of my people ... since the Ndalla killed my father in the Great Battle." He waited a moment for the clear sense of disdain he felt for the Ndalla to sink in.

Then, turning to the man beside him, he said, "This is Barei, a respected elder among my people." Barei stepped forward slightly and bowed his head, a gesture that the boy clearly did not approve of his having made to the queen of his enemy.

But I watched then as Ndalla bowed her head in return, and I saw the elder smile—in a kindly way, I thought.

"And this," he said, turning to introduce the young woman on his other side, the young woman who, I noticed, still stood slightly behind the boy, either out of fear of us or respect for him, I couldn't tell which, "is my sister, Mara." And with these words, I heard his tone, for the first time, betray his youth. Leader or not, his tone conveyed what I took to be any young boy's disdain for an older sister, one who perhaps, in this case, had even insisted on being allowed to be a part of the small group that would speak for their people.

His sister bowed her head slightly, as she had seen Barei do, but with her, there was an air of self-consciousness about the gesture.

Ndalla gave no indication that she had noticed the young woman's discomfort, though, and bowed to her just as she had to Barei. And I saw the young woman's neck and face grow pink in response to the beautiful smile that I saw Ndalla gift the young woman with as she raised her head again.

"We have come to hear what you have to say," said the boy, in a tone that was all business.

"Let us sit," said Ndalla, and I noticed that she waited for the boy to do so first.

When we were all seated, Ndalla spoke again.

"I appreciate your coming out to hear my offer. I was not sure when we approached the Daeika that they would be willing to hear me out. You have already made the journey worth the time it took my party to make it. And for that, I thank you."

The boy seemed pleased to hear gratitude coming from the mouth of his enemy.

"Is this your entire party, or do you have more warriors hiding in the woods around my village?"

I thought I saw Ndalla start to smile, but then she checked herself. "You are wise to ask such a question at the outset. This is not my entire party." And I saw the boy's expression betray his pride in having caught his enemy in an attempt at deception before his eyes became even more wary of us. "I have more warriors camped up on that ridge," she said, in a matter-of-fact tone, before adding, "along with several families, children, and elders who made this journey with me."

"You brought children and elders with you on this journey?" The surprise in his voice conveyed his disbelief that she would do such a thing.

"Yes," she said simply.

"Why?"

"They chose to come, to help me extend to the Daeika the offer of peace and friendship that I have come to extend to you."

"Yet you leave them camped in the hills. Is this how you show your trust of the Daeika?"

"I show my trust in the Daeika by having let so many of my people accompany me to your land so soon after having fought such a great battle with your people. It is the responsibility I feel for the safety of my people that led me to leave them camped in the hills until I had the chance to talk with you first and see if you are even interested in making peace with the Ndalla."

The boy considered this a moment before he spoke again.

"And what would your 'peace' consist of?" he asked, almost spitting the word out.

"It would consist of whatever the Daeika and the Ndalla decide together that it will consist of."

"You would have us 'work out' a peace between us, then?" he asked warily.

"Yes."

"Why?" he asked sharply, as though trying to catch her in a lie.

"Because I feel that is how both our people can benefit."

"You want something from us, then." His tone conveyed his certainty and his satisfaction that he had finally gotten to the bottom of things.

"No," Ndalla said simply.

And I watched as the boy's puzzlement spread across his face.

"We have come to offer you something."

He merely waited then for her to continue, clearly having exhausted his attempts to show her intentions to be something other than what she seemed intent on insisting they were.

"I know that all of your warriors were killed in the Great Battle." She waited a moment, perhaps out of respect for the fact that the boy—and the young woman too, for that matter—had lost a father in the battle she spoke of. "You are a people now without warriors to protect your young and your old. As such, you are a people that my people have left vulnerable to attack."

And here her voice softened as she said, "It was never our intention to leave you, as a people, so vulnerable to the attacks of others. The killing in the Great Battle went further than any of us could have foreseen."

She waited again, knowing—I am sure—how her words must be striking very close to the still-open wounds in the heart of both the boy and the young woman before her. "We have come," she said, "to offer you the protection that we have an obligation to offer you following such a battle. I can only hope you will consider accepting such an offer."

It was the elder who spoke at this point, perhaps aware that the young boy needed more time to consider the words they had just heard. "Your arm," he said, indicating the fact that it was obviously still bound, "was injured in the Great Battle?"

"Yes," she said, lowering her eyes slightly.

"It resists healing?"

"So far," she said. And then she added, "I feel certain that my arm—like the relationship between the Daeika and the Ndalla—will heal. It just needs time."

And I saw the elder nod in approval of her words. "What is it that you would have us do?" he asked gently.

"Go back and talk with your people. Explain to them what it is that we have come to offer the Daeika. And ask them if I may address them and extend to them in person the same offer I have explained to you here."

"That is all?" asked the elder.

"That is all," replied Ndalla.

Then the young woman surprised us all by speaking up. "My brother distrusts you and your people. He is sure you have come here to trick us in some way."

I couldn't tell by her tone if she shared his skepticism or was trying to embarrass him.

Ndalla then looked at the young woman before she answered her. "Your brother is wise beyond his years. He is wise to consider that we have perhaps come with some intentions other than what I have shared. To not consider this possibility would be foolishness on his part, and he is no fool.

I can see that."

She paused then, long enough to let the boy enjoy a small moment of victory over his older sister. Then she turned to look directly at the boy as she continued her reply to his sister.

"But to NOT consider now the possibility that we have come for just the reason I have stated would be even greater foolishness. And I trust that your brother is wise enough to know this too."

The boy raised his eyes then. I still read caution and wariness in his eyes now, but the pure disdain that had so colored his earlier words and gestures was somewhat diluted.

Ndalla then got to her feet, and the rest of us followed suit. "Your people deserve some time to consider what I have asked," she said. "With your permission, my party will camp out here in the open field, in plain sight of your village." Then she looked up to the sky. The moon was waning. "But if you have not returned to us by the time the moon grows to half its full size, to let us know that your people will hear my offer, we will return to our village, and we will respect the fact that the Daeika are not yet ready to reach out to the Ndalla in the spirit of peace, in which we have come." By my reckoning, that gave them a few days to get back to us.

"You will simply leave us then?" the boy asked, his disbelief apparent.

"Yes." It was all Ndalla said.

"Just like that?"

"We will leave you to live your lives as you choose," she said with a slight bow.

The elder stepped forward then and extended his arm. Ndalla took it in her left arm.

"We will share your offer with our people," he said. "And while I cannot speak for them, I believe your offer to be a sincere one. I will do what I can to encourage them to give you the audience you seek with them."

"Thank-you, Barei." And I saw their eyes meet in what seemed to be a measure of mutual respect and understanding.

The young woman then stepped forward and followed the example of her elder. Ndalla accepted her gesture of friendship and again made the young woman blush by gifting her with that beautiful smile. "And thank-you," said Ndalla, "for speaking so honestly with me."

Ndalla then looked directly at the boy, who, it was clear, was not yet ready to extend his arm in friendship. Ndalla made nothing of this, however. She merely said, "And I thank you, Daeikabah, for having the courage to listen to one that you clearly still see as your enemy. Such courage in men is rare in my experience. I look forward to future talks with you, if that is what is to be." After speaking these words, she bowed to him, a gesture he did not reciprocate.

The next few days passed quickly enough as our party of sixteen camped out in the open field while the rest of our party stayed camped up in the hills. We did not try to communicate with the rest of our group, as we feared that might cause some concern on the part of the Daeika.

We were blessed by the weather as we sat out in the open field with no shade to sit under. We would have baked under the sun if we'd had clear skies. But fortunately, clouds moved in the same day we talked with the three from the village. Clouds for which we were, at first, grateful.

It was not until the late afternoon of our third day of waiting that the skies became more ominous, and Ndalla said to us all, I think in an effort to encourage us not to lose our humor, "This will not be a pleasant experience."

We watched as the clouds gathered and the sky grew darker, and we listened as the thunder came closer, getting louder and louder still.

The first raindrops had already begun to fall when we saw three familiar figures make their way out of the village and walk—not run—toward our makeshift camp. Once again, Ndalla got to her feet as they approached in order to be able to greet them properly.

"Apparently, the Ndalla do not even know enough to come in out of the rain," the young boy could not resist saying by way of opening.

It was Barei who quickly stepped forward then, bowed slightly to Ndalla, and said, "My people are still considering your request. However, your party is welcome to move itself indoors until the Daeika have finished their considerations. We have two dwellings in our village—one for you and your immediate party and one for your warriors—which you are welcome to stay in while you continue to wait. We appreciate your patience."

"And we, your hospitality," said Ndalla.

"What of your people in the hills?" asked the elder.

"I assume they were able to find shelter already, well in advance of the storm. I would, however, like to send word to them to let them know that we will be a while longer."

"As you wish," said Barei.

Then, turning to the warrior closest to her, she said, "Tell our people that we are entering the village to await the answer of their people. The Ndalla are to stay where they are until I send word to them to join us." She paused a moment before adding, "No matter what happens."

"Yes, my queen." And with that, he left, and our party was down to just fifteen members.

Barei extended his arm then to escort Ndalla. But rather than take his arm, she gestured to Yolana and the healer to accept his offer.

To Barei, she said simply, "Please, help my friends first. I will follow."

"As you wish," he said.

And then, by way of introduction, she said to him, "This is the healer among my people, and this, Yolana."

He bowed slightly to each woman in turn, extending each an arm.

And to the women, she said, "Let Barei help you to get under cover as quickly as possible."

And so, the young boy, of course, led the way, with Barei and the two women following him closely. I fell in step on one side of Ndalla, who, I could not help but notice, was soon joined by Mara on the other. And Bakka led the warriors, who brought up the rear.

And so it was that our party entered the village of the Daeika on that dark and stormy night. Try as I might to stop it, my mind insisted on making the obvious connection between the storm raging in the outside world and the tensions I knew were still very much alive between our two peoples ... not to mention a certain tension I felt growing within at a more personal level, as I looked over at Mara and saw her eyeing Ndalla with a look I understood all too well.

CHAPTER 26

Entering the Daeika Village

Even with the rain pouring down, we could feel many eyes watching us as we made our way into the Daeika village. I sensed the warriors' uneasiness as I too considered the possibility that this might be a trap.

But Ndalla, if she felt fear, did not show it. She looked all around her as we entered the village, the rain streaming down her face. Her face conveyed neither fear nor pride, only open curiosity about this people who had made war on her people and who now held her own fate—and the fate of her people—in their hands.

Barei took Yolana, the healer, Ndalla, and myself to one dwelling while Daeikabah directed the warriors to another. I could see Bakka's uneasiness at this arrangement, as could Ndalla, who went over to Bakka and, within easy hearing of Daeikabah, said to him, "It is all right for now that the warriors stay here, apart from me. Stay with them tonight and reassure them that all is well. Then come to me in the morning. You will see that I am fine. The Daeika mean us no harm within the walls of their own village. I am sure of this."

He seemed somewhat reassured by her words and her gentle tone, but I could see that he was still uneasy. Even so, he did as he was instructed by his queen.

Barei came inside the dwelling with the four of us to make sure that we had everything we needed. It was a simple dwelling. Nothing extra, but it did shelter us from the rain and wind.

"We are bringing you—and your warriors—food and water tonight. I am not sure you had much to eat and drink while you were camped out in the open field these last several days."

"Thank-you, Barei," said Ndalla, and her smile conveyed her genuine gratitude. Barei seemed to be considering whether to say anything more.

He stole a quick glance at the doorway behind him before stepping closer to the queen and then speaking softly. "You have been most patient with my people," he said, "who have yet to be able to come to a decision about whether to even hear your offer."

"Tell me if there is anything I can do to help," she said in a tone to match.

"I am afraid it will take more time," he said. "Many of the elders are ready to hear your offer, but many of our young, who lost family members in the Great Battle, are still resisting the idea. Please be patient a little longer."

She reached out to him then and gently laid her hand on his arm. "I can be patient as long as you need me to be. And if the Daeika are not yet ready to consider my offer, Barei, know that I meant what I said: we will leave you to live your lives how you choose."

"I know," he said, his voice sounding almost sad, I thought. "That is exactly why we must convince the young to let you make your offer to the people."

"None of us should force another to do what he is not yet ready to do," she said simply.

"You are a wise leader," he said. And with that he took his leave of us.

Over the course of the next couple of days, I watched as Ndalla drew even further into herself during this time of waiting. The rain continued outside, keeping her from being able to go outside even if she'd wanted to. But I wasn't sure that's what she would have done anyway.

I found it very hard to read her as this difficult time of waiting passed ever so slowly. And the one thing I could read about her made me uneasy.

Increasingly, she showed signs of getting herself ready to receive another vision. And I began to wonder which would come first: the vision … or word from the Daeika that they were ready to hear her offer. What if word came from the Daeika just when she was unable to address the people of this village? What if she were in the middle of such a vision? Or still recovering from it? What then?

I wanted to ask her about these things, but I knew this was what she was referring to when she'd said to me, on the journey here, that she would not be able to explain things to me, things that she would have to rely on my ability to sense and try to understand on my own.

It was toward the evening of our third full day of waiting that we heard a knock at the entrance to our dwelling. Ndalla stood before it, calling, "Enter."

It was Mara who stood in the doorway, apparently alone, her arms filled with our evening meal. Yolana stepped forward quickly to help her, and even Ndalla stepped forward to help.

"You did not have to carry this all yourself," Ndalla said. "We would have been happy to come ourselves to at least help."

"I wanted to bring you your meal tonight."

And I noticed then that Ndalla stopped what she was doing and studied Mara's face a moment. "Do you want to stay and eat with us tonight?"

"Very much," said the young woman, her whole face brightening.

Ndalla seemed to consider her next question carefully before voicing it. "Are you sure this is all right with your brother?"

"Oh, he does not tell me what to do," Mara said dismissively.

"Even so," said Ndalla, "I do not want to do anything to displease him right now. I have asked him to do me a great favor by asking him to let me address his people."

"Do not worry," said Mara. "He will not even know I am here. He and the others who would decide this matter will be talking well into the night, as they have done every night since you first met with us out in the open field."

"Are you not, as sister of the leader of your people, involved in these talks as well?"

"Oh, I could be, but I choose not to be. I leave such matters to my brother." And then with a laugh, she added, "Of course, I reserve the right to tell him when I think he is wrong."

"I see," said Ndalla. And then, tentatively, she said to the young woman, "Do you not think you could be of more help to your brother if you sat in on these talks so that he would have someone to talk to, outside the group, should he find himself of two minds on the subject?"

Mara seemed to be considering Ndalla's suggestion seriously.

"Perhaps," she said.

"I do not know your brother as well as you do, obviously," said Ndalla. "But as a leader myself, I know the value of having such a person close to you, someone you can trust enough to speak your heart to when you are not even sure you know your own heart, when having to make such weighty decisions."

Mara seemed to still be considering Ndalla's words, even as Yolana finished laying the meal out for us.

"You are more than welcome to join us in our meal," said Ndalla, "if this is where you think you really want to be right now." And when the young woman still seemed unable to decide what to do, Ndalla added, "Or you could go and be with your brother now and come back again and join us for a meal when you are sure he has no immediate need of you." Then I saw Ndalla lay her hand on the young woman's arm. "I would like to have you stay for a visit, but only when you are sure you are not needed by your people elsewhere."

The young woman looked up at Ndalla then and smiled.

"Do you mean that?"

Ndalla smiled then and said simply, "The only words I speak are those that I mean."

After just a moment's more consideration, Mara said, "All right, then. I will go and sit in on these talks, and if my brother wants to know what I think, before he makes a decision, I will tell him. That will surprise him," she said with a laugh.

"I think he will appreciate that more than perhaps he will know how to say."

"I think you are right."

And with that, Mara was gone.

Much later that evening, long after we had eaten, Ndalla became ill. We got her to lie down. She was shivering violently, so we piled on her all the blankets we could find. I felt her head, and sure enough, I felt a fever. If this was a vision about to visit her, I remember thinking, it was like none I'd ever witnessed.

I looked to Yolana, who I knew had seen the queen go

through more vision sequences than anyone else, and even she seemed concerned.

I turned to the healer. "What is it that has come on her so suddenly?"

"I do not know."

"Can you give her anything?"

"I can give her something to help warm her and to fight the fever, but without knowing what brought this on, I hesitate to do so."

"Can you hear me?" I asked, bending down, closer to Ndalla. "Do you know what's happening? Can you tell us how to help?"

"It is a vision," she said. I could barely make out her words. "You must not leave me tonight, Julia. I will need your help to return."

"But where will this vision take you?"

And I saw the fear in her eyes even before she spoke the words.

"It is the Great Emptiness that calls me toward it tonight."

Do not go! I wanted to shout the words that filled my mind, but I did not dare.

"I must," she said in answer to my unspoken thoughts.

And with that, she passed out.

The queen's vision that night was unlike any that I had previously witnessed. Her body was eerily still for what I knew to be the passing of several hours. I began to fear that I would not know when the vision was over and when she needed my help to return to us. But then, I need not have worried, for as that night proved to me, we were connected at a level I need not have doubted.

I heard her voice, just barely, in my mind, as I had before when she needed such help.

And in my mind, I answered her call and kept calling to her, over and over again, until I could hear her voice growing just a little stronger.

I encouraged her, letting her know that I could hear her voice more clearly and urged her to keep moving in whatever direction she was moving.

I have no idea how long this continued. It felt like an eternity to me. Only after a very long time did I finally begin to feel her presence among us again.

And yet even once I felt her presence, she seemed to need still more help as she tried to make her way to us. It was as though a part of her had returned to us while another part of her still wandered, lost, in the Great Emptiness.

And even as I continued to call to her in my mind, I could feel a fear beginning to grow inside of me, a fear that the part of her that still wandered there was beyond even my reach.

I opened my eyes then and saw that Yolana was holding the queen's head up while the healer was offering her something to drink. I could see the relief on the two women's faces, even as I felt something cold and hard in the pit of my stomach.

"Has she opened her eyes yet?" I asked.

"No, but you can see that you have brought her back to us," said the healer. "See how she drinks of the medicine I offer her."

"Ndalla," I said as I leaned over her and whispered in her ear, "can you open your eyes? I need to see your eyes."

And as she did so, I could see that while she had done her best to return to us, she was not yet back from the Great Emptiness, not totally.

I called to her again in my mind.

And I heard her voice say the words that chilled my heart: "There is a part of me that cannot return just yet." And then I heard her say, "You must be patient, Julia."

386

The next morning, we were all still sleeping after our ordeal of the night before when we were awakened by a loud pounding at the entrance of the dwelling.

And then, even before anyone could say, "Enter," I saw Daeikabah standing before us, furious.

I looked beside me, where the queen still lay, asleep and unmoving. The sight of her appearing to rest so peacefully only seemed to infuriate the boy still more.

"The sun has already journeyed halfway to its mid-day height, and still your queen sleeps," he said, his tone clearly one of disdain.

"She was taken ill last night. Even now, you can see that she fights the fever," I said.

He came closer to see if I spoke the truth, and only then did he seem to accept the fact that she was, really, ill. Once he did so, he quickly stepped back, apparently afraid that whatever afflicted her might jump to him as well.

I thought of telling him he needn't worry, but then I thought better. Why ease his mind?

"When she awakes, you can tell her that you are no longer our guests. You are all our prisoners now."

I looked down at the queen, who seemed to be trying to rouse herself at the sound of the boy's angry tone, but she could not.

"Why," I asked. "What has happened?"

The boy turned, apparently to see whether or not Barei had followed him yet into the dwelling. He had, but only with what I could see was great reluctance. And then I saw that Mara too stood in the doorway, her face white, either with fear or shock.

"I will leave Barei to give you the details. I came only to make sure that you know you are our prisoners now. Tell your queen when she awakes that she and her warriors had better not try anything. My people and I are all too ready to seek revenge for what happened last night."

After the boy left, Barei came forward while Mara stepped just a little farther into the dwelling before deciding, apparently, to wait there.

"What happened to your queen?" asked the elder as he approached where she lay.

I debated how much to share with him. "She was taken ill last night, sometime after supper."

He laid his hand gently on her forehead.

"Tell me, if I may ask. Was her hair always this short? Or did the Daeika warriors do this to her?"

"The Daeika warriors."

"And her arm? It too was at their hands, was it not?"

"Yes."

"And—" He hesitated here, but I could see where his eyes went.

"It is her belief that she carries life within her as a result of what happened at the hands of the Daeika warriors, as well," I said.

And I saw him close his eyes. When he opened them, I could see the tears that he tried to hold back.

"And yet she comes to offer us peace?"

"It is what she believes the Forces have indicated it is time to do," I said.

He looked up at me suddenly, alarm on his face. He looked over at Mara then and gestured that she should close the entrance to the dwelling. She did so quickly before coming over to join us then.

"In my village, it is only the elders who still speak of the Forces as you just have."

"What do you mean?" I asked.

"Daeikabah's father," he began, and then he turned to the

young woman beside him before continuing. "Mara's father did not believe in the Forces, and so, as leader of our people, he had the right to decide that the Forces would not play a role in the lives of his people."

"So your young people—"

"They do not even know about the Forces," he said, finishing my sentence.

"This would seem to explain then why your people are so unwilling to trust the Ndalla, would it not?"

He only nodded, wordlessly.

I decided at that moment to trust the man and the young woman before me, even knowing as I did so that I was putting us all, particularly Ndalla herself, at great risk.

"Not only does the queen believe in the power and the wisdom of the Forces that she listens to, but she receives visions directly from the Forces and has the power to travel in and out of the spirit realm."

I could see that Barei understood what I was saying, even as a part of my mind registered pure amazement on Mara's face.

I also sensed uneasiness on the part of both the healer and Yolana, but to their credit, they maintained their silence, which I took to be a sign of their trust in the queen's trust in me.

"She had such a vision last night. It was a vision that took her into," and here I paused, knowing how my next words would upset the two women at my side, "the Great Emptiness."

I waited a moment before continuing. "It is where she believes the spirits of a number of your warriors had gotten lost before the battle, and it is also where she believes the spirits of a number of those who live among you are still lost."

I watched as he stroked her hair gently on hearing these words. "I knew your queen was wise. I could feel her wisdom in that first meeting. I see now that I did not see just how wise—and brave—she is."

Then, while keeping his hand gently on her, he asked, "What can I do to help?"

"Tell us what happened last night!"

"One of our youths was killed. It appears that it happened in his sleep. There are signs that his dwelling was entered and that he was stabbed as he slept."

"And your people believe that it was one of our warriors that did this?"

"How could they not think such a thing?" he asked, and I had to admit he had a point.

But still, I thought, they had to use some sense. What had we to gain by doing such a thing?

"Some of our youths," he went on to say, "are calling for the execution of all the Ndalla warriors that we allowed into our village, as we cannot know for sure which it was that killed the youth."

"They choose then to ignore the very real possibility that it was not any one of the Ndalla warriors that did this thing, that it may well have been one of their own people?"

"But why would one Daeika kill another?"

"I don't know. I just refuse to believe that it was one of our warriors," I said, trying not to give into my growing frustration.

I looked down then at Ndalla, and I knew instantly what to tell the old man. "Try to keep your people from doing anything they will regret. Give me this day, Barei. Let me talk with the queen. She will know what to do. Come back this evening, and we will work together to find a solution to the problem that the Forces have seen fit to present us with this day."

And with that, Barei and Mara left us.

It was sometime later that morning before we were

successful in getting Ndalla to open her eyes at all. And when we did, I could see that some part of her still had not yet made its way back from the Great Emptiness. Yolana helped her drink the medicines the healer prepared for her, and when she seemed able to understand my words, I shared with her what Barei had shared with us, but only the information about the killing, not that his people had lost touch with the Forces over the years. I saw her raise her hand to her forehead as she lay back down then.

She gestured to me to come closer, and when I did so, I heard her voice, weaker than I'd ever heard it. "I must go back, Julia."

"No!" I shouted as I sat back up. And I saw Yolana and the healer both jump at the sound of my voice, spoken in answer to the queen's words that I realized then they hadn't even heard. I bent back over Ndalla and whispered, "Please do not make this journey."

But when I sat back to read a response on her face, as I heard her say nothing, I realized that she had already left us again.

And so, just as we had the night before, we waited at her side, as her body stayed eerily still and quiet. I closed my eyes, determined to be ready to call her back the moment I heard even the faintest sound from her in my mind.

I waited and waited, but heard nothing. And still I waited, and still I heard nothing.

We waited the better part of that day. And then finally, not too long before sunset, I heard her faint voice calling to me, "Julia."

I knew it was her voice this time. All day long, I had wanted to hear her voice, and all day long, my mind had kept playing tricks on me. But this, I knew, was her voice.

And so, I called back to her in my mind. It seemed to me that she found her way back to me more easily this time. But even so, it was a painstakingly slow process that I could feel taking a lot out of me and that I knew had to be taking even more out of her.

Eventually, though, I could feel her presence filling the room, and this time, it did not feel to me as though a part of her had remained behind.

I saw her lungs fill with air as her body and spirit reunited, and I felt her reach up for me and hold on to me with her left hand, more tightly than I would have thought she had the strength to do. Then I saw her open her eyes, and I knew she had come back to us, fully this time.

"You made it," I said. "You are safe. You are among friends again."

She looked around at the three of us, smiled, and then cried tears of joy and relief.

When Barei and Mara returned that evening, the queen was resting quietly. "Is she no better this evening?" Barei asked, upon seeing her look much as he remembered having left her that morning.

"No," I assured him, "the queen is much better." I thought about sharing more with him, but then thought better and decided to keep things as simple as possible right now. "She asked to be awakened when you returned so that she could speak with you, Barei. However, she is very weak. You will have to listen closely in order to hear her." The old man seemed to understand. "Give me a minute," I said before going over to where Ndalla lay.

Within minutes, she was fully awake but still so weak that I hesitated even to tell her she had guests. Nevertheless, when she heard that Barei and Mara had returned, she tried to sit up.

"You are too weak," I said. "Save what strength you have

to be able to talk with them."

Somewhat uncharacteristically for her, she did as I suggested, without protest.

"Barei," she said, extending her arm in greeting as he approached where she lay. He took her hand and touched it gently to his forehead. "And Mara, too." The young woman smiled at being acknowledged. And then Ndalla gathered what little energy she had in order to share with them what she had to say.

"Thaeikus," she said, using a name I had not heard before, but Barei and Mara both seemed to recognize the name. Their faces registered their surprise at hearing her use it. The queen merely nodded and continued. "He was a friend of Daeikabah's, was he not?"

The old man nodded, his face betraying his astonishment at the queen's knowing the name of the Daeika youth who had been killed, something he knew he had not shared with us. "This will make matters difficult for Daeikabah," she said, almost more to herself than to us.

Then she continued. "But Thaeikus also had another friend, a very good friend. Thaeikus would not speak his name."

"You spoke with Thaeikus?"

"He made his spirit available to me today. I did not know if he would, lost as he is in the Great Emptiness," and her body shivered at the memory of where her spirit had traveled.

I raised the covers up over her more fully and tried to comfort her. "Do you want some tea before you continue?" I asked.

"Yes, please."

Barei helped her lift her head as I held the cup for her. She could not drink much yet.

As she lay back down, she continued, looking directly at Barei as she spoke.

"You know the friend of which I speak?"

"Yes," said the old man, and the young woman nodded as well.

"You must get Daeikabah to talk with this boy. If Daeikabah can get him to talk, the boy can bring to light what happened to Thaeikus. But Daeikabah must approach the boy gently, with readiness to hear what the boy wants to share."

"What do you mean?"

"Daeikabah cannot approach the boy in anger. That will only cause the boy to lie. The boy seeks Daeikabah's approval. That is why he and Thaeikus made the pact they made."

"What pact?"

She waved her arm weakly by way of dismissing the question. "It is for the boy to say, or not. But it was a pact that the two boys made in order to restore honor to the Daeika and also in order to dishonor the Ndalla. Daeikabah must understand that the boys meant to do what they thought was right. Only if he approaches the boy in this spirit will he get the truth from the boy."

And with that, it was clear that Ndalla could not—or would not—say more. In fact, she fell asleep instantly, as she finished these words.

I stepped outside then with Barei and Mara so that we could talk further and let the queen rest. "Can you get Daeikabah to approach the boy as she asked?"

"I don't know. Our young leader is very angry already," Barei commented honestly.

"I think I can get him to," said Mara.

"How?"

"I am his big sister, after all. I have my ways," she said with a smile.

But I knew this was no game, and I feared that if she mishandled the situation, it would be the Ndalla people—and in particular, the queen—who would pay.

"Mara, this is very serious. If Daeikabah is told that the queen believes in the Forces, which your father instructed your people not to believe in, that could be enough for him to decide to take action against the Ndalla. You must understand, we are at his mercy right now."

"I understand this," she said, her tone indicating that she did not appreciate being spoken to as though she were a child.

"Then how can you get Daeikabah to do as the queen has asked?"

"I do not know yet. I only know that I can. I will figure out how when the time comes."

I looked to Barei for some help in this.

"Let the two of us talk a while," he said to me. "Together, I think we can figure out a way to get Daeikabah to approach the boy as the queen has suggested he must if he is to get to the truth of what has happened."

I turned to Mara and was relieved to see that she seemed grateful to have the old man's help in figuring this out.

"I will leave the matter, then, in your hands," I said. "I have no other choice."

Part Six:
Finding a Way Forward

CHAPTER 27
Practicing Patience

That night, before she fell into what appeared to be a deep and restful sleep, Ndalla drank some of the healer's fortifying medicine, which—always before, anyway—had a way of helping her recover her strength quickly.

I had my doubts, however, that her recovery would be as fast this time. I had never seen the look in her eyes that I had seen following her first encounter with the Great Emptiness, nor had I ever had to work so hard to call her back from the spirit world as I did that time. And then for her to have found whatever it must have taken to return to such a place ... I couldn't imagine.

I couldn't help but wonder if the events of the past several weeks—months, really—could finally be catching up with this woman whose strength and resilience had always seemed to me to be so limitless. And that wasn't even taking into account the fact that some of her energy was now being used to support the new life that she was carrying.

I looked down at the strong young woman who had so mysteriously appeared in my bedroom ... how many months ago? Close to six months, by my reckoning.

I smiled to myself as I registered how easily my mind had shifted from looking for a calendar to considering the number of moon cycles that had passed: two back in my world and close to another four in hers.

She looked so much older to me now. Still, when I thought of what those months had held for her, was it any wonder that she appeared to have aged so?

In the quiet of the night that passed, I found myself reflecting on the "time of testing" that Ndalla had foreseen before she had journeyed to my world, all those months ago. She could not have been that much older than Mara when she first started foreseeing such a time approaching for her and her people. I considered that for a moment and found myself wondering what kind of courage it must have taken to face such a great unknown so bravely at such a young age. What exactly was it that she had foreseen, I wondered? And what would have happened to her had she not journeyed back to my world? Was I giving her the kind of help she needed from me right now? Or was there something more that I could be doing? And if so, what?

These questions, the more I thought on them, moved me to a melancholy place that I soon realized I had better get myself out of. What use could I be to her if I were to get lost in my own world of "what if's" tonight?

I fell asleep that night, half my mind wondering about the events in this world in which I found myself so caught up, and the other half telling myself to let go of such wondering and just be present to whatever it was that was about to happen and what it might require of me.

––––––

The next day passed quietly ... perhaps too quietly. Ndalla continued to rest and, with the help of the healer's medicine, to regain her strength, or so I hoped. Daeikabah did not burst in on us again, a fact for which I was extremely grateful.

However, we were not visited by Barei or Mara all day, a fact which caused me more than a little anxiety. What could be happening, I wondered? And should the fact that we'd heard nothing yet be taken as good news or bad? And what, if anything, had the Ndalla warriors been told about what was going on? How were they dealing with the news that they were now prisoners of the Daeika, whose warriors they had defeated so recently? And more troubling still, how were they dealing with the news that their queen was also being held as prisoner? And what were the Ndalla people still camping up in the hills making of this prolonged silence from their queen? Surely, they would have expected to hear something of her progress by now.

I realized then that if nothing else, I needed to try to get word to the warriors here in the village that they should be patient. The last thing the queen needed to deal with right now was a situation in which her warriors became a part of the problem. I was still convinced that none of them were responsible for the boy's death that had occurred the night before last. But I also knew that being held as prisoners for something they had not done would not sit well with such proud men as I knew the Ndalla warriors to be.

But how could I get word to them without making matters worse myself? Just as I was wondering this, I heard a knock at the entrance to our dwelling. It was quite late, and the sound of the knock made us all jump. I looked to Ndalla, and even she'd heard the sound. I could see her trying to rouse herself despite her extreme drowsiness.

"Rest," I said to her gently before I got up and went to the door to open it myself.

It was Daeikabah and Barei and Mara. All three of them stood there in the doorway, the expressions on their faces unreadable.

"The queen is still quite ill," I said as firmly as I could. "Can this not wait until morning? She should rest now."

I saw Daeikabah look over my shoulder as if to confirm the truth of what I'd claimed.

"While the news can wait until morning, I would rather talk with her now," he said before a nudge from his sister seemed to prompt him to add the words, "if I may."

I tried to gauge his tone but had trouble doing so. I looked to Barei for some sign of how best to proceed and read on the old man's face what I thought to be the suggestion that I should let them in. And so I did.

Barei and Mara stayed behind Daeikabah as he approached where the queen lay. She had fallen back into her sleep. Then I saw Barei step out from behind the boy and approach the queen himself. He took her left hand in his and then lay his other hand on her head and began stroking the hair back from her forehead, gently rousing her to wakefulness.

As she opened her eyes and recognized the old man and took in the gentleness of his touch, I saw her smile at him. She seemed genuinely pleased to see him again.

"All is well," he said before she had a chance to try to say anything. "Daeikabah is here with me and would like to speak with you tonight." I saw her try to sit up, but the old man had no trouble convincing her to just rest easy. It had to be clear, even to her, that she hadn't the strength to sit up. "He knows how tired you are, and he has promised to keep his words brief."

Barei moved aside then, just enough to let Daeikabah approach the queen, but the elder kept his one hand on her head, and with the other he held her hand while the young boy spoke.

"I have come to let you know that we have gotten to the truth of what happened the other night. You and your warriors are no longer prisoners. You are our honored guests."

Ndalla started to smile, as much as she had the energy to, at the sound of the welcome news. But it was clear that the boy had more that he had prepared to say. "I apologize," he said, clearly not used to using the word, "for doubting you and your people."

Once again, Ndalla started to respond, but between her profound weakness at the moment and the speech in the boy's head that he seemed intent on finishing, she couldn't seem to find her voice quickly enough. "We hope," he said, "that you will stay on here in the village now that this matter has passed, even though the storm outside has passed, while my people conclude their consideration of your offer to speak with them." And with that, he finally seemed to have gotten through what he came to say.

Ndalla took a moment to find her voice. "Thank-you for your generous offer to stay on here in the village," Ndalla said, speaking as loudly as she could. Even so, we strained to hear her. "We accept your kind offer." She stopped here to catch her breath before continuing. "And I give you much credit for getting to the truth of what happened so quickly."

It was clear to all of us just how much effort it took for her to get these words out. Even Daeikabah seemed to realize, perhaps for the first time, just how weak she was. And I thought I saw him show concern, despite himself. If so, I attributed it only to his concern that the leader of such a great people might die in his village, something that would cast into doubt again the honor of his own people.

"You are very weak," he observed. "I will send my healer to you. You must regain your strength if you are to address my people."

"Thank-you, Daeikabah. But my healer has made the

journey with me. She knows well how to help me regain my strength. We will do our best," she said with a slight smile.

And then she said, more seriously, "I would like to talk with you further about all of this, Daeikabah. Perhaps we can do so tomorrow, though? I would like very much to rest now."

"Yes," he said. "Of course." And he got up to leave. "Will you be strong enough by tomorrow evening to share a meal?"

You've got to be kidding, I said to myself.

But I heard Ndalla say, "I will try to be ready to enjoy the evening meal with you tomorrow. Thank-you, Daeikabah."

And with that, the boy headed out, with Mara close behind him.

Before she released Barei's hand, however, Ndalla turned to him and said, "And you. Will you return tomorrow as well so that we can talk some more?"

"Whenever you want me to return, I will be here."

"Tomorrow morning?" she offered.

"Are you sure you shouldn't just let yourself rest?" he asked.

Then she smiled at him and conceded, "Late morning then."

"Very well, I will stop in not too long before mid-day, and we will share a late morning pot of tea together if you feel up to it."

"Thank-you, Barei."

"No," he said. "It is you to whom my people owe a debt of gratitude they do not even realize yet." He stroked her hair tenderly a couple more times. "Try to rest now," he said as he stood to leave.

As I walked him to the doorway, he said to me, "I have already let your warriors know the same news that Daeikabah just shared with your queen. They were greatly relieved, as you can well imagine. One of your warriors—Bakka, I believe was his name—wanted to come and speak with you tonight. I told him I would stop in and let him know when he could do that. Would now be all right?"

"Yes, please. And thank-you, Barei, for all that I know you have done to help this matter be resolved as quickly as it has."

"I did very little," he said. "It was your queen who did much, as you well know."

"Does Daeikabah know anything of her role in helping sort this out?"

"It is late. Let us talk of this when I return tomorrow morning, if that is all right with you."

Only then did I see just how tired the old man looked, and I wondered then if he'd gotten any rest since leaving us last night. "Yes, certainly," I said. "Go and get some rest yourself."

"Good-night, then," he said. "I will send Bakka over to speak with you."

When Bakka arrived, I assured him that the queen was all right, just extremely tired.

He asked if I thought he should send a warrior back to the people camped in the hills with word about all that had happened since we had entered the Daeika village, and I suggested that it would be wiser to wait until it became a little clearer to all of us just what had occurred.

He agreed. Then I told him to come back again in the morning so that the queen could see for herself that he was well and so that he himself could assure her that her warriors were well and that they had gotten through this time of waiting without incident.

Even though Ndalla felt better when she awoke the next morning, it was clear that she was still extremely weak, weaker than the healer thought she should be, considering the various medicines she'd administered to her queen already.

"She does not seem to be responding to the medicine as

quickly as she has in the past," said the healer. The concern in her voice was clear.

Although I said nothing, I thought of the many times that the healer had given the queen these same medicines in the past. Perhaps, as with any medicines a person takes over time, the queen's body was simply unable to respond the same way it was once able to. Perhaps, I thought to myself, the "magic" had worn off at last. Or, perhaps, the fact that Ndalla was pregnant made some sort of difference.

Or—and I didn't like to consider this possibility at all—perhaps Ndalla had simply gone too far this time, subjected her body—and spirit—to something she was just not up to handling. Perhaps she had misjudged her own capabilities this time and had pushed herself farther than she should have.

Perhaps, like her shoulder that seemed unable to heal properly, some part of her spirit had been damaged beyond repair as a result of her venturing into the Great Emptiness. Perhaps she had simply risked too much this time and would now have to pay a price she had not foreseen having to pay.

I spoke none of this aloud, though. And then I thought of Daeikabah's offer.

"Would you consider consulting with the Daeika healer?" I asked. The look that I got left no doubt that the healer considered my question an insult to her abilities.

I tried to restate my question so as to take back the offense I'd unintentionally given.

"I do not doubt your abilities," I quickly added. "You are the best healer I know."

"I am the only healer you know," she said, and I was happy to see that at least she still had her sense of humor.

"I only meant that if you could talk with another healer, you might perhaps consider something that you might not otherwise consider. At least that's the way it is with me. You know the old expression, 'Two heads are better than one.'"

She looked at me as though I myself had two heads at that moment, and I realized that this was one "old expression" that had not yet made its way to her world.

Still, she considered what she understood me to be suggesting. I could see that it was a matter of pride with her. After considering the idea a while, she said, "Tell Barei when he comes that I will meet with the Daeika healer if he will introduce us."

I knew how hard it was for her to say that. All I could think to say was, "Thank-you."

When Bakka came to see the queen, she praised the warriors and asked Bakka to share with them her gratitude for having shown such restraint through such a difficult time of waiting.

Then she assured him that she was well and asked that the warriors be patient just a little while longer.

"Go this day, yourself, to our people camped in the hills," she said. "Do not worry them with details of what has occurred. We will share the whole story with them when we understand it better ourselves. Share with them only that we are all well and that we will need them to wait a little while longer. Ask them to be patient. Then return here." She smiled before adding, "I feel safer with you here in the village with me."

"Yes, my queen." And I could tell that he took her words to be a great compliment.

After Bakka left us, she closed her eyes again and rested until Barei arrived. As he had earlier, he went to her side when he arrived and woke her up as gently as he had the night before.

And once again, he was gifted with that beautiful smile of hers when she opened her eyes and saw who it was. "Barei. Thank-you for coming to see me."

"Are you any stronger this morning?" he asked in a gentle tone.

"A little," she said.

"Are you feeling strong enough to drink a little tea with me?"

"I will try," she said, indicating that she needed some assistance in order to sit up.

Once she was settled and Yolana had brought the tea over, Ndalla surprised me—and Barei as well, I think—by starting the conversation with, "How is Daeikabah this morning?"

But then Barei surprised me as well by hesitating in his answer. "He—"

"His speech seemed too practiced last night, Barei. There is much he is not saying to me yet," said Ndalla.

"There is much I am sure he is not saying to any of us, I fear."

"Was it he who went and talked with the boy?"

"Yes."

"Did he go alone?"

"Yes."

While Barei seemed willing to answer the queen's questions, he offered no more.

"Tell me, Barei." Ndalla set down the cup in her hands before she asked, simply, "Does the boy Daeikabah went to talk with still live?"

Barei hesitated only a moment before answering. "No." Both Ndalla and the old man closed their eyes and looked away from each other, clearly sharing the same reaction.

"Was it at Daeikabah's own hand?"

The old man could only nod, wordlessly.

Then I saw Ndalla double over, I thought first in pain; then I realized that the pain was not of the body. When at last she could speak, she asked, "Does he keep to himself now?"

"Yes, other than the little bit of time he spent with us

408

preparing what he would say to you last night."

She looked to the healer then. "Healer, I must regain my strength faster than this. I wish to go to him."

I could see that the healer was uncertain how to handle the situation, so I said, "Barei, our healer has expressed a willingness to consult with the healer of your people, to see if there is some stronger medicine that she might offer the queen at this time. Will you show her where to find your healer?"

"I will take you to him now," offered Barei, speaking directly to the healer.

The healer turned to her queen first, either for permission to leave or for approval of her plan to consult with another healer; I could not tell which.

Ndalla merely nodded.

"With your leave then," said Barei. And he escorted the healer out.

After they left, I went over to Ndalla. "You really must try to rest now and forget about Daeikabah. You can be of no help to him until you are stronger."

I could read the frustration on her face that she had not recovered her strength as quickly as she was used to recovering it.

"Is there anything I can do to help?" I asked.

She merely shook her head. I reached over to touch her and was surprised to feel her pull away from me. I debated a moment before getting up to leave her alone. While I was willing to consider that she didn't need my help right now as much as she needed the help of others, I did not want to turn away from her feeling angry or hurt.

"I will leave you alone then to rest," I offered.

And then, as I rose to my feet, I heard her say, "Please, Julia. You too must be patient just a little longer." But when I turned to look at her, I found that she was fast asleep already.

The two healers returned together not too long after that, and Barei with them.

To say that the Daeika healer was much older than I expected would be too great an understatement. He appeared more wizened than I thought anyone still living could look. And he moved extremely slowly, a characteristic that I soon discovered would drive me crazy if I had to be around him for any length of time.

I looked to our healer to gauge, if I could, her assessment of her colleague, but I could not. She seemed intent on following his movements closely, as he approached the queen and slowly made his way around where she lay so as to look at her from every angle possible.

When, at last, he seemed satisfied that he had looked at her long enough, he set down his walking staff and surprised us all by getting down on his knees beside where she lay.

Holding both hands out over her body, then, he began in earnest what I can only assume was his examination of her.

He began on the queen's right side, and when his hands passed over her shoulder, not even touching her, she winced in pain. "Hmmm," he said and paused there a while, apparently considering what he had found, before continuing on.

When his hands passed over her abdomen, again the queen moved, although not in any pain or discomfort this time. It was clear, though, that her body could feel something as his hands remained over her, not making any physical contact. We watched then as his wrinkled face twisted itself into what I took to be a smile. "A child," he said. "Very healthy and strong."

Then, with some help from both Barei and our healer, the old man got to his feet, retrieved his walking stick, and slowly made his way around to the queen's left side, and once again, he put his stick aside and got down on his knees again.

This time, he took even more time before he extended his hands over the queen's body.

Closing his eyes, he stayed there, rubbing his hands around each other for what seemed an interminable length of time, before finally he extended his hands once again.

No sooner had he extended them, though, than the queen's body nearly jumped off the floor where she lay, this time in obvious pain.

I felt my body move toward him. But before I could move more than a step or two, I felt our own healer's hands stop me. "Wait, traveler. He knows what he is doing."

I watched helplessly as the queen rolled over toward him, doubled over, in obvious agony as a result of whatever the old healer had triggered with his mysterious touch. He gestured to the healer, whose hands were still restraining me, that he needed her to roll the queen back over on her back so that he could continue his examination.

Before she would let go of me, though, the healer shot me a warning glare. Then she went over to the queen and gently repositioned her on her back.

The old man continued his examination, this time carefully avoiding the one spot that had triggered such a reaction from the queen.

When he was satisfied, he gestured to Barei and the healer that he was ready for their assistance again as he got to his feet. Then he turned to the healer, who still stood at his side, and said, "Come. I know now what we must prepare." And with that, the two healers left.

The queen never awoke during this strange examination, nor did she awake during the hour or two they were gone. When they returned, they had a couple of people from the village in tow to help them carry their potions and poultices.

We all watched silently as the old healer, with our own Ndalla healer assisting him, carefully positioned one of the poultices they had prepared on the spot on the queen's left side that had triggered such a reaction earlier. While still she did not awake, once again, her entire body jumped, and she cried out in her sleep as the poultice made contact with the spot he'd located earlier that evidently was so tender. It was everything I could do to not reach out and stop him from continuing.

Then we watched as the old man, ever so slowly, made his way around to her other side. When he got there, he and our own healer worked to remove the binding that had held the queen's right arm still for so long now. And once it was free of the binding, he applied the other poultice that they had prepared to her shoulder. This time, the queen moaned softly at the touch of the poultice, but still she did not wake up.

"Now," he said, "we must get her to drink this. I do not want to wake her, though. Who is it here that can speak to the queen in the spirit world?"

I stepped forward.

He indicated that the person who had carried the cup should now hand it over to me.

Then he turned to Barei and the healer next to him. "Hold her head up, just enough that she can swallow what is in the cup." And they did as instructed.

"Now," he said to me, "do not call her to wakefulness. Only tell her to drink. Reassure her that this will give her the strength she seeks and that she must drink it all and then let her body rest. When she awakes, she will feel the benefit of the medicine. Assure her. Do it, now."

And so, I did as instructed after first glancing over at our own healer to make sure she was in accord with what the old healer instructed. When I saw that she was, I proceeded to call out to Ndalla and got her to drink the medicine, even though it smelled so foul that I almost got sick just holding it. I could tell that her body balked at the taste, not to mention the smell of the stuff, too. But she did as she was told, and together we got the entire drink into her somehow without her waking up.

"Now she must rest completely," the old healer said.

Just then, there was a knock at the entrance.

When Yolana opened it, Daeikabah stood there. It was only then that I remembered that he was scheduled to return that night to share an evening meal with the queen. He was clearly surprised to see the Daeika healer there.

"Have you come to see her?" the old healer asked the boy.

Daeikabah nodded, his eyes on the queen, as though still trying to take in the seriousness of her situation.

"Come back tomorrow night. By then, she should be up to receiving you. But now she must rest." Then, turning to the rest of us, he said, "I will return tomorrow at mid-day. We will wake her up then. And only then," he added as though cautioning us all to obey his instructions.

Then, turning to the boy in the doorway, he said, "I will walk with you, Daeikabah."

The boy did not seem his old self at all. I considered that it was only the queen's concern for him, that I had witnessed earlier, that made him seem different to me that night, but he was clearly troubled. There was a blankness in his face, suggesting a kind of numbness that I had not seen in him before as I saw him wait patiently at the entrance to the dwelling for the old Daeika healer to join him.

Before the old healer left, he turned to our own healer and reached out for her hands. Once he held them in his own, he said, "We have together solved the mystery of your queen's loss of strength. Know that. You are a wise healer. I look forward to learning much from you. Try to get some rest yourself tonight. Good-night now."

I did not talk with the healer that night, although I wanted to know more. She seemed to want to keep to herself, apparently still deep in thought about all she had witnessed that day.

It was not until the next morning, over a light breakfast, that I felt comfortable asking her if she would talk with me about what had happened when she got together with the old healer.

She merely shook her head, indicating that she was still not ready to talk about it. But she did offer, "He is a much more knowledgeable healer than I am." I did not hear hurt pride, only a kind of amazement and perhaps admiration on her part.

"He is a great deal older. Perhaps he has only had the chance to see more in his years."

"That is part of it," she said. "But there is more. He understands things about the spirit world that even our queen has not yet had the chance to learn in her young life."

"Then it is good that you consulted him yesterday," I said, trying to make her see that she too had shown her own wisdom yesterday.

"Had he not intervened, I am not sure the queen would have ever regained her strength."

The seriousness of her words caused me to doubt once again Ndalla's resilience.

"Do you believe she will recover fully now?" I asked.

The healer smiled at me.

"Yes. It will take some time, but I believe she will." Then, after a moment, she said, "There is much I can learn from this healer."

"He indicated last night that the same is true in reverse, that there is much he can learn from you."

Her attempt at a laugh suggested that he was only being kind.

"You have served the queen well all these years," I said. "You know how highly she values your knowledge and wisdom, do you not?" But it was clear that yesterday's exposure to the old healer's knowledge of things that she did not yet know had put her world off-balance.

I searched my mind for something to say that would comfort the woman but could not find it. I knew that if Ndalla were awake and aware of the healer's frame of mind, she would know just what to say in order to restore order to the old woman's world. But I did not have Ndalla's wisdom when it came to dealing with her people. And so, our conversation ended.

The healer said, "I will go now to the healer's dwelling so that when he is ready to come, I can walk with him." And she left.

The Daeika healer arrived at mid-day, as he said he would, escorted by our healer. As he had done the previous day, he took his time, just walking around the queen, observing her from every angle. She had not moved all night or all morning. The poultices were exactly where he had left them. *What could he possibly be taking such time to look at?* I wondered impatiently.

Then he gestured to the healer at his side, and together they removed first the poultice that had rested on her shoulder and then the other.

Then once again, I saw him position himself carefully before he set aside his walking stick and got down on his knees, starting once again on her right side. We watched him go, ever so slowly, through the same routine he had the day before.

Once again, I watched the queen wince in pain as the old healer's hands passed over her shoulder. Once again, he held his hands over her abdomen and again seemed pleased that he sensed a healthy young life growing there. And once again, he got up and walked around to her other side and got back down on his knees again; he took his time, rubbing his hands before extending them over the spot that had apparently been so tender the day before.

This time, though, as he held his hands over the spot, the queen's body did not jump. She let out a soft moan, much as she had when the pain in her shoulder was triggered, but I was surprised to see that the extreme tenderness associated with the spot merely hours ago was gone!

Then he reached up and touched her forehead. As she started to wake up, he gestured to the healer and to me; then he noticed Yolana and gestured to her as well.

We helped the old man to his feet.

Then he said, "Your young queen will be very sore when she wakes up, and she will find it difficult to move. Give her plenty of water to drink and let her rest a little longer this afternoon. By this evening, she will feel more like her old self."

"You are leaving?" I asked.

"Your queen and I will talk, but our talk can wait a few days until she is stronger."

Then he turned to the old woman next to him and put his hand gently on hers before he spoke. "Until then, you will know what, if anything, your queen needs."

And with that, the old healer left us.

CHAPTER 28

Daeikabah's Questions

As Ndalla came to herself, it was clear that she was very sore indeed. Even so, there was no doubt that something significant had changed in terms of her energy level. While she was still shaky from her extended time lying in bed unmoving, nevertheless, there was a light in her eyes that I'd begun to wonder if I would ever see again, and she was even able to hold her own head up as she drank thirstily from the cups of water that Yolana offered her, one after the other.

"You have done well, healer," she said when, at last, she stopped drinking long enough to speak. "I feel much stronger. Thank-you."

"It was not my medicines this time that helped you recover your strength, my queen," said the healer. "It was the Daeika healer who knew what to do."

Ndalla's face seemed to register some alarm at hearing this.

"He did not attend to me alone, did he? You worked with

417

him, did you not?"

"Yes, I assisted him," said the healer, reassuring her queen that she had not left her side throughout the old healer's time with her. "But it was his knowledge of things in the spirit world that enabled him to know what to do."

"Knowledge of things in the spirit world?" asked Ndalla, clearly intrigued to know more.

"He will be back to share with you what he discovered was keeping your body from healing, but not tonight. He said you should rest now," said the healer.

"Come," said Ndalla abruptly, gesturing to the healer to come closer to where she lay. And when the healer was close enough, Ndalla took the old woman's hands in her own before she spoke again. "It sounds as though there are things this healer can teach us both," she said, her eyes lighting up. "We are fortunate to have made contact with him at this point in our lives."

"Yes, my queen." But it was clear that the healer still felt, at the very least, some measure of disappointment in herself and perhaps feared that the queen might be disappointed in her too.

"My old friend," said Ndalla, squeezing the old woman's hands still tighter. "You did not think that the Ndalla had grown so wise that we could not learn from another people's wisdom. Did you?" The healer shook her head, somewhat reluctantly, it seemed to me.

"What you have done, by accepting the Daeika healer's help in this matter, took much courage."

The healer raised her eyes then and looked at her queen, who said, "Your act of courage will stand as an example of what I want all of my people to do as we open our hearts and minds to these people. There is much, I believe, that we can learn from them, and they from us. Thank-you, my old friend, my dear friend, for showing my people what it is that we all must be willing to do from this day forward."

And I saw the healer positively beam at the sound of these words from her queen.

After Ndalla had swallowed all the water she could and even gotten up to go outside and relieve herself—the first time she'd been on her feet in days—she agreed to lie down and rest until later that evening. More than once, she surprised herself by finding out just how tender was the spot that the Daeika healer had found and applied the poultice to the night before.

"Healer, what is this?" she asked, not understanding how her body could have sustained such an injury without her having been aware of it.

"That is part of what the Daeika healer will explain to all of us when he returns," said the healer by way of an answer, which—much to my own surprise—seemed to satisfy Ndalla.

It wasn't until we were getting her comfortable in bed again that she sat up and said, "Daeikabah!" apparently remembering that she was to have shared the evening meal with him.

"He came last night—" I started to say.

"Last night?" she asked. And then I realized that—between the medicines that had been administered to her and all the time she'd slept—she had lost all track of time.

"—just after the Daeika healer was finishing up attending to you," I said, finishing my sentence. "The old healer suggested that the boy come back tonight as he knew the medicines that he and our own healer had given you would make you sleep through the night, last night, which you did."

I saw her rub her head as she tried to re-orient herself in time, given this new information.

"It was two nights ago, then, that Daeikabah came with the offer that we could stay on in his village ... as his guests again?"

"That's right," I assured her.

"And it was yesterday morning, then, that I asked Bakka to go and talk with our people camped in the hills?"

"Yes."

"Has he returned yet?" she asked with sudden concern.

"He has," I said gently, trying to reassure her with my tone of voice.

"And our people in the hills?"

"—are fine," I said. "Everything is fine. Now you must rest."

"Will you wake me when Daeikabah arrives?"

"Certainly. I will not let you miss his visit. Now rest. Please." It was not easy getting her to do so, but we finally succeeded in getting her to close her eyes, and once she did, the tiredness of her body took over, and she was asleep within minutes. It was the knock at the entrance to the dwelling, several hours later, that woke her. She needed no help from us.

When I opened the door, I saw Daeikabah standing there, alone, looking disheveled and exhausted. I almost didn't recognize him. I heard the concern in Ndalla's voice, as well, when she saw him.

"Daeikabah," she said, making the effort to sit up entirely on her own. Yolana hurried to adjust the bed so that her queen had something to lean back against.

"Please come in," said Ndalla, and I thought for a moment she was going to try to get out of bed herself to guide him across the room. Clearly, she wanted to. But she could see that I had him, and she could feel, I'm sure, her own limitations still.

I helped him sit down beside where she lay and left the two of them to talk.

"Yolana, bring us both some tea, please," she said. And then, turning to the boy, she softened her tone. "I'm glad you came back tonight. I'm sorry I was not able to be with you before now." I could see that she wanted to put her hand out and touch the boy, but she stopped herself, unsure how best to reach him right now.

"Thank-you, Yolana," she said, offering the boy a cup of tea, which he expressed no interest in whatsoever.

"Please," she said. "I could use some myself. But I cannot drink alone in front of a guest who will not accept my hospitality."

He looked up at her, then, making eye contact with her for the first time, before reaching out and taking the cup she offered. She waited then, indicating that she would not drink before he did so first. And so, even though it was clear he registered no thirst of his own, he drank.

"You have not slept for days, have you?" she said to the boy.

His eyes met hers again, apparently debating on whether or not to reply. In the end, he merely shook his head, wordlessly, as his eyes fell.

"You have not eaten either." It was spoken, not as a question, but as an observation that needed no confirmation. "Nor have I. We will eat together tonight, Daeikabah. I must," she said, "to regain my strength. And as with the tea, I cannot eat if you, my guest, refuse to."

And then, I thought I saw the boy smile just a little, despite himself. "You are quite insistent for one who has recently been so ill," he said, clearly smiling now.

"I have been a leader of my people all my life. I suppose I have grown accustomed to having my way. I am sorry if my tone offended you," she said, softening her tone a little.

"Not at all," he said quickly. And then, after considering a moment longer, he added, "I will eat with you tonight. After all, you are my guest too, and I have an obligation here." Then he smiled a little wider. "The truth is, I am hungry, and I too need to regain my strength."

"Good," she said, indicating that Yolana should bring them both some food.

We left the two of them to eat alone and to talk together without an audience.

We stepped outside, the three of us—Yolana, the healer, and myself—and ate our meal just outside the dwelling, where I must admit, I listened to much of the conversation going on within, despite my intention to give them privacy.

I heard her ask him if he had found anyone to talk with yet about what had happened when he had gone to question the boy who had taken the life of Thaikus. The silence I heard in response told me he had not.

Then I heard her say, "A leader's responsibilities are heavy—too heavy to bear all alone, some think."

And then, after a moment, she said, "As leader of the Daeika, you have been handed a burden that you are strong enough to carry. Even so, until you have a chance to become accustomed to its weight, I wish you would allow me to be of whatever help I can be to you."

"You carry such a burden without anyone's help." His words were not offered as a question but rather as an observation and—or so it sounded to me—as a challenge to what she was telling him.

"For many years, I did. I became queen at my birth. I never knew my mother ... in the physical realm. What I know of her comes to me from the stories that my people have told me about her and from what I have come to learn of her from visiting her in the spirit realm."

I listened carefully at that point, curious to hear the boy's response to her words about a realm that Daeikabah's father not only had renounced for himself but also had his people deny any knowledge of. But if the boy made any reaction, the queen did not acknowledge it, as she continued what she was saying.

"And so, for many years, at least here in the physical realm, I carried my burden alone. My people were very good to me and helped in the ways that they could. But essentially it was my burden to carry alone."

"Then surely I can carry my burden alone," I heard the boy say, and while I heard some of his former defiance in his voice, it sounded to me as though he was asking a question at the same time.

"But that was during a time when my people were not at war with another people," the queen said in a low tone of voice before continuing.

"As the time of collision between our two villages approached, it became clear to me that I needed to make a journey, to open myself up to new ideas and feelings and even people that I could not know by staying always within the confines of my own village. And so I went on such a journey. And I brought back with me one in whom I can confide, one who can help me in ways that others among my people cannot."

"Tell me: how is it that you knew such things, that the time of collision approached, and that you had to make such a journey. Who told you these things?"

"No one told me. The Forces helped me to feel it and know it, just as our bodies allow us to feel our own hunger when it is time to eat."

"The Forces?"

I knew then that Ndalla had to be taking in the fact that Daeikabah knew nothing of the Forces. And I listened as she took a moment to consider carefully how to proceed with this new knowledge. "I did not mean to speak of things that perhaps your people do not honor," she said.

"What do you mean? Tell me of these Forces that help you to feel and know such things."

"But if this is not the way of your people—"

"It is my place now to determine what is the way of my people."

As he spoke these words, I heard a strength in his voice that I suspect hadn't been heard by anyone for days. Ndalla had to have heard it too and had to have been encouraged by it.

"I would be happy to tell you more about the Forces," she said. "But I do not think I can do it all in one evening's conversation." I could hear the smile in her voice as she spoke these words. "Come back tomorrow night, after you have rested a little, and perhaps too after you have spoken with the Daeika elders to find out why listening to the Forces has not been your people's way. Then, when you have taken the time to know this, if you still want to hear more, I will tell you whatever you want to know."

The two ate a while in silence, and I could well imagine Ndalla's relief to see the boy's appetite having returned. When next they spoke, it was of Daeikabah's encounter with the boy who had killed Thaikus. Daeikabah started out by sharing with her that Barei had shared with him what Barei had learned from Ndalla herself regarding the boy's role in Thaikus's death.

"From me? But I—" I could hear Ndalla's discomfort at having been discovered to have had a role in the matter.

"Do not be angry with Barei," said the boy. "He did not tell me that he learned what he knew from you. Your own reaction just now did, though." I could hear the smile in the boy's voice. And from his next words, I could tell that Ndalla must've returned his smile. "There is clearly much I do not know about your ways and the ways of your people. I would like to know these things."

"Yes," she said. "There will be much sharing between us now, I think." And I heard in her voice what I took to be great relief.

424

"I would ask you to speak of one more thing this evening, though," the boy said. "And then we will speak of it no more."

"What is it?" I heard Ndalla ask.

"You met my father on the battlefield, did you not?"

"I met the leader of the Daeika warriors on the battlefield, yes." And with that memory, I could hear her voice become somewhat strained.

"He was a brave warrior?" asked the boy.

Ndalla did not answer right away. And when at last she found her voice, she spoke haltingly.

"He was ... one of the ... fiercest warriors I ever encountered on the battlefield. He was very sure of himself, very protective of his people's right to live their lives as he saw fit."

"Was it your hand that killed him?"

"No, Daeikabah. I was in no condition to raise a hand to anyone when your father was killed. My warriors killed him in order to save my life."

"He would have killed you then?"

"Or worse."

"What could be worse than death?"

Once again, Ndalla did not answer right away.

"Your father envisioned for me a life of captivity, away from my people, a life not lived in accord with my beliefs. This 'death in life' is far worse than any physical death that allows us to pass into the spirit realm. So I believe."

"Was it he who injured your shoulder so that it does not heal, even now?"

After a silence, I heard her say, "Daeikabah, it is hard for me to speak of such things."

"Please. I must know. And then we will not speak of it again."

"To learn of such things, you must speak with one of my warriors. I will take you to one who will be able to tell you what it is you want to know. Tomorrow, if I am strong enough."

"I have heard that my father did terrible things to you. I must know—"

"Whatever your father did, he did on the battlefield, where life is not what it is off the battlefield. Do not judge him by standards that are unfair to him. What he did, he did not do to me as a person. What he did, he did to me as a fellow warrior and as the leader of my people."

"Even so, you would not have treated him as he treated you." It was spoken as a statement, yet there was a question behind it as well.

"No, I would not have. That is not my way. Or the way of my people."

"You think he acted wrongly." Again, it was a question spoken as a statement. I could only imagine the toll this line of conversation was taking on Ndalla.

After another silence passed, I heard her say, "I cannot judge his actions, Daeikabah. Every person must act as they see they must."

"But still—"

Ndalla interrupted him, her voice conveying her insistence that they speak no more about this. "He acted with hatred and violence. Such things can blind one's better judgment. And that is all I will say, Daeikabah." And then I heard her tone soften. "I will not speak against your father. Listen to me, Daeikabah. Yes, it was your father's dragging me as roughly as he did and as long as he did that injured my shoulder. And it was either his own violation of me or that of one of the many warriors he invited to do the same that has resulted in the life I carry within me now. These are hard truths about your father if you want to know them. I cannot tell you about how he died because I was unconscious by that time."

The softness of her tone as she spoke of such things must have left the boy undone, for I heard him say nothing. And I felt myself undone, hearing her speak of such things.

"Come," she said. "These are things we need never speak of again unless you choose to. They are things for which you bear no responsibility whatsoever. You must know that."

I looked inside then and saw her take the boy in her arms and hold him for a very long time. If he cried, I could not tell from where I sat looking in on them.

All I know is that it was a long time before she released him, and when she did so, he looked both better and worse than he had when he'd first arrived at the entrance to our dwelling earlier that night. I had no doubt that he'd heard more than he'd bargained for, yet there was something about him that seemed satisfied that he'd heard at last what others had not had the courage to tell him about his father.

"Now you must go and rest," she said to him at last. "And I must do the same."

"May I come again tomorrow night and visit?"

"Do not wait until tomorrow evening. Come at mid-day."

And then I heard her laugh before adding, "I think, given the amount of rest we both need, we will only then be ready for a morning meal."

And I heard him laugh a little too.

"We will talk more tomorrow," she assured him.

And with that, he left.

The three of us entered the dwelling then. Yolana cleaned up the remains of the queen's meal, and the healer went over to the queen to check on her one more time. Then the queen said good-night to both women.

It was only when we were alone that I sensed that Ndalla might be ready to talk further, but I could not be sure. I knew her conversation with Daeikabah had taken much out of her.

"How do you feel tonight?" I asked, taking her in my arms as I lay down beside her.

"Very tired." Then I could hear the smile in her voice as she snuggled up against me and said, "But it is a good tired. I feel I will regain my strength very quickly now."

"You had a good talk tonight?"

"I believe it was a good start." And then I could hear her smile even wider as she said, "I could feel you listening to us."

"Did you mind?"

"No, Julia. I am glad you did. Now I can ask you to share your impression of the boy."

I didn't know where to begin. "He seems genuine in his desire to understand things."

"Yes," she said. "His desire is genuine. But what do you think of his readiness?"

"To understand such things?"

"Yes."

"That I cannot gauge. He is still so young," I said.

"Yes. But I believe he is ready to assume his responsibilities. He has proven that already in his handling of the matter of the boy who killed Thaikus."

I couldn't believe my ears.

"Because he has taken a life, you judge him to be ready to be ruler of his people?" I asked, incredulous. I felt her pull away from me then as she sat up to face me.

"To take such a life, the life of one of your own people, is no small matter. It requires more strength than anyone can know," she said, sounding almost hurt by my apparent inability to appreciate this. And I thought then of the times she'd found herself having to take such action.

"I'm sorry," I said, trying to take her back in my arms. She came but not willingly. I knew she was tired and needed rest, so I said, "You are right, of course."

But rather than help her relax, my words had the opposite effect. Again, she pulled away from me and sat up, not facing me, though.

"What is it?" I asked her back.

"You say I am right only to get me to relax and perhaps even to rest. But you do not mean it. I have never known you to use words with me that you did not mean." And still, she did not turn to face me. But her tone told me what I needed to know, even without being able to see her face: how hurt she was by my apparent lack of honesty with her.

I sat up behind her. But I knew better than to try to touch her right then.

"You are right about the boy's readiness," I said. "I know this even if I cannot fully understand these things of which you speak. If you sensed that I did not mean the words I spoke, I am sorry. It is only that there is so much that I do not understand. Please believe me when I say, I believe that you are right in this matter."

She turned then, not all the way to face me, but enough that I could see her profile.

And still I waited, unmoving.

"I am sorry," I heard her say softly, "if I misjudged you."

"Come," I said. "You are trying so hard right now to be present to so many different people. And you haven't even the strength it would take me to be present to just one person. You owe me no apology. You are only speaking what you feel to be the truth. That is all you have ever given me: the truth. I know this."

And this time she came back into my arms willingly. We lay back on the bed then and got comfortable again. After a while, I heard her voice, very sleepy. "Julia?"

"Hmmm?" I answered, feeling just as sleepy as she sounded.

"I do not think I could be queen now without you; I have come to rely on you so."

"I'm not going anywhere," I said, happily.

And then I felt her move even closer to me. I was just about to drift off to sleep when I heard her voice again.

"Julia?"

"Hmmm?"

"When we return to Ndalla, and I can return to the clearing, when my mind is not so distracted with all that we must attend to here in Daeika, I would like to ask the Forces if it would be all right to declare my commitment to you openly, in front of my people."

I waited, not knowing what to say in return.

"Would that be all right with you?" she asked. "My people," she went on to say, "already understand the strength of the connection that joins us, Julia. But even so, I would like to make the commitment if the Forces indicate that it would be all right."

"And I? Might I do the same?" I asked.

"If the Forces indicate that it is all right, then we will undergo the joining ceremony that is the way of my people. It is a public recognition of the connection we feel. Among my people, such a ceremony is very joyful but also very solemn," she said. And then she asked, with some concern in her voice, I thought, "Is it so in your world also?"

"It is so in my world as well," I assured her.

"I do not know where our paths will take us, Julia. But I know the sacredness of the connection I feel with you."

"And I with you."

"Then we will consult with the Forces when we return to the clearing in Ndalla."

Even as she said this, I remember wondering what need there was to consult with the Forces. If we felt the sacredness of the connection, as we had just admitted we did, then how could the Forces indicate any other course of action would be appropriate for us?

I wanted to ask this question at the time but thought better of it. I knew she needed her rest. And I knew too that she'd already indicated that this was not the time to resolve such a matter anyway. There were more important matters to attend to here in Daeika.

And so I held her in my arms that night and let myself dream of that moment in the not-so-distant future when—or so I believed that night—we would stand before her people together and have the connection we shared recognized by her people in a very public ceremony.

CHAPTER 29

Sharing More Than a Meal

When Daeikabah arrived the next day about noon, Ndalla was already awake. Not only that, but she was up and out of bed and eager to head outside with him, partly because she was so tired of having been shut up inside for so many days, I'm sure, but partly too, I believe, because she wanted to see, first-hand, the people of Daeika.

"Would it be all right?" she asked the boy once she had expressed her wish.

"Are you sure you are strong enough?" His concern sounded genuine.

"Yes," she said simply in a tone that indicated she wanted no further discussion on the matter. She then rested her hand on his arm, and the two headed out.

They were gone all afternoon. In fact, Yolana was just debating on whether or not to prepare an evening meal for them when they returned, at last, accompanied by Barei and Mara. The queen invited all three of them to stay and eat with us. Not only that, but she asked Yolana and the healer to go and find the Daeika healer as well. "See if he will join us for our evening meal as well. Then our party will be complete," she said. Daeikabah agreed.

It was clear that Ndalla and Daeikabah had come to feel very comfortable in each other's company over the course of their day together. I noticed that she looked tired but very happy indeed. The boy, although clearly tired from the toll the past several days had taken on him, seemed as relaxed and happy as Ndalla. While we waited for the healers and Yolana to join us, Ndalla and Daeikabah told us about their day together, and it soon became clear why she looked so happy and relieved despite her tiredness.

According to Daeikabah, his people had been completely won over by Ndalla's kindness as the two of them had made their way through the Daeika village.

"She had to stop and talk with everyone, I think," said the boy with a smile and an exaggerated look of exhaustion. Then he sat up straighter and composed himself before saying to her, "My people found in you what I have found: a caring person, generous with her time and herself, one who knows how to listen to others and to hear what they are trying to share."

Ndalla smiled, and I saw a slight blush start to rise on her neck, but she quickly controlled her body's reaction to the boy's words as she paid him a compliment of her own.

"You must know that it was the fact that you were there, demonstrating your trust in me, that enabled your people to open their hearts to me. They trust you and look up to you already, Daeikabah, and trust whomever you indicate you trust."

Daeikabah then announced to the group that he had invited Ndalla to formally address the Daeika people. "It is my belief," said the boy, "that such an occasion will mark the beginning of a long time of peace and friendship between our people. There is no need for us to go forward from here as anything but friends. The time of fighting is past now."

But Ndalla cautioned the boy not to dismiss the past time of fighting so quickly. "Those who would dismiss the past too quickly, in their rush to move forward, risk bringing the past back into the future to be lived again, only more slowly this time." Then, seeing the puzzled look on the boy's face, she turned to him. "My people believe that the past and the future are very strongly connected, that the one informs the other, and that if we do not learn from the one, we are destined to be given the opportunity to learn the same lessons from the other."

"But what are we to learn from this time of fighting that is now behind us, other than that we need not fight anymore?" he asked.

"I believe there is still much that is to be learned, Daeikabah, by both the Ndalla and the Daeika. And I believe that what there is to be learned will not become clear to us until we slow down enough that we can talk with each other about what brought our people to blows with one another in the first place. Only when we have considered carefully what lessons have been made available to us in the course of this terrible experience will we be in a position to truly move forward through the passage offered to us by the Great Unfolding of Time."

He remained silent as he considered Ndalla's words before saying at last, "Surely you are not suggesting that we should dwell on what caused our people to distrust one another in the first place. This would only keep alive such feelings of distrust, would it not?"

"You are right to want to see the feelings of distrust between our people disappear, Daeikabah. Such feelings, if we allow them to live on, will only jeopardize the future that we both want for our people, one that involves cooperation and trust. But to dismiss those feelings of distrust without truly understanding what enabled them to grow in the first place is to invite such feelings back into our lives again in the future, and probably when we least expect them and are least prepared to deal with them productively."

"But what is it that you are suggesting then?" He seemed willing to consider the truth of what she was suggesting but was clearly at a loss as to what exactly it might involve.

She put her hand gently on his arm. "You and I, Daeikabah, have not the wisdom to figure this out between just the two of us. We are leaders of our people, yes. But even leaders need the counsel of those wiser than themselves. This is a matter that I think our elders should be asked to consider," she said, looking to Barei, perhaps for confirmation that he agreed.

But Barei made no visible sign that he felt one way or the other. In fact, if anything, the elder seemed to avoid Ndalla's direct gaze.

Daeikabah, following the queen's eyes, looked at Barei then. "Is this a matter that the elders would be willing to consider, Barei?"

Barei hesitated. "Your father, as I'm sure you know, disbanded the Council long ago."

The boy considered this a moment before speaking.

"Did the Council do something that offended my father?"

"The Council disagreed with him on a matter of some importance."

"And because the Council disagreed with him, he disbanded it?"

"Yes," said Barei, clearly uncomfortable at being asked to discuss the matter, perhaps all the more so in front of people from outside the village.

"This does not seem to have been a wise decision on the part of my father."

The silence in the room echoed. It was evident that Barei was in no way prepared to offer an opinion on the matter, even if he were asked for one directly.

"I agree." The words were so shocking that it took us all a moment to get past the words in order to realize who had spoken them. It was Mara. "I think you should reinstate the Council of Elders," she said to her brother.

Daeikabah looked at his sister, without any clear emotion that I could read, and then turned again to Barei. "What was the matter of importance on which the Council disagreed with my father?"

Barei took a deep breath and looked briefly in the direction of the queen before speaking.

"There were many matters on which the Council disagreed with your father. Over time, your father came to see a great many things differently from the way the Council saw them. But there was one matter that made your father come to the decision he did, and that was the matter concerning the Forces and the role your father said they would play in our lives." Then, looking at both Daeikabah and Mara, he said simply, "Your father did not believe in the Forces."

"And because he did not, he said his people would not?" asked the boy, for clarification.

"Yes," said Barei.

"And because the Council of Elders disagreed with him on this, he disbanded it?"

"Yes," he said again.

The boy seemed to be considering his next words carefully. But before he could speak, the two healers entered the dwelling, followed closely by Yolana and a number of people from the village, all of them helping to carry in the evening meal for our party, which was now complete.

"We will finish this conversation after we have eaten," said Daeikabah, as he welcomed the old healer to the group and

436

made sure that everyone knew everyone else. Our party of eight consisted of four from the Daeika village—Daeikabah, the old healer, Barei, and Mara—as well as the four of us from Ndalla—the queen, the healer, Yolana, and myself.

The eight of us made a good group for casual conversation, and the meal was one of the tastiest we'd enjoyed since having entered the village. Under Ndalla's gentle influence, the boy proved to be as good a host as Ndalla herself, the two of them content to keep the conversation during the meal light and upbeat so that everyone could enjoy both the good food and the good conversation.

It wasn't until after we'd finished the meal that Daeikabah brought up again the subject of his father's having disbanded the Council of Elders. It did not take the old healer long to realize what conversation he'd missed just before having arrived for the evening meal, nor did it take him any time at all to pick up on Barei's uneasiness with the line of conversation.

"Daeikabah," said the Daeika healer, "it is good that you want to understand more about your father and the decisions he made, years ago, that set our people on the course they are now on. But perhaps you should call the Council together and speak with them yourself about these matters. It was a long time ago that these events unfolded, and perhaps it is not fair to ask Barei to speak on behalf of a group of which he himself was just one member, and so very long ago."

After considering the old man's suggestion, the boy said, "Then let us make this happen. Barei, will you call together the elders and tell them I want to meet with them?"

"Yes, certainly. When?"

"As soon as possible. Let us meet tomorrow evening." Then, turning to Ndalla, he asked, "And how soon would you like to address my people?"

"Whenever you like." She paused a moment, looking at

first Barei and then the old Daeika healer before continuing. "Perhaps you would consider asking the elders for their opinion in this matter. The decision, of course, would be yours. But they may have some good ideas to offer."

"Yes. I will do that. Come, Barei, we have much to talk about. Will you excuse us?"

"Certainly," said Ndalla, getting to her feet. "Thank-you, Daeikabah, for all the time you gave me today. I will always remember today and my first impression of your people, who have been very kind to me, as has their leader," she said, bowing slightly.

He took her hand in his then and returned the gesture.

"If I do not see you tomorrow, I will come and see you the next day, after my meeting with the elders," he said. "We can talk then about when you will address my people."

"As you wish."

Then he turned to Mara. "Come, sister. I would like your advice in some of these matters as well." And with that, he and Barei left us.

Mara, trailing behind, came over to the queen then and said quietly, "If it is all right, I will come and visit you tomorrow."

"I would like that. Come whenever it is convenient for you. I look forward to your visit."

After they'd left and Yolana had also taken her leave of us, the four of us who remained sat down to talk further, the two healers sitting opposite Ndalla and myself.

It was the old healer who started the conversation. "You look much better than when I saw you last," he said, addressing the queen with a smile.

She returned the smile and said, "I feel much better, as well. Thank-you for sharing your knowledge in these matters with my healer, who has always known what to do to help me regain my strength at such times."

"I gather this time was a little different," he said, smiling at the old woman seated beside him. Then he turned to Ndalla before asking, "Do you know why?"

She shook her head, the curiosity on her face clear to see.

"It was the journey you took it upon yourself to make into the Great Emptiness."

I could feel Ndalla, beside me, shiver at his mention of the place. So could the two healers. "Even now," he said, "the mere memory of your journey there frightens you, does it not?" And then, without waiting for an answer, he added, "As well it should."

He studied her a moment. "You are perhaps, only now, beginning to realize what a great risk you took in traveling there," he said. "Do you know how fortunate you are to be back among us and not wandering there still, lost?"

Her silence was her only answer, and it was a solemn one at that.

"You are indeed fortunate to have one in your life with the power to help you find your way back," he said, nodding in my direction. "Even so," he said, "you took a greater risk in going there than I think you still realize." His tone softened. "You will always carry with you the shiver of recognition you felt when I mentioned the place just now."

He smiled then what seemed to me a very sad smile as he said, "Therein lies the paradox that makes its home in the events that are a part of the Great Unfolding of Time. Because of their own foolishness and pride, some of the Daeika lost themselves in the Great Emptiness. And you, the Ndalla, ended up becoming their enemy because of their being lost there. Now, in your effort to try to re-establish the peace between what you know to be these two great peoples, you have journeyed into the Great Emptiness yourself, and in so doing, you have made yourself more vulnerable to its pull than ever you were before you visited it. In this way, you have joined your fate to that of those who called themselves your enemy."

My heart went out to Ndalla, who seemed to me to still be shaken by the memory of what she'd encountered in the spirit world and now by the seriousness of the old man's words as well. I could not contain myself.

"Was it your intention, healer, to frighten the queen tonight and to make her regret her actions, undertaken with only the noblest of intentions? If so, then you must be satisfied that you have done your job well," I said, making no effort to hide the intensity of my own feelings.

The anger in my voice brought Ndalla back to herself. "Julia!" she said in alarm.

"The protectiveness you feel for the queen is clear to see, traveler," said the old man, addressing me directly now, his voice just as calm as when he'd begun speaking. "Your own healer has shared with me some of what you have done in the short time you have known the queen to ensure her safety." He paused a moment before continuing. "But as I am sure the queen herself knows, there are certain considerations for our own safety that no one but we ourselves can bear responsibility for." He paused again. "While it was not my intention to frighten the queen, it was my intention to impress upon her the serious consequences of the choice she made to journey as she did into the Great Emptiness."

Before I could find my voice, I heard Ndalla's voice, low and controlled. "I appreciate your willingness to speak of these things with me, healer. I still have much to learn about the spirit world in which I have traveled all my life."

"You know a great deal already," he said. "More than most people my age. I stand in awe of your ability to move so easily between the spirit and physical realms."

She bowed slightly in recognition of the old man's compliment before saying, "But ease of movement between the realms is of little use if I know not where it is safe to go and where it is not safe."

"Well spoken," he said with a smile. "But you knew the Great Emptiness was not a safe place to travel to. Why did you go?"

"The Forces indicated that there were answers to be found there to questions that would arise as we attempted to establish peace between the Daeika and the Ndalla."

"As indeed there were," he said. "But still, the Forces themselves would have made you aware of the tremendous risk. And still you went."

She nodded silently.

"I think," he said, "pride played a part in your decision to go." She flashed him a look then that I had not seen cross her face in some time. But she did not speak.

"Pride," he said again. "And something else: trust in something that you felt, very deeply." He considered a moment. And then he said, "Ah, I see."

I looked to Ndalla then, sure that she would ask him to explain himself, but she did not. And I did not feel it my place to ask him to do so. And so the question went unasked.

"I would talk with you about your wounds now, with your permission."

I saw Ndalla take a deep breath before indicating that he had her permission to do so.

"The wound in your side, which you sustained while you were in the Great Emptiness, and your shoulder wound, which is taking longer than usual to heal, have this in common: they are both wounds that you sustained in the spirit realm."

Surprised, Ndalla looked at him then, unspeaking.

"If you consider carefully your feelings," he said to her, gently, "you will see that a part of you has known this but was unwilling or unable to recognize it."

She sat in silence for a while before speaking. "Yes," she said at last.

"Your shoulder wound was sustained here in the physical

realm, in the heat of the Great Battle between our peoples; that is true. But it was also sustained at a much deeper level. Your very spirit was wounded by the treatment you received at the hands of the Daeika. And so that wound will not heal until you can come to terms with the spiritual damage that was sustained.

"The other wound, there," he continued, indicating her left side, "was actually sustained in the spirit realm. I have heard of such wounds but never before encountered one. When you returned from the Great Emptiness, you did not even know you had sustained a wound. Your healer could not know it either, as it had not yet manifested itself as a physical wound.

"Nevertheless," he continued, "the toll that wound, left untreated, was taking on your physical body was what was keeping you from regaining your strength as you—and your healer—were used to your having done in the past. Once that wound was allowed to manifest itself as a physical wound, it then became treatable. Only then could you begin to regain your strength."

"But I fought no battle when I journeyed to the Great Emptiness," said Ndalla.

"You didn't have to," he said simply. "Again, I do not think you know how vulnerable one's spirit becomes when one journeys into the Great Emptiness."

He paused a moment. "You encountered the spirit of Thaikus there, did you not?"

Ndalla nodded.

"And he showed you his wound, did he not, in the course of telling you the story of how he sustained it."

She nodded again.

"Your own empathy for his wound and for his misguidedness in having sustained it made you vulnerable to feel its impact in your own body in ways you could not have foreseen."

As Ndalla sat in silence considering this, he then turned to our own healer, sitting silently beside him, and spoke directly to her. "You could not have known of that wound. The queen herself did not even know of it, and there were not yet any physical signs of it that you could have seen. And as for her shoulder, you have done all that a healer can. The rest of the healing that is needed there will be up to the queen herself."

"Can you be of help to her in this?" the old woman asked him.

"I do not know that I can." Then, turning to speak directly to Ndalla, he said, "In many ways, you are far ahead of me when it comes to matters of the spirit, young queen. But I will do what I can."

"Thank-you," she said.

And shortly after that, the old healer asked to take his leave. "It is late, and this old man is tired."

Ndalla got to her feet and approached the old man. "You have been most helpful to me tonight, healer. How can I thank you?"

"You already have, young queen. It is clear that you have found a way to befriend the young ruler of my people. He has needed a friend for some time. More than that, he has needed a mentor. In you, I think he has been fortunate to find both. You have given him good advice in the short time you have known him. Let us hope, for the sake of both of our peoples, that he has the courage necessary to follow it."

"Good-night, healer," she said, extending her hand to the old man. And turning to her own healer next to him, she said, "And good-night to you, my old friend."

"I will see that he gets home safely," said the healer, offering her arm to the old man for support.

And with that, the two healers left us.

CHAPTER 30

Offering a Suggestion

As I held Ndalla in my arms that night, my mind kept hearing, over and over again, the old Daeika healer's words to her. And I found myself fearing for her future safety as I recalled his having said that she had joined her fate to that of those who had called her their enemy.

Is it any wonder then that I was confused when at last I heard her voice and she was saying, "I find myself encouraged, do you not, by Daeikabah's attitude tonight."

My mind hadn't been on that earlier conversation at all.

"Yes," I said at last.

She sat up and looked at me then. "Your thoughts were far away just then. Where were they, Julia?"

I hesitated to bring my own dark thoughts into the conversation, as she seemed to be so relieved by what really did seem to be Daeikabah's improved frame of mind. But I could not be dishonest with her.

"I was thinking of the old man's words to you about the

tremendous risk you took," I said at last, "and about the tremendous danger you have put yourself in." I looked at her. "Even now, as I hold you in my arms, you carry within you the powerful memory of that place. It has a hold over you that I fear can draw you back into it at any time."

"You forget, Julia. You yourself encountered the Great Emptiness."

"Not as you did."

"No, I journeyed farther into it and encountered a spirit who was lost there." And I felt her shiver again as the memory of that experience came alive inside her. "But you did encounter it. The Emptiness is something that surrounds all of us, always. We cannot deny its existence."

And then, seeing that I was still not comforted, she said, "Julia, I am here. I am not lost there. I do not intend to go back. Ever. I only went there because I thought I could learn things that would help us achieve the peace we sought with the Daeika."

"And something else. The old healer said there was something else that entered into your decision."

"My own pride," she said, turning away from me.

I had forgotten that. "No. It was something else. He said," and I searched my memory for his exact words. "He said, 'trust in something that you felt, very deeply.' What was that?"

She turned back to face me, her eyes searching mine. "You do not know?"

"Your connection with me?" I ventured.

"I knew that our connection would enable me to return," she said, smiling.

"You knew no such thing. You only hoped it would." I could feel myself getting upset at what I saw as her failure to recognize even now what a tremendous risk she'd taken.

"I believed it would. And it did." She reached up then and touched my face. "Why are you so upset, Julia?"

"Because you refuse to see how great the risks are that you take, and I fear that someday you will take too great a risk, and I will lose you." There. I'd said it.

She withdrew her hand then from my face and put her head down a moment before raising her eyes and locking in on mine before speaking.

"Perhaps I do take great risks, Julia. Perhaps you are right." Then she straightened her back before continuing. "But I will live my life as queen of my people, the only way I know how. I cannot afford to second-guess myself. If I do, I will not have the sureness of myself that I need when it is time to act. This I know. I will not apologize for it. I cannot."

"I'm not asking you to apologize for anything, certainly not for the way you live your life. From the moment I met you, back in my world, I've admired you for the way you live your life. It's just that," and I paused here, not sure how to say what I meant.

"What?" she asked, and I heard tenderness in her voice.

"You are more than just a queen now. You spoke last night about our undergoing the joining ceremony of your people. And you will be a mother soon. Do these connections you feel mean nothing to you?"

She turned away from me, hurt.

"I didn't say that right. I know the connections you feel— to me, to the child—mean more than words can say. It's just that you must consider these connections too when you consider taking such risks."

"You are suggesting that I no longer act as the queen I have been all my life, that I change how I act now that you are in my life and now that I am to be a mother?"

"Yes."

"You ask much, Julia."

"You are worth much to me."

Looking me straight in the eye, she said firmly, "I will not compromise the promise I made to my people long ago to be the best leader I could be." Then she turned away from me again. "I will consider what you ask. When we get back to Ndalla, I will spend time in the clearing. I must be clear myself about what all of these changes in my life require of me."

"That is all I ask," I said, taking her in my arms.

It was much later that night before I could feel her body start to relax and later still before I was reassured by her steady breathing. Even so, I could feel a distance between us that left me feeling uneasy. When I awoke the next morning, she was gone. When I asked Yolana where the queen had gone so early, she said only, "She left before the sun came up. She said she needed to be alone for a time this morning."

"Did she seem okay?"

Yolana looked at me, clearly unable to understand my question.

"Did it seem that a vision might be coming on?" I asked.

"The queen said nothing more than what I have already shared with you." It seemed to me that Yolana knew more than she was saying. And yet, as I looked at the woman, another part of me felt sure that I was just being foolish. "Can I get you some breakfast?" she asked.

"No, Yolana. Thank-you. I will wait for the queen to return before eating."

She seemed to start to say something, then stopped herself and left me alone with my thoughts. It was mid-day before my solitude ended, and when I was finally joined by someone, it was not Ndalla, but Mara, who had come to visit the queen.

As Yolana showed Mara in, I heard her say to the young woman, "Please wait here. I will go and let the queen know that you have arrived."

There was an awkward moment, then, as Mara took in what I could only assume was my unexpected presence. I decided to take the initiative. Stepping forward, I said, "You will want to visit with the queen alone, I think. I will excuse myself."

But just as I got to the entrance to leave, Ndalla herself was there. I tried to read her face in a moment's glance. She seemed well-rested and relaxed. And then, upon seeing me about to leave, I read something else on her face I could not quite identify. "You are leaving us, Julia?"

"I thought you might prefer to visit alone with Mara." I looked over at the young woman and had no doubt that she was eager to see me leave.

"I would prefer—" Ndalla started to say, but she stopped herself. "Have you eaten?" she asked instead.

"No, but I—"

"Then please, Julia, stay and eat with us." And then, perhaps sensing my hesitation, she reached out and took my hand and said, "I would prefer that you stay and join us."

"Are you sure?"

She smiled then and said very softly, "Have you ever known me to be otherwise?"

She waited to see my smile in return before she gave my arm a gentle yank. "Come now. Let us not keep Mara waiting any longer. It was so good of her to come and see us."

And so, the three of us sat down to eat.

Ndalla asked Yolana to join us as well. And much to my surprise, I found myself drawn into the conversation, and the meal was more enjoyable than I would've thought possible.

I found myself won over by Ndalla's charm as she did her best to make sure that Mara was comfortable and that I, too, was gradually brought out of myself and into the conversation.

Throughout the meal, I felt Ndalla's hand on my own as she seemed intent on assuring me that all was well despite our not having had the chance to see one another all morning.

The only time I saw Ndalla falter was in response to Mara's question about the child she was carrying. Mara's innocent question about when the baby would be born stopped Ndalla in her tracks.

I heard a faint gasp escape Yolana's lips, and I saw Ndalla reach over to reassure her lifelong friend that it was all right; then she took another moment to gather her thoughts before saying, "My people believe it is best for the mother not to speak of such things. We believe the bond between mother and child to be one of the most sacred. And to honor the sacredness of that bond, the mother maintains a silence on the subject until the baby is born. To break that silence is to tempt the Forces to take the child away from the mother."

Whether in an effort to change the subject out of respect for what she'd just heard or perhaps because she really was curious to know more about the Forces themselves, Mara said, "These Forces seem to play a role in every part of the lives of your people."

"We believe the Forces are at work in our lives constantly, and to not consider Them as we make decisions about how to act is to blunder through Life in a way that is most unfortunate for all concerned."

"Why do you think my father did not believe in the Forces?"

Ndalla smiled slightly, a forced smile, it seemed to me. "I could not say," was all she offered.

"Now that my people are free to talk about the Forces, it seems to me there are a great number of our elders who have believed in them all along, even though they did not speak of them while my father lived."

"It does not seem to me that a leader's dictate to 'not believe' in something will ever have the power to change what an individual believes in his heart," said Ndalla.

"I think my father might have been a better leader had he had the chance to meet you."

Again, I saw Ndalla smile, and this time it seemed to hold

some genuine amusement.

"You forget. He and I did meet. On the battlefield."

"But that was too late. I mean, before that, when he might have been able to talk with you and learn from you."

"Your father did not strike me as a man who was interested in learning from anyone, least of all me," Ndalla said, clearly amused at the thought. "But I understand what you are saying, Mara. And you are right. Let us hope that our people can listen to each other and learn from each other from this time forward."

"But what can your people learn from us? We know nothing of these Forces."

"I suspect your elders know more than many in your village know they know! You forget: It was your own healer who knew enough to help me recover recently. He knew about things my own people did not. You have only to listen carefully to your own people to discover how much wisdom they have already, Mara."

Mara seemed willing to consider this. But then she seemed to be willing to consider the truth of everything she heard Ndalla say. There was no doubt that she found herself in awe of the young woman who was not that much older than herself in actual years but far beyond her in terms of the wisdom she'd gained during those years.

"Can I come back again tomorrow at this time and visit with you again?"

"Certainly, Mara. We are glad for your company."

And with that, the young woman left, as did Yolana after cleaning up the remnants of the meal.

As the two of us found ourselves alone, then, I looked at Ndalla, uncertain where things stood between us. Only then did I see a tiredness around her eyes that I hadn't seen before.

"You did not sleep well?" I asked. She shook her head. "If you would like to be alone to rest, I will leave you," I offered.

She looked up at me then, and I could see what I thought to be uncertainty in her eyes.

"I would prefer that you stay."

"Then I will stay," I said, taking her in my arms. "Come," I said, leading her to the bed. "You must rest now."

I felt her snuggle up against me. "And what about you, Julia? What is it that you need now?" I heard her ask as I felt her whole body start to relax.

"Me? Only to hold you in my arms as I am right now." And I meant what I said. It felt so good to hold her so.

We must have both dozed off then, for when I awoke, it was much later, and Ndalla was still asleep in my arms.

Yolana came with supper, and I asked her to leave it for us. She smiled at me as she did so, and I thought I read in her expression some relief, perhaps just at seeing her queen sleep, but it seemed to me that there was more that her expression took in. I thanked her, and she left.

When Ndalla started to stretch herself to wakefulness, sometime after Yolana left, I waited, enjoying the opportunity to watch her.

"Julia," she said when she realized I had been awake as she herself was just waking up. "Did you not sleep?"

"I did. I woke up just a little while ago. Yolana has brought us some supper," I said, indicating the food that awaited us.

"I am not yet hungry," she said. "Are you?" I shook my head, indifferent to the subject of food. "I would like more than anything to just be with you this evening," she said with a smile.

"I would like that."

"You are not angry with me then?" she asked.

"Angry? Why in the world would I be angry with you?" I was genuinely at a loss.

"You seemed so when I came back here today and found you about to leave."

"Oh, that. I just was uncertain what to do. I'm pretty sure that Mara wanted to be alone with you. And I wasn't sure how you felt about anything when I first saw you. That's all."

"Why would Mara want to be alone with me?" she asked, apparently at a loss.

"She is attracted to you," I said with a laugh. "Can you not see that?"

"She is an attractive young woman herself," Ndalla said with a smile.

But before I could react, she had me in her arms. "But why would that concern me? I have already found the woman I feel connected to."

And then I felt her lips on mine. And I felt her body begin to move with mine in ways that left no doubt about the connection we both felt to each other.

The next morning, when I awoke, I was pleasantly surprised to find Ndalla still by my side. And for a change, she was already awake by the time I opened my eyes!

"Good morning, sleepy-head," she said with a smile as she watched me stretch myself awake, something she didn't often get the chance to do.

"How long have you been awake?" I asked.

"Not long," she said with a laugh. "But I awoke before you for a change." Then she pushed me back gently onto the bed as though to indicate she'd won some sort of contest. "Not only that, but I feel very good this morning. Well rested and hungry, first thing in the morning!"

"Too hungry to take the time to come here and say good-morning properly?" I asked her teasingly.

"Not at all." But I heard no teasing in her voice, only seriousness as she bent over and gave me a good-morning kiss that was not designed to let us move on to breakfast anytime soon.

It was sometime later, then, when we got out of bed and Ndalla called for Yolana to bring us some breakfast. True to her word, she ate a good breakfast, the best I'd seen her eat since ... I couldn't even remember when! And as soon as we'd both eaten our fill, she led me back to the bed again, where we ended up staying for most of the morning, enjoying each other's company and sharing so many of the things there had been no time to share during our stay in the Daeika village, although, as I recall, not many words were spoken that morning.

Around mid-day, Mara came to share the mid-day meal with us as she had the day before. Unlike the day before, however, I felt relaxed from the start of the meal, sure within myself of Ndalla's affection. While I could still see just how taken the young girl was with the queen before her, I felt reassured this time by the hours that Ndalla and I had spent together, both that morning and the night before. And I could see that Ndalla, while gracious, did nothing to encourage the young girl's infatuation ... other than be her naturally charming self, that is.

At one point, Mara started to share news about how her brother's meeting with the elders had gone, but Ndalla stopped her politely.

"Thank-you for offering to share such news. But your brother will share such news with me himself when he is ready. We must respect his right to share with me only what he chooses."

"Oh, he will choose to share this news!" said Mara excitedly.

Ndalla studied the young girl a moment. "I wonder if I might ask you a question. It is somewhat personal."

I saw the young girl blush. "Certainly," she said, only too happy, I thought, to get into personal territory with the queen who sat before her.

"Have you considered what your role will be as your brother steps further into his role as leader of your people?"

"My role?"

"As his sister, you are in a position to be a great help to him if you choose to be."

"How?"

"You are, I think, closer to him than anyone else at this point in his life, are you not?"

"I suppose."

"As a leader myself, I know how lonely such a life can be. He will need people in his life that he can trust, people he can talk to, people whose opinions he respects. It does not seem to me that he has had the benefit of too many of these people in his life up until now. If he starts to rely on the Council of Elders, I believe he will find there mentors that he can trust. But as for friends, a leader," and here she hesitated a moment, "cannot have many. Some can have none at all."

"But why?"

"It is hard for me to explain, but I will try."

Ndalla took a moment as she struggled to find a way to say what was on her mind. "A leader's first responsibility is to his people, all of them. And if he chooses to allow himself to befriend some and not others, this will put him in a difficult position to act as he must and to make the kinds of decisions he must be willing—and able—to make."

"But you have friends."

"Not as many as you seem to think, Mara," she said with a slight smile. "And those that I have, I have come to recognize as friends only recently. For many years, I had no one in whom I could confide. And it is only now, looking back on my younger life, that I can see how hard that made my life, in ways that I would not even let myself recognize at the time."

She then shifted the focus of the conversation away from herself and her own life.

"I do not know your brother that well yet. But already I sense in him the potential to be a great leader. He seems to have handled this recent episode, involving the killing of one of his own people, with the courage and strength of one who is born to lead. But what was required of him took a toll on him that even he cannot let himself recognize. The fact that he was friends with the boys who were involved only made it more difficult for him than it would have been otherwise."

She hesitated then a moment before continuing, giving the young girl time to absorb what she seemed to want her to understand. "Your brother must be careful to surround himself with the kind of people who will provide the right influence on him as he grows in his awareness and understanding of his role. I believe you can help him in this. As his older sister, you know him, perhaps better than he knows himself at this point in his life. You know what kinds of strengths are his to draw on, and you also know the shadow side of those strengths."

Again, she paused and waited to see if the young girl seemed to be following her. "You are in a position to exert a tremendous amount of influence over how your brother grows into his role should you choose to do so. The more aware you are of this position you hold, the better you position yourself to be able to use your influence for the good of your people."

Ndalla then reached forward and took the young girl's hand in her own for a moment before continuing.

"I never had a sister, Mara, so I cannot speak of these things from personal experience. But I have observed family life among my own people, and I know big sisters can do their little brothers much good—or harm, depending on the choices they make. The more aware you are of the choices that are yours to make, the better choices you can make." And then she said, "That is all I meant to say."

455

"But you have said much," said the young girl.

"Perhaps more than it was my place to say."

"No. I am glad you spoke what was in your heart. I will consider what you have said."

After Mara left, I turned to Ndalla. "You care for Mara and her brother a great deal."

"They have not had anyone in their lives to help them find their way," she said with some sadness in her voice. "Despite that, they have both managed to hold onto much of the wisdom they came into this life with. That says much about what they have to offer their people as they grow, each into the role that they have been offered to take up."

"They are fortunate to have you come into their lives."

But Ndalla dismissed this compliment with a wave of her hand as she called Yolana to help us clean up after the meal.

Daeikabah arrived shortly after Mara left then, to share with Ndalla what had happened during his meeting with the Council of Elders.

This time I really did give them their privacy and did not listen in. Even though I had no doubt that Ndalla would not have minded my staying close by, I respected the fact that it was important to her to make the boy feel as comfortable as possible when he was with her, and I figured he would probably prefer to do his sharing with her one-on-one.

It was quite a bit later in the day, then, that Ndalla caught up with me walking through the Daeika village.

Daeikabah had been right the other evening about her popularity with his people, for until the queen fell in step beside me, I'd been able to walk through the village with relatively few interruptions, despite my being a visitor in their village. But the moment Ndalla joined me, it was a different story. Everyone we passed, it seemed, had something they wanted to share with the young queen from the neighboring village who had come all this way to befriend them.

I was glad when at last we made it back to our dwelling and were able to enjoy a moment alone. I took her in my arms as soon as we were inside.

"Are you as happy as you appear?"

"Yes." And I could hear the mix of excitement and relief and happiness in her voice as she spoke that one simple word. "I will tell you about it over our evening meal. Yolana!" she called, and when the woman appeared, Ndalla asked her if she'd seen the healer that day.

"No, I have not."

"Go and find her and ask her if she will join us for dinner. And you join us as well, Yolana. The four of us have much to talk about."

Over dinner that night, Ndalla shared with us that Daeikabah's first meeting with the Council of Elders had gone well, at least according to Daeikabah's own account.

"He found the elders eager to meet with him and to share with him their thoughts on the subjects that he asked them about. He asked that the group start meeting again regularly and that the first matter they take under consideration be this matter about the Forces and what role they might play in the lives of the Daeika from this point forward."

"Did he ask them about the timing of your address to the Daeika people?" asked the healer.

Ndalla nodded. "It will occur very soon," she said. "The day when the sun stays in the sky the longest approaches. Our gathering will happen that evening, when the time of darkness is the shortest. I have already asked Bakka to bring our people down from the hills tomorrow. They can spend some time getting to know the Daeika people before the night of the gathering."

Ndalla seemed relaxed and happy as she shared with us

more of what Daeikabah had shared with her that afternoon, all of it good news as far as she was concerned.

But my thoughts wandered away from the group for a time as Ndalla's words sunk in: "The day when the sun stays in the sky the longest approaches. Our gathering will happen that evening." I realized she was referring to the Summer Solstice, and my thoughts flashed back to the Summer Solstice that I'd been anticipating the night before she'd arrived in my world ... just six months ago. My old world, that is, for surely this, Ndalla's world, was my world now.

"He will make a good leader of his people," I heard her say. She was speaking to Yolana and the healer. Her words brought me back to the group. "His head and his heart are both in the right place. He has only lacked good council up until now, and that need not continue to be the case, now that he has called for the Council of Elders to reconvene."

"And now that he has you to consult with," I added, trying to rejoin the conversation.

"I have only encouraged him to listen more carefully to his own inner wisdom, which is plentiful, especially now that he is listening to his own elders again." I could see that she'd made the decision not to accept any credit for the boy's success, and so I let the matter drop.

After dinner, I helped Yolana clear away the meal, as I thought I saw that Ndalla wanted to have some time alone with the healer. The two of them even stepped outside to talk a while, and when she came back inside, she was alone, her mood somewhat changed, I thought, although I could not say exactly how.

As we lay there in bed sometime later, I asked her about the healer. "Is she all right?"

She turned to me before she answered. "What I share with

you, I share in confidence."

"Absolutely," I said.

After a moment, she said, "She is worried about the old Daeika healer."

"Is he not well?"

"It is his age that concerns her."

"Concerns her how?" I asked.

She hesitated a moment, apparently unsure how to help me understand what the healer had shared with her in confidence. "There is much that she wants to learn from the old healer. She said she has already learned much from him in the short time they have been together."

"But I don't follow," I said. "Is she concerned that, because he is so old, they will run out of time before she learns all that she wants to from him?"

Then I saw a look pass over her face that I saw only when she was blushing, but it was too dark to see whether her cheeks had colored.

"No," she said in a tone that told me she had, in fact, been blushing. "She is attracted to the old man in a way that goes beyond what she wants to learn from him."

It took me a moment to take in this idea. The only emotional response I'd registered while in the old man's presence was my own impatience at how slowly he moved.

As I took in the idea of the two of them together in that way, all sorts of thoughts ran through my mind—not all of them kind, I'm afraid—and I thought it best to just wait for Ndalla to make the next comment.

"She is uncertain how to act right now," Ndalla said at last. "She does not want to do anything to make him feel uncomfortable. But she wants to let him know how she feels."

I kept my thoughts to myself a moment longer.

Finally, I asked, "How did you advise her?"

Ndalla looked at me then. "I advised her to follow her

heart," she said simply.

I rolled over toward her and propped my head up so that I could see her more clearly. And I was gifted with that wonderful smile of hers.

"Is that what you did?" I asked, taking her hand in mine and sliding it up above her head where she lay, looking so beautiful and so relaxed.

She did not answer right away, seeming to enjoy the moment of intimacy before she spoke. "Yes," she said in a voice that made me feel weak inside.

Then I felt her other hand start stroking my side in a way that took away any resolve I might have had to continue talking before we moved on to other things.

"Julia," I heard her say just as I bent over her to kiss her.

"Hmmm?"

But instead of words, she met my lips with her own, and we spoke no more words that evening.

CHAPTER 31

Recognizing a Calling

The next day, Ndalla once again awoke early. She looked well-rested, and her appetite was apparently good too as she shared a good breakfast with me before indicating that she would spend the morning with Barei if she could find him. "I want to get his sense of how Daeikabah's meeting with the elders went the other night," she said as she was leaving.

Then she stopped in her tracks and came over to me. "Our people should arrive this afternoon. Will you stand with me to welcome them to Daeika?" she asked, touching my face gently with her hand.

"Absolutely," I said.

Then she flashed me that beautiful smile and left, saying, "I will meet you back here for the mid-day meal."

"Will Mara be joining us?" I hollered after her.

"I don't know," she called back. And with that, she was gone.

I was still trying to decide how I would spend my morning

when I was surprised by an early morning visitor.

"Come in, healer," I said, inviting her in.

"Traveler," she said by way of greeting, a little more gruffly than usual, I thought.

"Would you like some tea?"

"Perhaps," she said. "Is the queen here?"

"No, she left not too long ago. She was going to seek out Barei, if she could find him, to get his sense of how the meeting of the Council of Elders went the other night."

"Ah," said the woman, just as Yolana came into the room with some tea.

"Thank-you, Yolana," I said. "Come, healer, sit." But I could see she wasn't sure if she wanted to just yet. Clearly, she had come to see her queen, not me. "The tea is fresh and hot."

"Perhaps I will have a cup with you, traveler."

Yolana left us.

"The queen has awakened early the last two mornings, feeling well-rested and having a good appetite," I offered by way of a conversation opener.

The healer offered what appeared to be a genuine smile of relief at the news.

"The old Daeika healer seems to be very knowledgeable," I said, introducing the subject I figured was on her mind. "We are fortunate to have had him come into our lives when he did."

"Yes," she said before taking a long drink from her cup.

"The queen said that you have already had the chance to learn much from him in the short time you have known him," I offered, trying to get the conversation jump-started somehow.

"Yes." And again, it was all she said.

After another silence, I ventured, "What kind of a man do you find him to be, healer?"

And in answer to the rather sharp look of alarm I received,

I quickly added, "I have never known someone with so many years of living behind him."

She let herself smile a little then. "Yes," she said. "It is his years that have given him his great knowledge of things."

And then I saw her lose herself a moment as she thought of him, her smile widening ever so slightly. "And other things, too," she said softly.

Somehow I knew she would not appreciate the rather blunt "Like what?" that was playing over and over in my head, and so I said instead, "He seems a very gentle man, very patient, too."

"Yes," she said, letting herself make eye contact with me for the first time.

I decided then not to ask any more questions and to respect her right to keep her feelings about the man to herself. An easy silence was just beginning to settle in between us when I heard her say, "He is like no other man I have met."

I struggled not to drop my own cup as I reached for the pot and poured her another cup.

I thought it best to maintain my silence again, and I kept my eyes focused on the cup I held in my hand.

After a moment, I heard her ask, "Did you not think him a very good-looking man, traveler?"

I raised my eyes then and looked at her. She was positively beaming.

"Yes." And then I added the honest observation, "A very striking presence he has."

"Yes," she said, with a smile and a nod. "Very striking."

I was just beginning to wonder how long I could sustain this conversation when I looked up and saw that Ndalla had arrived. She looked as surprised to see the healer sitting there talking with me as I was to see her standing there.

"I am sorry. I did not mean to interrupt," she said, turning to leave us.

I looked to the healer before jumping to my feet.

"No, don't leave," I said. "The healer and I were just having some tea. It was you that she came to see, isn't that so?" I asked, turning to the healer for confirmation.

The healer, while clearly not wanting to hurt my feelings, was obviously relieved to see her queen. "Yes," she said. "It is so."

"I'll leave you two to talk then," I said. "I wanted to spend some time in the village this morning, anyway. I'll be back for the mid-day meal," I said, turning to Ndalla. "Perhaps the healer can join us too. It's been good talking with you," I said to the healer. And I left.

When I returned for lunch, I found not only the healer there, but Barei and Mara as well.

Ndalla got up when she saw me enter and came over and said quietly, "You were very kind to the healer this morning. She does not know that I shared with you what I did. And I thank-you for that," she said, putting her hand on my arm. "She told me that you said some very kind things about the Daeika healer this morning, and that meant a lot to her. Thank-you, Julia, for being so kind to her."

"It was the least I could do," I said with a shrug. "She has been a good friend to me in the time I have known her."

"Even so. I thank you." And I saw in her eyes how much my small kindness to her friend had touched her. She turned then to escort me over to join the others.

"Barei was not available this morning, so he was good enough to join us for our mid-day meal," she said by way of explanation to me. "I have sent word to ask Daeikabah and the Daeika healer to join us, as well."

She had no sooner gotten the words out than we turned to see the two of them standing at the entrance to the dwelling.

She reached out to greet the boy first, and he accepted the gesture with a smile and came inside. "It is good to have a chance to meet with you today so that we can talk about how best to celebrate the arrival of your people in our village this afternoon," he said.

Ndalla smiled and nodded before turning then to greet the old man, who said, "Thank-you for your invitation, young queen. You look as though your strength has decided to return to you at last."

"Yes, it has, thanks to you," she said softly. "Come, join us." Then turning to take in how large our group had become, she said, "This has turned out to be quite a gathering!"

She turned to me then and asked, "Will you help Yolana and ask her to join us as well?"

"Certainly," I said.

"I will help too," offered Mara, getting to her feet.

And so, the eight of us, who had shared a meal just a couple nights earlier, did so again.

As I looked around where we sat, I was amazed to witness how comfortable with each other we'd gotten, even in so little time. And I knew exactly who it was that deserved so much of the credit for how well things had gone since our party had entered the Daeika village. And I knew too that were I to suggest as much to her, she would quickly deflect that compliment as she had the others I'd tried to give her recently. She was so focused on doing all that she could to build the nascent trust between the Ndalla and the Daeika, that she refused to step back, even for a moment, to consider her role in making it possible. That was not important to her; I could see that. What was important to her was that the trust had begun to take root.

I looked over at Ndalla then and saw her in conversation with Barei and Daeikabah, both the old man and the young boy intently engaged in what she was saying. The two healers were, of course, deeply engaged in their own, much more private conversation. And even Mara and Yolana, who at the last dinner had just begun a friendship of sorts, seemed to be enjoying an animated conversation of their own. And I? I was just happy to be an observer of all of it.

And I recognized in that moment, the way one sometimes recognizes such things, that it was very right for me—at this particular moment—to be nothing more or less than an observer. I was also aware of a certain solemnity as I registered this moment. As I was puzzling over what that feeling might signify, I happened to look up and see Ndalla steal a moment, while Barei and Daeikabah were in conversation with each other, to look up at me and smile. And something inside me knew that she too had felt what I'd just felt and that her smile was a recognition of what it was I'd just felt. And I knew, too, that we would speak of this moment when next we found ourselves alone. I smiled as I felt my eager anticipation of our next private conversation.

That afternoon, the people of Ndalla, who had been camped in the hills for the past many weeks, entered the village and were greeted enthusiastically by the people of Daeika.

Ndalla and Daeikabah stood at the front of the crowd, she taking the time to introduce her people to the boy, who then, in turn, saw that the family just introduced to him was handed off to one of the elders, who would help the family connect with whatever Daeika family they would be staying with for the next several days while we prepared for the solstice. There were no words said publicly, either by the Ndalla queen or by the young Daeika king. The time for ceremony and formal words had been set and would not happen until then.

What I witnessed on this day was simply people meeting people. The Ndalla were grateful, I think, to come down out of the hills and finally meet the people they had traveled so far to meet, and the Daeika, for their part, seemed genuinely happy to finally get to meet other families like themselves, as, up until now, the only people of Ndalla they'd had in their midst were either warriors or various members of the queen's own party.

Ndalla was clearly pleased to have so many of her people around her again, and she took the time to visit with each family who had made the trip, and she visited as well with each elder in turn, making sure that everyone was well and that their time in the hills had not been too hard on any of them. Then she gathered her warriors and told them that she wanted them to meet with Daeikabah and herself that after-noon.

As she was leaving with her warriors, though, she took the time to stop and talk briefly with me. "I do not know how long I will be tonight, Julia. You should plan on sharing your evening meal with someone other than me," she said, a little sadly, I thought. Then she added, brightening a little, "I will make myself available to Daeikabah as long as he might have need of me tonight. He has many responsibilities right now, and I would like to help him if I can."

"I understand."

And then a look flashed across her face that I could not read.

"Perhaps," she said after a moment, "you would like to share a meal with the storyteller tonight. I am sure he would be a ready listener if you want to share with someone all that has happened in the time we have been here."

And the memory of that moment, when it had felt so right to be an observer, flashed before me. And I wondered if the same thought had occurred to her. But there was no time to talk of such things just now, so I said, "I will see if I can spend some time with him."

And then, before she left, I took her in my arms. "Will I see you tonight, though?"

"Yes," she said with that wonderful smile of hers. "I do not know how late I will be, but I will be there." And then, before she left, she looked up at the moon, still in its fullness tonight, a week or so before the solstice would occur. "This is not unlike the time when I first came to visit you in your world, Julia. We are in that moment between the time of the moon's fullness and the longest day of the year. There is a significance to this time that we will honor tonight."

That evening, I shared my evening meal with the storyteller, as Ndalla had suggested. We sat out under the stars to eat, as did the rest of the people in the village, each group only a few feet—and sometimes mere inches—away from the group next to it. It was like a huge informal gathering with lots of sharing, from one group to the other, going on: sharing of food, sharing of conversation, sharing of whatever a group happened to be in need of.

As for the old man and myself, however, we found a relatively quiet spot at the edge of the open area where so many had gathered. We both seemed to know that we wanted to be able to sit and talk without interruption, and the groups around us seemed to sense that as well and so were good enough to leave us to ourselves that evening.

"Your eyes and ears have witnessed much during this important time, traveler."

"Yes," I agreed. "A lot has happened in a very little time." I looked at the old man then, who was clearly not used to having to ask for stories to be told to him. "I will do my best to share with you what I have witnessed so that you will know it too," I offered.

The old man nodded, either to communicate his approval of the idea or his gratitude; I could not tell which.

And so I began the story ... going all the way back to the

day that we approached the village and the queen called out for one who would speak for the Daeika to come out and join our party in the open field. I shared with him every detail I could recall of the past weeks.

And as I recalled these details to share with him, I found that the moments came to life in the very act of sharing them in a way I could never recall such memories coming to life. I could recall with certainty that it had been late in the afternoon of our third day of waiting in the open field that the skies had become so ominous, and I could hear again in my mind the queen's exact tone of voice when she had turned to us and said, in an effort to encourage us not to lose our humor, I thought, "This will not be a pleasant experience." It was as though I was reliving the experience myself as I brought it to life again for the old storyteller. I had never really had this experience. I had always written of such things, not spoken of them. I found that in speaking such memories aloud, with an engaged audience right before me, I was able to access them in a way I had not known was available to me before.

The storyteller was an excellent listener. He was extremely interested in everything I said; he was attentive and alert, and he looked as though he was allowing the sights and sounds I was sharing with him to play freely in his own mind, exactly as I presented them to him. It was as if his attentiveness to what he was hearing and seeing in his mind's eye fueled my own attentiveness to what I was recalling and sharing. My memory of the events became, in an instant, his memory. I felt as though there was no translation process; the transmittal of images and feelings between us was instantaneous, and I was assured by a feeling that my telling of events was absolutely error-free as well. It was an amazing experience.

At several points in the story, the old man asked me to pause. And we took such occasions to eat and drink a while, and he also commented on what I had shared so far.

And so, he taught me something that night about pacing, as well.

His questions and comments during these pauses only encouraged me further in my certainty that the process was working as well as it felt to me that it was. It was quite late then when I concluded the tale, ending with the meal that the eight of us had shared earlier that day.

I hesitated to inject into the tale such a personal note as a description of the feeling I'd had about the rightness of my finding myself in the role of observer during that meal. And yet even as I hesitated, I could sense his awareness that I was holding something back from him. He said nothing, and yet I could tell he was waiting for me to share that feeling as well.

And so I did, trying to put into words as best I could the feeling I'd registered, knowing at the same time that I was failing miserably, at least by my own estimation.

The old man smiled as I finished what I was saying ... or trying to say, anyway.

"You are a born storyteller, traveler. And as with every storyteller I've known, you will always find it easier to shine a light on those around you than to shine it on yourself. That is nothing to apologize for. A storyteller has the honor of holding up a great light that allows his people to see themselves through their own stories told back to them. Do not regret that the light shines best in only one direction. That is part of the honor you are granted in holding it up."

And with that, the old man got stiffly to his feet. "It is late, and I must head to my bed. I thank you for the many stories you have shared with me this evening."

Then he looked at me a moment longer, unspeaking. "I do not know whether to say, 'Good-night, traveler,' or 'Good-night, storyteller,' for surely you are both now in my eyes."

I let myself register the pride I felt as he spoke those words to me.

And then, not knowing what to say in response, I heard myself say, "You could call me simply by my given name: Julia."

"Only the queen calls you that. Her people honor you—and the special relationship you share with her—by not using that name."

"I did not know."

"You are learning, traveler. You are learning," he said with a smile. "When you have learned enough, I will call you 'storyteller.' Until then, I will say, 'Good-night, traveler.' Sleep well. And let yourself feel tonight the peace that comes when you are finding your way through Life as the Forces intend."

When I got to the dwelling that night, I found Ndalla lying in bed, awake, waiting up for me. She could see my happiness when I settled in next to her, and she asked me to tell her all about my evening. And so I did. I told her how much I had enjoyed sharing with the storyteller all that had happened while he and the others were camped up in the hills. And I shared with her also his kind words toward the end of the evening, about my "finding my way through Life as the Forces intend." She could see how much hearing those words meant to me, and I knew in my heart already how much they meant to her.

"These words of the storyteller's resonate within you?" she asked.

"Yes!"

"I can see that they do," she said with a smile. "And yet you needed to hear them spoken by someone outside yourself in order to know them."

I did not know if she was asking me a question, as though for confirmation, or making an observation.

"I suppose I did," I said at last.

And then I looked at her. She was positively radiant.

"What is it?" I asked.

"I am happy for you, Julia. Ever since I have known you, you have been seeking your path through Life. Even back in your own world, you seemed uncertain which path was yours to take. I am happy to see that you are finding such a path, and happier still that it is a path here in my world."

She sat up then before continuing with what she was about to say. "Do you recall the feeling you had at our mid-day meal earlier today?" Of course I did, but I hardly knew how to talk about it. "You felt it so strongly that I felt it myself as well," she said, smiling.

I recalled then the look we had exchanged during the meal at that moment when I had been struck by how right it felt to be an observer. And I recalled too my anticipation of the chance to talk with her about that moment. Here, now, however, I found myself unable to speak.

"Julia," she said, and her voice became very serious. "To be a storyteller is a great honor among my people. If that is what you feel yourself called to do, then I encourage you to spend as much time as you can with the storyteller. He can teach you much, both about the storyteller's ways and also about the great responsibility the storyteller has to his people."

Then she smiled. "Your role is not only to be the queen's companion." And I felt her arms around me. "Although you do that very well." I returned her embrace. "No, Julia, your role in life is much bigger than that. I sense it. And I know you sense it too."

On the night of what, in my old life, I would've referred to as the Summer Solstice—six months after that same Solstice had occurred back in my old world—Ndalla stood before the people of Daeika in the center of their village. Her people, the brave

Ndalla who had made the journey with their queen in the spirit of friendship, stood in the crowd, shoulder to shoulder with the Daeika.

It was a beautiful evening. The moon, which had started to wane almost a week earlier, nevertheless shone clear above her as she prepared to speak. Daeikabah stood beside her. And then she stepped forward to speak, and the crowd quieted itself.

"I, Ndalla, queen of the Ndalla people, stand before you, the people of Daeika, in the spirit of peace and cooperation that now binds us together." A cheer went up, and she waited for the crowd to quiet itself before speaking again.

"While we faced each other as enemies not too long ago and fought a fierce battle that cost many warriors their lives, we have taken from that time the knowledge that is ours to take. We have learned from that battle the lessons that Life itself would have us learn: that we are, after all, more alike than we are different, that there is much we can choose to learn from each other, and that we owe a debt—each to the other—that we will spend the rest of our time in both the physical and the spirit realm repaying. We, the people of Ndalla and the people of Daeika, are bound together now. Fate has tied the lines of Time around us, bound us to one another, and we will honor what Fate has decreed." She stepped aside then as the people cheered, and Daeikabah stepped forward.

"I, Daeikabah, leader of the Daeika, stand before you now, Ndalla and Daeika alike, and on behalf of my people, I accept the hand of peace and cooperation extended to us by the Ndalla people. I thank the people of Ndalla who made the journey here to extend this offer. And I thank the queen of the Ndalla people, most of all, for what she has already given us in her time with us. I have learned much from her in this brief time, and I look forward to learning more."

He turned to her then and extended his hand in a gesture

of friendship. She grasped it firmly, and they embraced. I recalled the brashness he had exhibited when we first arrived at his village, just a month earlier. Thanks to Ndalla's gentle influence and—I had to admit—his own willingness to be influenced by her, he was a different person now. A much better person. And a much more capable leader of his people.

Then he stepped aside, and she stepped forward once again. This time, before she spoke, though, she reached out and put her arm around him.

"On behalf of both Daeikabah and myself, I ask that we all, Ndalla and Daeika alike, embrace our role in the events that make up the Great Unfolding of Time. I ask that we all seek the wisdom to see clearly as far as we need to see to be able to do our work well and in the spirit of both humility and pride that befits Ndalla and Daeika alike."

And then, as she had before on such occasions, she closed, saying, "Let us each consider carefully tonight our place in the Great Scheme of Life and ask for the strength to do well that which it is our place to do."

Epilogue

There is, of course, more to the story. But I will end here for now, for this is an ending of sorts. And as such, it is also a beginning, as all endings are.

Long ago, such a paradox might have seemed too simple to be able to hold any real truth for me. But then, long ago, I would have had a hard time accepting that I would have to travel such a long way through time, to Ndalla's world, and then again from her village to the village of the Daeika, a village whose warriors had violated her so during the Great Battle, in order to find my own voice as storyteller, a voice I could not find in my own world. But there you have it.

I have more stories to tell of my life with the Ndalla and the Daeika ... of how they learned to live together, in a new world in which they were no longer enemies; of how Makei fared back in my old world for a time; of how, when it came time for him to return to Ndalla, that journey was made; of the new life that Ndalla brought into the world, a life born of both the Ndalla and the Daeika; and of how I came to write these stories ... in a land where reading and writing have no place.

And I also have more stories to tell ... of my life with Ndalla, the woman with whom I traveled through Time itself, the woman who gave me access to the Spirit Realm that she knew so well and that had always surrounded me without my knowing, the woman I now know I have known throughout Time, the woman to whom I always was and always will be connected.

But I am in no hurry to tell those stories. They will be told in the fullness of Time.

I close this book, grateful for my role as storyteller and queen's companion ... and any other role that I might be called upon to play in my journey through the events that make up the Great Unfolding of Time and ask for the strength to do well that which it is my place to do.

Acknowledgements

I want to thank the following individuals, each of whom contributed in some way to getting this book into your hands:

Irene, whose gentle soul inspired the fictional character of Julia, whose story this really is.

My good buddy Penny, whose enthusiasm for this story when she read it in draft form fueled my energy to see it published.

My long-time friend Betty, who has always believed in me … even when I didn't.

My editor, Asata, who helped me make this book better than it was the first time she saw it, by encouraging me to continue asking many of the same questions I was already asking … and also to find the courage, confidence, and commitment to pursue the answers to those questions!

My friend Gay, who helped me work my way through a revision process that was sometimes very disorienting and that threatened to overwhelm me at times.

My parents, who have inhabited the spirit realm for some time now. While alive, they encouraged me, each in their own way, to follow the path that they knew I would find … eventually. Since they have passed, I continue to feel their energy supporting me.

My sister, Patty, who has always challenged me in ways that have helped me find my way.

My partner, Pat, whose support and encouragement sustain me more than she'll ever know ... and whose passion for photographing the moon was instrumental in the cover design of the book.

My son, David, the best guy I know, who reminds me, as often as he needs to, that if my dreams don't scare me, they're probably not big enough!

About Atmosphere Press

Atmosphere Press is an independent, full-service publisher for excellent books in all genres and for all audiences. Learn more about what we do at atmospherepress.com.

We encourage you to check out some of Atmosphere's latest releases, which are available at Amazon.com and via order from your local bookstore:

Tsunami, a novel by Paul Flentge

Tubes, a novel by Penny Skillman

Skylark Dancing, a novel by Olivia Godat

ALT, a novel by Aleksandar Nedeljkovic

The Bonds Between Us, a novel by Emily Ruhl

Dancing with David, a novel by Siegfried Johnson

The Friendship Quilts, a novel by June Calender

My Significant Nobody, a novel by Stevie D. Parker

Nine Days, a novel by Judy Lannon

Shining New Testament: The Cloning of Jay Christ, a novel by Cliff Williamson

Shadows of Robyst, a novel by K. E. Maroudas

Home Within a Landscape, a novel by Alexey L. Kovalev

Motherhood, a novel by Siamak Vakili

Death, The Pharmacist, a novel by D. Ike Horst

Mystery of the Lost Years, a novel by Bobby J. Bixler

About the Author

Recently retired, Beth is enjoying having the time and energy to focus on the twin passions that have teased, haunted, and sustained her for decades. Writing has always helped her "see" more clearly what she is trying to see, and since she began sculpting a few decades ago, playing with clay has given her another way to "see" the world—and particularly the people in that world—around her more clearly. She is gratified to offer this story, originally drafted over a decade and a half ago, as her first published novel.

Please visit the author's website,
www.writerandsculptor.com

Made in the USA
Monee, IL
22 July 2022